# PRAISE FOR M1

"With her wonderful characters and resonating emotions, Melissa Foster is a must-read author!"

—*New York Times* bestseller Julie Kenner

"Melissa Foster is synonymous with sexy, swoony, heartfelt romance!"

—*New York Times* bestseller Lauren Blakely

"You can always rely on Melissa Foster to deliver a story that's fresh, emotional, and entertaining."

—*New York Times* bestseller Brenda Novak

"Melissa Foster writes worlds that draw you in, with strong heroes and brave heroines surrounded by a community that makes you want to crawl right on through the page and live there."

—*New York Times* bestseller Julia Kent

"When it comes to contemporary romances with realistic characters, an emotional love story, and smokin'-hot sex, author Melissa Foster always delivers!"

—*The Romance Reviews*

"Foster writes characters that are complex and loyal, and each new story brings further depth and development to a redefined concept of family."

—*RT Book Reviews*

"Melissa Foster definitely knows how to spin a tale and keep you flipping the pages."

—*Book Loving Fairy*

"You can never go wrong with the heroes that Melissa Foster creates. She hasn't made one yet that I haven't fallen in love with."

—*Natalie the Biblioholic*

"Melissa is a very talented author that tells fabulous stories that captivate you and keep your attention from the first page to the last page. Definitely an author that you will want to keep on your go-to list."

—*Between the Coverz*

"Melissa Foster writes the best contemporary romance I have ever read. She does it in bundles, tops it with great plots, hot guys, strong heroines, and sprinkles it with family dynamics—you got yourself an amazing read."

—*Reviews of a Book Maniac*

"[Melissa Foster] has a way with words that endears a family in our hearts, and watching each sibling and friend go on to meet their true love is such a joy!"

—*Thoughts of a Blonde*

# THE MR. RIGHT

## Checklist

# MORE BOOKS BY MELISSA FOSTER

## LOVE IN BLOOM
### BIG-FAMILY ROMANCE COLLECTION

### SNOW SISTERS
*Sisters in Love*
*Sisters in Bloom*
*Sisters in White*

### THE BRADENS AT WESTON
*Lovers at Heart, Reimagined*
*Destined for Love*
*Friendship on Fire*
*Sea of Love*
*Bursting with Love*
*Hearts at Play*

### THE BRADENS AT TRUSTY
*Taken by Love*
*Fated for Love*
*Romancing My Love*
*Flirting with Love*
*Dreaming of Love*
*Crashing into Love*

### THE BRADENS AT PEACEFUL HARBOR
*Healed by Love*
*Surrender My Love*
*River of Love*
*Crushing on Love*
*Whisper of Love*
*Thrill of Love*

### THE BRADENS & MONTGOMERYS
*Embracing Her Heart*
*Anything for Love*
*Trails of Love*
*Wild, Crazy Hearts*
*Making You Mine*
*Searching for Love*
*Hot for Love*
*Sweet, Sexy Heart*
*Then Came Love*
*Rocked by Love*
*Falling for Mr. Bad*

### BRADEN NOVELLAS
*Promise My Love*
*Our New Love*
*Daring Her Love*
*Story of Love*
*Love at Last*
*A Very Braden Christmas*

### THE REMINGTONS
*Game of Love*
*Stroke of Love*
*Flames of Love*
*Slope of Love*
*Read, Write, Love*
*Touched by Love*

## THE WHISKEYS:
## DARK KNIGHTS AT REDEMPTION RANCH

*The Trouble with Whiskey*

*Freeing Sully: Prequel to For the Love of Whiskey*

*For the Love of Whiskey*

*A Taste of Whiskey*

*Love, Lies, and Whiskey*

## BILLIONAIRES AFTER DARK SERIES

### Wild Boys After Dark

*Logan*

*Heath*

*Jackson*

*Cooper*

### Bad Boys After Dark

*Mick*

*Dylan*

*Carson*

*Brett*

## HARBORSIDE NIGHTS SERIES

*Catching Cassidy*

*Discovering Delilah*

*Tempting Tristan*

## STAND-ALONE NOVELS

*Hot Mess Summer* (romantic comedy)

*Chasing Amanda* (mystery/suspense)

*Come Back to Me* (mystery/suspense)

*Have No Shame* (historical fiction/romance)

*Love, Lies & Mystery* (three-book bundle)

*Megan's Way* (literary fiction)

*Traces of Kara* (psychological thriller)

*Where Petals Fall* (suspense)

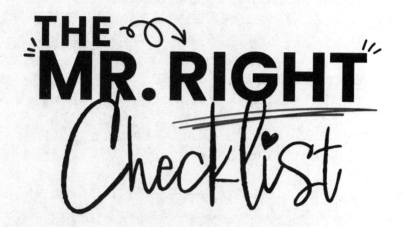

# MELISSA FOSTER

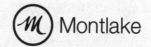 Montlake

Published by Montlake, Seattle

www.apub.com

Amazon, the Amazon logo, and Montlake are trademarks of Amazon.com, Inc., or its affiliates.

ISBN-13: 9781662507977 (paperback)
ISBN-13: 9781662507960 (digital)

Cover design by Hang Le
Cover photography by Michelle Lancaster PTY LTD
Cover image: © KVASVECTOR, © TWINS DESIGN STUDIO / Shutterstock

MELISSA FOSTER® is registered in the U.S. Patent & Trademark Office.

Printed in the United States of America

*For everyone who believes in love, and even those who don't*

# Chapter One

## DESTINY

"I finally did it, Molly," I say excitedly to my favorite client as I give her a trim. "I put up my website and handed out flyers to start my marriage-proposal business last week, and I already booked my first client. I have been dreaming about this for so long, I can hardly believe it's *finally* happening. Guess what it's called! Get the Yes! How cute is that?"

"It's better than Let Destiny Do It," Ruby, my best friend since childhood and my boss, calls out from the other room.

"That was a great name," I call back.

"It made you sound like a sex worker," Ruby says with a laugh. "What does Molly think of your plan?"

I look at the big, lovable Bernese mountain dog I'm grooming. "She's as excited as I am. Aren't you, Mol?"

As if on cue, Molly barks.

I kiss her snout and grab a brush to finish grooming her as Ruby breezes into the room with Chipster, a rascally white labradoodle who's covered in dried mud *again*. Ruby, on the other hand, looks as stunning as always, and it has less to do with the clothes she's wearing under her grooming apron, her flawless dark skin, or her chic buzz cut that makes her high cheekbones and dark eyes stand out and more to do with her inner beauty, which radiates from her heart in endless patience and support.

"How are you doing on time?" Ruby asks. "Should we have Laura call Molly's dad and let him know you're running late?" Laura runs the front desk of Ruby's pet grooming business, Perfect Paws.

"Nope. I'll be done in time." I went to a neighboring town to drop off flyers before work and have been running behind all day, but the last thing I want is for Laura to call Grumpy Gus and make him even grumpier. The man barely says two words to me as it is. "Did you happen to see the picture of the Chiffon Park gazebo at sunset that I posted on my social pages last night?"

"*Yes.*" She settles the pooch on the grooming table. "The bouquet of white roses was a nice touch. It made me want to get married again." She'd met her husband, John, while attending college in New York. I'd helped John plan the perfect scavenger-hunt proposal, and they'd had a simple wedding in our hometown of Rosebell, Georgia.

"I will happily expand my business to include vow-renewal proposals."

"Once you're established, you should put together the ceremonies, too. I bet you'd make a killing. Think about it. You'd double your income from working with the same couple." Ruby glances over as she brushes Chipster. "Have you told your dad yet?"

My chest constricts. I lost my mom when I was eleven. My father raised me alone, and we were as thick as thieves. I was beyond devastated when he passed away unexpectedly a little more than a year ago. I continue to pay his cell phone bill just so I can hear his voice when I miss him or want to share news, or even talk something out like we used to—when I'd ramble and he'd listen. I'd never admit the whole cell phone thing to anyone else, but Ruby is like a sister to me. Which is why, three months ago, after a year of Ruby's urging, I moved to Harmony Pointe, New York, to start over in the same town where she and John live. So far I love it here, with its cobblestone streets, brick-front eclectic shops, and old-fashioned streetlights.

"I called him as soon as the site went up and the flyers were printed. I know he's smiling down on me. I'm so excited, I feel like I'm vibrating inside."

"*Really?* I couldn't tell." She giggles.

"Hush up, you pest."

"I saw someone pick up one of your flyers at La Love when I was getting coffee earlier, and Heaven said she and Echo have been talking you up to customers." La Love Café & Gift Shop is located a few doors down from Perfect Paws, in the center of town. It's owned by the Love family and run by Heaven Love and her brother, Echo.

"They're the best."

"How's your first big job coming along? I still can't believe you agreed to plan it in such a rush. I mean, a week? That's asking a lot. You should've charged double and gotten it all up front."

"I know you think so, but I need the experience. As far as the timing goes, it has to be done that fast." I didn't even have time to meet with my client in person because the timeline is so tight. We've done everything over the phone and through email. "She said after this weekend she won't see her fiancé for a few months because of their schedules, and she wants to put a ring on it before that happens. Did I tell you *she* is giving *him* a ring?"

"No, but that's cool."

"I thought so, too. Why wait for the guy to make the move? Anyway, I've got the whole thing planned for Saturday. A champagne picnic in the park right by that massive oak tree near the trail. That tree is so beautiful. It's going to be stunning with draped white silk along the low branches. I bought a white chalkboard and put it in a gold frame on a gold stand, and I'm going to write *Be Mine Forever* on it in red chalk and decorate the top of it with roses and greenery and baby's breath." I shiver with excitement.

"That sounds wonderful *and* expensive."

"It's pricey. I've already spent way more than the initial deposit, but it'll be worth it. Did I tell you I got the six dozen red roses I wanted?

I'm lucky the florist could help me out on such short notice, and they said if we do enough business together, they'll give me a discount. They referred me to a photographer named Ha-Joon. I'm meeting him tomorrow at lunch, and he's already said he's available to photograph the event. He was expensive, too, but his social pages are to die for."

"I've seen them. He's well known around here. He does great work, but are you charging enough to cover his fees, too?"

The truth is, I've already spent more than I'm charging for the event, but I don't want to worry Ruby, so I play it off casually. "I'm not making any money off this one, but it's a good learning experience, and I want everything to be just right. She has already given me permission to use some of the photos on my website and in marketing materials. That's saving me from buying stock images, so please don't lecture me. I know what I'm doing, and everyone in this town has been so kind and receptive to my flyers. Get the Yes is going to be a huge success. I can feel it in my bones. I checked my website this morning, and it's already had more than a hundred views. That's not bad without any paid advertising, right?"

"I think it's great, but why aren't you advertising? Between your dad's life insurance and selling his auto repair business, you can afford to run a few local ads."

"I know, but I want to start slow and grow my business organically while I iron out all the kinks."

"I get that, but you could—"

"*Rubes*," I warn. Ruby is as organized and efficient as I am a fly-by-the-seat-of-my-pants kind of girl. She would be a great resource for all things business related, but she'd take over without even trying. It's just the way she is, bless her heart. I adore her, but she'd drive me crazy, wanting everything meticulously planned out to the nth degree five years into the future, like she's done with Perfect Paws. Our friendship is too important to me to risk ruining it over this. Plus, she and John are trying to get pregnant, and it has been a heartbreaking few months for them. She doesn't need added stress.

"Fine," she relents. "I'll zip it about that, but you do realize you'll have to gussy up for potential clients, right?"

"Why? You don't think they'll hire me if I show up covered in pet fur?" My words drip with sarcasm as I glance in the mirror at my cuffed jeans, yellow socks with colorful paw prints on them, and dirty-blond hair that I swear has a mind of its own. It's in a ponytail right now, but there are wayward strands poking out everywhere, like I walked through a wind tunnel. I don't know how that happens when I've been indoors this whole time, but it always seems to, and my pink sneakers have definitely seen better days.

"I'd hire you, but not everyone loves fur babies."

"You're right. I'm not looking forward to that aspect of the business, but I'm still my mama's daughter at heart. I can be a pretty, proper Southern belle when necessary."

"You're always pretty, but proper? *Well . . .*"

We laugh. I can be unfiltered and outlandish, but I like who I am and so does Ruby, and that's all I need.

"What are you doing tonight?" she asks as we groom the dogs.

"I have a few things to do for the event, but they shouldn't take too long. Beyond that, I don't know yet. Why? Do you want to hang out?"

"I was just curious. Sorry, but I can't hang out. I will be busy having wild, dirty, hopefully baby-making sex with my husband."

"I'm jealous." I can't remember the last time I had sex, and it wasn't with someone who loved me like John loves Ruby. According to Ruby, that brings sex to a whole new level.

"You want to have sex with John?" she asks with a tease in her voice.

"*No.* Gross. He's yours."

"Did you just call my husband gross?"

"I didn't mean *he's* gross. It's just that he's yours, and that's sacred. Besides, he's not my type."

"You mean he doesn't meet all the ridiculous items on your Mr. Right Checklist? What a surprise. No man alive can live up to all that."

"What can I say? I know what I like, and it's not organized and careful Ken dolls. I'm more of a G.I. Joe girl. I'm into rugged, dark, and spontaneous guys who roll with the punches and are comfortable in any situation and can fix anything."

"I *know*. No highfalutin egos for you, and you would kick Chris Pine or Ryan Gosling out of bed for their hair color alone, which I think is nuts. They're my hall passes."

"Yes, you've made John and me well aware of that."

We continue chatting while I finish grooming Molly. When I'm done, I grab the box of bows. "Okay, Mol, your daddy is going to be here any minute. What color should we go for today?" I hold up the box, and Molly sniffs a pink bow. "A girl after my own heart. Maybe pink will get a smile out of your grumpy daddy." I pluck two pink bows from the box.

"Fletch isn't grumpy."

"Who's Fletch?" I ask as I put the first bow in Molly's hair.

Ruby's brows shoot up. "Molly's *owner* . . . ?"

"Why do you say it like I should know his name? Nobody calls him that. Even Laura calls him Molly's dad."

"Whatever. He's not grumpy. He's just reserved."

"If you say so." I pet Molly. "But I'm pretty sure this big, beautiful girl is the only one Stuffy Steve smiles for." Molly pants happily.

Ruby laughs. "You're a lost cause."

"It's not my fault Aloof Adam acts that way."

The intercom on the wall buzzes, and Laura's voice comes through. "Destiny, Molly's dad is here."

"I'll bring her right out." I flash a victorious grin at Ruby, who rolls her eyes.

Grumpy Gus is standing in the middle of the reception area, his expression as stoic as ever. His arms are crossed over his broad chest, legs planted shoulder width apart, thigh muscles flexing against his dark slacks. His dirty-blond hair is short on the sides, slightly longer on top, and so thick it reminds me of plush carpeting. His scruff is perfectly manicured, as usual, and his light blue eyes are narrowed, like he doesn't trust me. Laura is sneaking peeks at him, but he seems oblivious to her appreciative glances. His gaze falls to Molly, and a smile blooms across his face, softening his hard edges for a second, until those baby blues land on the pink bows in Molly's hair, and his jaw tightens again.

He grumbles, "*Bows.*"

"Molly loves them. She chose pink today." I hand him the leash.

"She's a dog," he says flatly. "She doesn't know what a bow is."

"Then she's lucky I do, because she's a pretty girl, and she deserves to look her best."

He frowns. "The last time she *ate* one, and it cost me a few hundred dollars at the vet."

My stomach sinks. "*Oh no.* I'm so sorry. I wish you had noted that when you made this appointment. I'll just . . ." I quickly and carefully remove the bows, whispering to Molly, "Sorry, Mol." I tuck the bows into my apron pocket. "I'll avoid bows from now on, and I'll pay for the vet bill if you'd like."

"That won't be necessary."

"If you had said something—"

He arches a brow. "I thought *please don't put bows in her hair* was pretty clear."

"I assumed you just hated bows, and you'd get over it," I say a little too defensively.

His lips twitch into a semi-grin. "You know what they say about assuming. I hope you don't make a habit of ignoring your clients' requests."

"I didn't ignore it. I just didn't think you meant it."

He shakes his head. "Thanks for taking them out. We'll see you in a few weeks."

After the door closes behind him, Laura sighs dreamily. "*God*, he's cute."

I watch him through the window as he walks toward a Range Rover. Two women are openly checking him out in the parking lot, but he doesn't even look their way.

Ruby walks in and puts a folder on Laura's desk. "Gawking at Molly's hot daddy?"

"Yes," Laura says.

"*No.* I'm just trying to see what you guys see. I mean, he's tall and fit, and he's handsome for a blond, but he has no swagger." I watch him guide Molly into the SUV. He grabs her big head and plants a kiss on her snout, earning *Aw*s from Ruby and Laura. "Okay, that *was* cute. I'll give you that, but his personality is so far from my checklist, it's in another country."

# Chapter Two

## Fletch

My phone vibrates with a text, and I look up from the paper I'm grading.

**Talia:**

Where are you?

*Shit.* I was supposed to meet her for coffee five minutes ago. Talia Dalton is one of my closest friends, as well as my colleague at Beckwith University, where I teach sociology. She was one of the first people I met there nearly a decade ago, and we clicked right away. Like me, she takes her job seriously and avoids drama, and with the exception of me and her husband, Derek, she has a general lack of trust in the opposite sex.

**Fletch:**

On my way. Sorry.

**Talia:**

My phone rings as I head out of my office, and I put it to my ear. "Sorry, Tal. I was grading papers."

"What are you late for this time?" my younger brother, Jimmy, asks.

"Coffee. How's it going?"

"Better than it is for you. I'm working through my jobs for the wedding." Jimmy is marrying his childhood friend, and girlfriend of the last few years, Beth Peterson, next month. Our older brother, Chuck, and I are sharing the honor of being his best man.

"That doesn't sound fun." I regret it as soon as the words are out of my mouth, because Jimmy is so in love, I know he'll give me an overly enthusiastic lecture about how good it feels to be engaged to the love of his life. I, on the other hand, would rather drink tar than ever get married again, so I cut him off at the pass. "And don't tell me about how great it is to marry Beth. I'm happy for you, but I'm on my way to meet Tal, so what do you need?"

"It *is* great," he says with an audible shit-eating grin.

"*Jim*," I warn.

He laughs. "Did you get your tux?"

"Did I say I would?"

"Yes, but you're also late for meeting Talia for probably the tenth time this month."

"I got it."

"Great. Beth wants to know if you have a plus-one yet."

"Why would she even ask that? She knows I have no interest in dating." My family has been annoying the hell out of me lately, telling me it's been long enough since my divorce and I need to get back out there. My mother has even started texting me pictures of her friends' daughters, asking if I'll accompany them to one event or another. The other day she texted a picture of a barista and said she could pass along my number, like she's some kind of wingwoman.

"Because she loves you, dude. You know your dick will fall off if you don't satisfy it with something other than your hand every now and then."

"Just because I don't date doesn't mean I'm celibate." Though it has been several months since I've entertained a woman.

"I'm only giving you shit. We love you, man. It's not about sex. It's about *connection*. We'd like to see you let a woman into your life as more than a friend. Don't you miss that?"

"No. Why don't you bother Chuck with this nonsense?"

"Because he doesn't give off a get-the-fuck-away-from-me vibe around women, like you do. He goes out with plenty of them. When's the last time you planned a week away with anyone other than your dog?"

"Molly doesn't annoy the shit out of me or bitch about everything I do." Molly and I spend a week at my fishing cabin every August, and I enjoy our annual long weekend away at a dog retreat, where Molly gets to play with her own kind.

"Know what else she doesn't do? Stroke your ego or that other body part you like to ignore."

As I round the corner toward the food court, I see the bane of my existence, my student Cecilia Ulman. *"Fuck."* I turn around, heading back the way I came as fast as I can. I'll take the long way to the food court.

"What's wrong?"

"Stalker." There are always a couple of guys and girls in each class who get student/professor crushes and try to reel me in with excessive eye contact or unnecessary questions before or after class. But Cecilia is disturbingly relentless.

"Come on. She's got a harmless crush. You're used to that."

"This one feels more like a fatal attraction. The other day I found a rose on my windshield with a note about having a drink with her, and before you ask, *yes*, I've told her that I don't get involved with students."

"Take it as a compliment."

"I became a professor to educate and shape young minds, not to get compliments from women who are barely out of high school." I glance over my shoulder and breathe easier when I see she's not behind me. "What else is going on? Are you going to show up Sunday, or are you blowing us off again?" Jimmy lives in our hometown of Sunnyvale, and

Chuck lives in Port Hudson. Both are neighboring towns to Harmony Pointe. They try to make it into town for a basketball game with me and my buddies once or twice a month on the weekends.

"Hey, if your wife came out of the bedroom in lingerie, you can't tell me you wouldn't blow us off just as fast."

"If a woman calling herself my wife came out of my bedroom, getting laid would be the last thing on my mind." I walk into the food court, and spot Talia sitting at our usual table by the windows. I head in that direction. "I've got to go. Try to show up tomorrow if you can."

"Will do. Tell Talia I said hello."

I end the call and pocket my phone as I approach Talia. Her wavy dark hair is tidily pulled back at the base of her neck, her makeup and attire are demure and professional, and her smile reaches her eyes, despite my tardiness.

"Your coffee is probably lukewarm by now." She nods to the coffee she bought me.

"Sorry. I was grading papers and lost track of time." I sit down and motion to a pink-and-gold flyer on the table. "What's that?"

"It's for a company that does marriage-proposal planning. I thought I'd give it to Scott, since he's planning on taking the plunge." Like Talia, Scott is an English lit professor.

I pick up the flyer and quickly scan it.

Get the Yes!

Your personal romance concierge.

Let our love expert create a magical and unforgettable proposal just for you and your forever love.

We'll make your big moment stress-free and beautiful.

We do the prep. You get the yes!

"Are you kidding? Now guys need other people to do their bidding?" I scoff and push the flyer across the table.

"I think it's a great idea. It has to be stressful figuring out just the right proposal."

"No, it's not. Look at how Derek proposed to you. He didn't put on a show, and you were walking on air for weeks." I always thought Talia would fall in love with a great guy one day, but Derek took us all by surprise. He'd been a long-haired bartender and a dancer at a club back then. How he'd convinced Talia, who didn't like bars and blushed at the thought of watching a guy dance onstage, to go out with him was a wonder in and of itself. But here they are, two years later, happily married with a little boy named Evan.

She grins and glances at her rings. "It was the perfect proposal. How did you propose to your ex?"

I grit my teeth, not wanting to think about Elaina, the proposal, or the way our marriage ended. "I don't remember."

"Which means you don't want to talk about it." She holds up her coffee cup. "Here's to leaving the past in the past."

I toast with her and sip my tepid coffee. "How's your day been?"

"Not bad. The end of the semester is always exciting and trying. Nobody really wants to be here, including me. But I do have new pictures of Evan to show you." She shows me several pictures of her adorable dark-haired toddler.

"He gets cuter every week."

"He really does." She sets her phone down. "He's into everything these days, but you'll see for yourself this weekend, when you come to our dinner party."

"I believe I already turned down that invitation." Ever since falling head over heels for Derek and having Evan, Talia has been trying to set me up with women, which is infuriating, since she knows better.

"Yes, but you didn't really mean it. It's not like you have anything better to do."

"Do I have some kind of sign on my forehead that says 'Don't believe me when I speak'? This is the second time in two days this has happened. That know-it-all dog groomer said the same thing to me about putting bows on Molly, and I was *perfectly* clear when I asked her not to. You know me. I'm always clear, and she has the nerve to argue with me about something every damn time I pick up Molly. As if she knows me at all. It's fucking irritating, and she talks with a Southern drawl. I thought Southern women were supposed to be sweet and passive."

"That's a gross generalization, but she sure gets a rise out of you. Maybe I should invite her to the get-together."

I give her a deadpan look. "She wears socks with paw prints on them."

"You noticed her socks? *Interesting*."

*Yes, I noticed her damn socks.* I also noticed the dimple in her left cheek when she smiles and the way her mouth looks too wide for her face. I've never tried to notice those things any more than I've tried to notice the way she looks at Molly with genuine affection—and at me with contempt. Or at least dislike. I have noticed way more than I want to, and her feisty attitude has been invading my thoughts for far too long.

"You're getting as bad as my family." I eye Talia as I take a drink. "I liked you a lot more before you fell in love."

"Because I was as cynical as you are?"

"Exactly."

# Chapter Three

## DESTINY

I fell asleep on the couch Friday night, and much to my lazy cat Clementine's dismay, I was up at the crack of dawn Saturday morning, stressing over every detail for my first official proposal event. I took Ruby's advice and wore a floral halter dress with cute strappy sandals and spent extra time on my hair and makeup. I arrived two hours early to get everything set up so Ha-Joon, the middle-aged, serious-but-friendly photographer, could take pre-event pictures. My client looks like the epitome of a bride-to-be in a white sundress, her loose and lovely blond hair falling to the middle of her back. Her boyfriend is meeting her in twenty minutes, and Ha-Joon is moving stealthily around us, capturing her first look at the elaborate and romantic setting for her proposal.

Her eyes dance with excitement as she takes in the white silk I've draped over the branches of the stately oak tree, the picnic blanket with red rose petals scattered around it, and the antique wooden boxes, which I lined with white fabric that has red hearts on it. I filled one box with grapes and baguettes and the other with flowers and mason jars full of strawberries and blueberries. The charcuterie board is tastefully done, and the pastries are displayed on a mint-green pedestal cake stand beneath a clear glass dome. A bottle of champagne and two fancy glass bottles of water on which I've written their names in silver sparkling ink are chilling in a silver ice bucket. An open wicker basket with wildflowers tucked into the corners holds the champagne flutes, plates, silverware, and fabric napkins. I added a romantic, old-fashioned lantern for effect and tucked a few pink flowers around the base.

"This is so much more than I could have hoped for," she exclaims.

"I'm glad you're happy with it. I had a lot of fun putting it together."

"I *love* all the little touches. The wooden boxes, the wicker basket, the chalkboard. I feel like I walked into an Instagram photo shoot."

"You did," I say with an easy laugh, as Ha-Joon captures our smiles. "The pictures are going to be gorgeous." Which I'm thankful for since I'll be using them to promote my business.

She peers into the glass dome at the pastries. "You even got the treats Ryan loves from that bakery in Sweetwater. You listened to *everything* I said."

Molly's dad's voice tramples through my mind. *I hope you don't make a habit of ignoring your clients' requests.* The snarky voice in my head says, *See? I listen.* I push those thoughts away and focus on my client. "Of course I did. You hired me to give you the perfect, stress-free proposal. I wouldn't be very good at my job if I didn't listen." I glance at the time on my phone. "Ryan should be here any minute. I'm going to be watching from right over there." I point to a wooden bench by the paved path that snakes through the park.

"I'm so nervous." She touches her hair. "Do I look okay?"

"You look beautiful, and you're going to do great. Good luck." I give her a quick hug and head over to the bench, giddy with anticipation.

I take a deep breath as I sit down, thrilled with how things are going so far, and look up at the sky, imagining my father's loving dark eyes watching over me. "This is it, Dad," I say just above a whisper so my client doesn't think I'm nuts. "I'm going to make you and Mama proud."

Movement in my peripheral vision draws my attention, and I see Molly bounding down a hill. Happiness bubbles up inside me at the sight of my favorite four-legged client, and then I see Grumpy Gus a few beats behind her, and my joy deflates. It's strange seeing them outside of work, and it takes a few seconds for me to realize Molly is bounding directly toward the picnic blanket.

I scramble to my feet, running after her and calling out, "*Molly!*" just as my client shrieks and Molly tramples onto the blanket, knocking over the pastries and lantern as she lowers her big mouth over the charcuterie board and snatches up a hunk of cheese. "*Nooo!* Molly, come back!" She bolts back the way she came, and I chase after her.

My client is screaming, Molly's dad is calling Molly's name, and Molly doubles back and barrels into me, knocking me off-balance. Grumpy Gus grabs my arm, and suddenly his eyes lock on my client, and he grits out, "*Shit.* I need your help. Just go with this."

"With *what?*"

"A kiss," he says urgently, eyes pleading.

Shocked, I stammer, "Um . . . *oka*—" My voice is lost to the hard press of his warm lips as he tugs me closer. His arms circle me, holding me tight against his hard body, and *boy* does he feel good. He even smells good. *Spicy.* His tongue glides over the seam of my lips, and I open for him, allowing him to take the kiss deeper. He tastes like coffee and mint, and his tongue sweeps slowly and possessively over mine. Holy cow, the man can *kiss.* Desire prickles hot and enticing inside me, and just as I give myself over to the kiss and my thoughts fall away, Molly's big paws land on my side, jarring me from my blissful state.

I stumble back in horror at what I've just done, but he's still holding me, pulling me closer as my client's angry shouts cut through the air, and Molly runs around us barking.

"What kind of business *is* this?" she fumes. "You're making out with my boyfriend!"

"I . . . *What? This* is Ryan?" My head is still spinning, and I can't make sense of any of this.

"I'm *not* her boyfriend," he seethes through clenched teeth.

"I'm so confused," I mumble, and pull my arm from his grip. "She hired me to put all of this together so she could propose to you."

He looks mildly disgusted. "*You're* the person behind those proposal flyers?"

I lift my chin. "If you mean Get the Yes, then yes, I am."

"Why am I not surprised?" he mutters with blatant irritation.

I huff out a breath. "Didn't your mama ever teach you to be nice?"

"Didn't yours ever teach you to do your homework?" He motions to Cecilia. "She's a student of mine at Beckwith."

"Ryan, don't pretend—"

"Cecilia, *stop*," he demands. "And it's *Professor Fletcher* to you."

"Wait. You're not even dating her?" I ask incredulously, and before he can respond, I turn on Cecilia. "You made all that up? He doesn't buy you red roses every week? He doesn't take you to antique shops on the weekends? Sweetie Pies *isn't* his favorite bakery?"

"Hell *no*," he growls, and the reality of what I've done hits me like a truck.

"That's not true!" Cecilia whines. "I heard you tell Professor Grant Sweetie Pies was your favorite."

"The only reason you overheard that is because you've been stalking me, and it ends *now*. I've told you multiple times that I don't get involved with students. Now I'll let the police and Beckwith administration handle you." He puts his phone to his ear.

Cecilia shoots me a death stare. If looks could kill, I'd be pushing up daisies right now.

"You ruined *everything*," she snarls and stalks off as Ryan tells the police our location, Molly goes paws up against my stomach, and Ha-Joon captures it all for my first-and-worst event memory book.

## FLETCH

I'm trying to focus on the policeman as he explains what I need to do to file a restraining order against my student, which sounds like a big fucking headache to me, but I can't take my eyes off the woman behind this fiasco, Molly's groomer, in that short floral halter dress that makes her look about nineteen years old. I have no idea how old she is, but nobody gets that kind of confidence without a few years of real life behind them. She's making several trips to her car, arms full of decorations, food, and whatever else she has over there, and my dog is trotting along behind her. I've tried calling my fluffy monster, who licks the girl's face every time she crouches to pick something up. Groomer Girl looks frazzled. She keeps dropping things and looking up at the sky, talking to herself. Molly thinks it's a game. She picks up some of what's been dropped and takes off with it. That's the only time Groomer Girl's too-big smile appears, and for some reason it sends my mind straight back to that freaking kiss.

I panicked when I saw Cecilia. I intended to just give Molly's groomer a quick peck to get Cecilia to back off. I don't know what happened. I must have lost my mind. I like tall women with meat on their bones. Soft womanly curves, breasts that more than fill my hands, a nice round ass, and ample hips made for holding on to. This girl is maybe five four and skinny as a bird. But Jesus, that hot, willing mouth of hers drew me right in. I watch her climb into her car and drive away, and thoughts of what else I'd like to do to that mouth taunt me.

*As if I need that headache in my life.*

"So you'll come down to the station?" the policeman asks, jerking me from my thoughts.

I clear my throat in an effort to clear my mind. What the hell is wrong with me? It was one kiss with a woman whose name I don't even know. "Yeah." I motion to Molly sniffing around the big oak tree. "I'll be there after I drop my dog off at home."

With a nod, the policeman walks away.

I silently chastise myself for that kiss. I imagine Groomer Girl telling her friend at the front desk of Perfect Paws about the kiss and realize I have to find a new groomer for Molly. Just one more headache to deal with. I whistle for Molly. "Come on, girl!"

Molly runs toward me with something red in her mouth.

"Whatcha got?" I give her a pet and take the wallet from her mouth. As I pull out a driver's license to see who it belongs to, a second one comes out with it—one local, one from Georgia—and I'm met with those Julia Roberts smiles. Groomer Girl looks like she's smiling for cameras on the red carpet, that alluring dimple in full force.

I look down at Molly. "You couldn't have given this to *her*?" Molly barks and takes off again. What is it with females? Even my dog is defiant.

I glance at the name, address, and issue dates on the licenses and realize with irritation that Groomer Girl lives around the corner from me. "You're a long way from Rosebell, Georgia, Destiny Amor. What happened? Did you get chased out of Georgia for setting up too many stalkers with their victims?"

# Chapter Four

## Destiny

I'm still trying to wrap my head around everything that just happened as I carry the picnic paraphernalia into the house I'm renting a few blocks from Main Street and the park. I bump the door closed with my butt and drop the last of the supplies from my epic failure on the floor by the living room. Between my mess from prepping for the event and my usual casual lifestyle, my place is kind of a disaster.

Clementine jumps off the couch and prances over. His soft tail brushes my leg as he winds around my feet. Sighing, I scoop him up and kiss the scar where his left ear should be. I don't know what happened to it. It was missing when I found him.

"I love you, sweet pea, but now is not a good time. Mama's life dream was just turned upside down."

I set him on the floor and pull my phone out of my dress pocket. I briefly consider calling Ruby, but I don't want to bum her out, so I call the person I've always turned to in times like these, instead. With a heavy heart, I put the phone to my ear. My father's craggy voice takes my anxiety down a notch as I listen to his message. "Hi, Daddy, it's me. I am sorry to report that it was an utter disaster." I pace by the stairs, my pulse quickening with agitation. "The girl lied about *everything*, and the guy she *said* was her boyfriend turned out to be a grooming client, and he was madder than a cat on a hot tin roof." Disappointment swamps me. "I don't know if I'm cut out for this. I want it so bad, but . . . I don't know. I wish you were here. I wish you could send me a sign and let me know if I should cut and run or stick it out."

A knock sounds at my door.

"I really believed this was it for me, you know? I thought I could do it," I say as I head over to answer the door. I pull it open, and my chest constricts at the sight of a stoic-faced Ryan or Fletch or whatever his name is, standing on my front porch with Molly. A dozen thoughts race through my mind at once—*I kissed him! Why is he here? How does he know where I live?*—and I realize I know *nothing* about this man. Embarrassment and worry trample through me. "I gotta go, Daddy. Love you." I end the call, holding Ryan/Fletch's gaze. "How do you know where I live? Are you a stalker, too? Are the police with you?" I lean out the door looking for them as another concern hits me. "Am I going to be arrested as an accomplice to your stalker? Is that a thing? Because I didn't know."

A rough laugh tumbles past his lips, *and* now I'm thinking about those lips and that scorching-hot kiss again.

"It's probably a thing," he says. "But no. You dropped your wallet at the park. I'm just here to return it." He holds up my wallet.

My relief rushes out. "Well, butter my butt and call me a biscuit. For a minute there, I thought I was in trouble. Thank you." I reach for my wallet and feel Clementine's tail on my leg.

Molly lunges for him, yanking the leash from Ryan/Fletch's hand as she sprints after the cat. "Molly!" we shout in unison, and as Ryan runs after her, I slam the door and follow.

Molly chases Clementine across the couches at breakneck speed, trampling over the pillow and blanket I slept with last night, and leaps over the side after the cat, knocking a lamp off an end table. Ryan/Fletch yells for her as Clementine scurries under the coffee table and Molly tries to do the same, knocking the dishes, and everything else that's on the table, to the floor. We both go for her leash, but Clementine bolts upstairs and Molly races after him.

Ryan/Fletch curses as we run for the stairs, landing on the same one, side to side, and get stuck. "*Sorry*," he grumbles at the same time I say it, and we both turn sideways, freeing the other to move forward just as Clementine darts down the hall past the steps and Molly barrels after him. We both hurry up to the next step, getting stuck again, and I laugh, because *come on*. What are the chances? He looks at me with such a serious expression, it makes me laugh even harder.

"It's not funny," he snaps. "She's making a mess of your house."

"Have you seen my house?" I ask through my laughter.

"She's a monster. She could *eat* your cat."

"Molly is *not* a monster. She's a bit of a bull in a china shop, but she's a sweetheart, and Clementine can fend for himself. Maybe *you're* the monster."

"*Yeah*," he says sarcastically.

"Well, you never smile—"

"Shh." He holds up his hand, stopping me from moving.

"*Rude.*"

"Listen," he demands, and looks upstairs.

I listen to the silence. "I don't hear anything."

"Exactly. That can't be good." He waves me on, and this time he waits for me to go first.

When we reach the landing, it's eerily quiet. I know Molly ran to the right, but I glance into the guest room on my left to assess the damage. Grumpy *Monster* Gus peers over my shoulder. The bed has clearly been trampled over, but nothing else is out of place.

Molly barks, and we hurry down the hall to my bedroom. Molly is in the middle of my bed in prime pounce-and-play position. Her chin is on the mattress between her forelegs, and her big furry butt is up in the air, tail wagging. She's staring at Clementine, who's sitting at the head of the bed, staring right back.

"I told you Clementine could fend for himself," I say as I walk into the room. "The only thing he's afraid of is thunder."

"Clementine's a *boy*? Never mind. Did you not notice your cat's ear is missing?" He grabs Molly's leash, and she's so excited to see him, she bursts to her feet on the bed and covers his face in slobbery kisses.

I stifle a laugh. "Molly didn't eat Clemmie's ear. It was missing when I found him. He was a scraggly one-eared stray hiding beneath a truck full of clementines."

"You might want to check to be sure he has all four legs." He looks at Molly. *"Down."*

Molly licks him again, and he shakes his head, glowering at the dog, but there's an undeniable softness to that glower, like the way my dad used to look at me when he was angry at something I did, and it warms my heart.

Maybe Ryan/Fletch isn't such a monster after all.

## FLETCH

*"Down,* Molly." I give her leash a yank, embarrassed that my frigging dog has gotten fur all over Destiny's bed, freaked out her cat, and turned her house upside down. Molly jumps off the bed, heading for Destiny. "No way, troublemaker." I tug her back to me and begin using my free hand to brush her fur off the sheets. Why isn't there a blanket or pillow on her bed? Destiny's cat stares at me like I'm the devil from her perch at the head of the bed, where the pillows should be. "I'm sorry about this. I'll help you clean up. If anything's broken, I'll pay for it."

"It's *fine.* Just leave it." She loves on Molly, leaning closer to my slobbery beast as she speaks to her like they're best friends. "You were just doing what dogs do, weren't you, Mol? And Clementine is no worse for wear."

I go back to swiping at the furry sheets.

"I'm the one who should be apologizing," Destiny says. "I'm mortified about what happened at the park. I had no idea you were the guy we were meeting, much less that you weren't dating Cecilia. There has to be something I can do to make it up to you."

I turn to face her, and my gaze catches on three colorful lace bras and matching panties hanging on a rope strung between hooks on either side of the windows. My mind skips right over the odd rope/hook situation to ways in which she can make it up to me. I grit my teeth, trying to shut those thoughts down. The fact that I'm thinking about this mouthy mayhem of a woman that way proves what I already know.

It's been far too long since I've satisfied those urges.

I lift my chin in the direction of the lingerie. "As much as I like your decorating, mind if we talk downstairs? It's a bit distracting."

She looks over her shoulder, and her eyes bloom wide, as if she is surprised by the lingerie. Her cheeks pink up, and she starts snagging the bras and underwear off the line, her words rushing out. "Yesterday was laundry day. I was drying them in the sun."

"I'm sure your neighbors across the street love that." I head for the hall with Molly, chuckling.

"Can you just forget you saw those?" she pleads, following me downstairs.

"Probably not."

*"Brat."* She swats my shoulder from behind. "I've had enough embarrassment for one day."

"Speaking of embarrassment, how could you not realize Cecilia was talking about me? Didn't you do any due diligence or ask for pictures of her boyfriend?" I ask as we head into the living room, which looks like it was hit by a tornado. I turn to Molly. *"Sit."* She obeys. *"Stay."* My beast grins up at me like she didn't create the mess surrounding us.

"Don't worry. I don't think Clem will come down while you're here."

I arch a brow. "You sure?"

"Would you come down if you just got chased by a new friend who was ten times your size?"

*A new friend?* "Good point." I unhook Molly's leash so she doesn't get caught on anything, and give her a pet. "Lie down." Molly slides down to her belly and rests her big head between her paws.

"To answer your question, even if I *had* seen pictures, it wouldn't have changed anything. It's not like I know who you're dating."

"But if she didn't have any pictures of us together, it might have tipped you off that something was wrong." I pick her laptop up off the floor and set it on the coffee table, hoping it didn't break, and begin picking up the dirty dishes that are now strewn across the floor as Destiny rights a lamp.

"Maybe, but probably not. Cecilia was my first client, and I was so excited, I didn't even realize I hadn't asked for pictures or proof of her relationship until the whole thing blew up."

"Your *first* client? You just started this business?"

"Yup. I know you must think I'm crazy after everything that happened, but I've dreamed of being a proposal planner since I was a little girl." She starts gathering what look like craft supplies and papers that are scattered around the floor. "I was sure I could be the best proposal planner ever to walk this earth. But now . . ." She shrugs and sets what she's picked up on the coffee table.

I tell myself to let it go and get out of there. That it doesn't matter that self-doubt sounds wrong coming from such a confident woman or that her hazel eyes, which have been dancing with delight every other time I've seen her, even when she's argued with me, are shadowed with sadness. But apparently my brain didn't get the memo, because "Why this business? Why marriage proposals?" comes out before I can stop it.

She looks at me as she picks up a few notebooks from the floor, and her eyes warm. "Because I *love* love, and what could be better than helping people get to their happily ever after?"

"So you're an expert on love?" I pick up a blanket to fold and realize it, and the pillows on the couch, match the sheets in her bedroom. I wonder why she slept on the couch. *Lovers' quarrel?*

"I'd like to think I am."

I glance at her left hand. "I don't see a ring. Have you ever been engaged or married?"

"Well, *no*." She moves to the other couch and starts folding another blanket.

This woman has got me all kinds of confused. "Have you ever been in love?"

"*No*," she says softly. "But I've *seen* love and I've *felt* it." Her entire face brightens. "I know what true love looks like, and it's the most beautiful thing you can imagine. We didn't have much when I was growing up, but we had an abundance of love."

"Loving your family and being *in love* are two different things."

"How do you know? Have you ever been in love?"

"Yes, a long time ago. I did the whole engagement-wedding thing, and it didn't end well. I'm never drinking that Kool-Aid again."

"*Never?* That's sad."

"It's really not. It's called preserving my sanity." I put the folded blanket on the couch and pick up the throw pillows from the floor.

"You just haven't met the right partner yet. *I* can't wait to fall in love. Want to know why I think I'm an expert on love? It's because of my parents. They were crazy about each other. You couldn't walk by them without feeling their love emanating around them. It was like another person standing with their arms around them, buffering them from everything else, keeping their love safe. Even the way they met and fell in love was romantic." She barely slows down to take a breath as she snags things off the floor. "My mama had gone through a bad breakup, and on a whim she closed her eyes and jabbed her pencil tip on a map of the world. That's how she ended up on a ten-day trip to Braga, Portugal. She didn't know a soul, and she couldn't speak the language, either, but she wasn't afraid to go alone. She met my dad on her first day there, and he spoke English, which had to be fate. She'd been riding a bike she rented, and it got a flat tire. She walked two miles to his family's auto shop to see if they could fix it. The way they told it, they took one look at each other and felt something absolutely magical." She presses her hands to her chest and looks up at the ceiling, dreamy eyed and sighing.

Her excitement is endearing, making her hard to look away from.

"They spent every day together and fell madly in love. But at the end of those ten days, they couldn't see a way to be together. My mother was all my grandmother had, and they lived together in Georgia, so she went back home to be with her, and my daddy stayed in Portugal. They didn't exchange phone numbers or addresses or anything. My mom told him it would be too painful to hear his voice and know they couldn't be together. But privately, I asked if she'd tried begging him to go with her, and she said, *Smart girls don't beg for love, and true love doesn't require beggin'*. She cried the whole way home. I asked her what that was like, and she said she felt like a falling star. Lost and alone. I couldn't imagine her ever feeling that way, because if you knew her, you'd know how confident and capable she was. She set out on that adventure to Portugal alone and unafraid, but she said when she got home, she couldn't figure out who she was without him. *Ten days* was all it took to forever change her."

Her enthusiasm has me invested, and I need to know what happened next. "If they didn't exchange numbers or addresses, how did they end up together?"

"That's the best part. Two days later, my father showed up at the lake where she'd mentioned she walked her dog. He'd been waiting there for *twelve* hours, afraid if he left, he'd miss his chance to find her. They were married two months later, and you know what? He gave up *everything* to be with her. His parents told him if he left their family and the business that had been in their family for generations to follow a woman he barely knew, they'd never speak to him again. Can you imagine having to choose between your family and the woman you love?"

"No, but I'd never choose a woman over my family." *Never again. Been there, done that.*

"Well, I'm sure glad he did, Mr. Naysayer. My mother followed a whim, my father followed his heart, and they found true love. They always said they were destined to be together, which is why they named me Destiny."

*Destiny Amor with her head in the clouds. It's perfect.*

Her smile falters. "But then my mom died when I was eleven, and my dad and I became the falling stars."

She tears up, and I feel a tug deep in my chest. "I'm sorry to hear that."

"Thank you." She breathes deeply, fanning her face. "*Sorry.* I still think about her every day, but don't worry, I'm *not* gonna cry." She lifts her chin, and a dim version of her smile appears, as if to prove her point. "I learned how to buck up and be strong right quick after that, because I knew two falling stars could crash and burn. I had to be there to push my daddy back up when he got too low, and of course he tried to do the same for me."

She wears her heart on her sleeve, and I've had mine locked down for so long, I don't even know what to do with it. "That would be difficult at any age, but I can't imagine what it was like for you at eleven."

"It wasn't easy. I did a lot of lying to myself, telling myself I was fine. But my best friend, Ruby—the woman who owns Perfect Paws—was there for me, and remember that thing I said about growing up with an abundance of love? My family was everything to me. They still are, and their love pulls me through the toughest times. I used to get real sad when it would rain because my mama and I used to dance in the rain, and I just couldn't do it after she was gone. But a few months after she died, it was rainin' real hard, and I swear I heard her calling me from outside. I went out there and I felt her *all* around me. I will never stop dancing in the rain, because I still feel her in every drop."

She's endured so much grief, my throat thickens at the weight of it.

"I believe my mama was smiling down on my daddy and me back then. Nourishing us with her love from the heavens above. I know I did her proud by taking care of my father and staying in Rosebell after high school."

"That was a thoughtful thing to do. I probably would have made a similar choice. Did you go to community college?"

She shakes her head and sinks down to the couch. "No. My mother didn't have life insurance or anything, and my father didn't have a lot of money, so I followed in my mama's footsteps and became a hairdresser. I enjoyed it, and all that really mattered was that I was close to my dad. He and I were like this." She crosses her fingers. "I could always count on him to listen to me and give me advice and just to be there, you know? He always knew how to make me feel special and pick me up when I was down or sick. For as long as I can remember, whenever something big happened, he'd bring me pink carnations. They're my favorite flowers, and when I was sick, he'd read me my mom's favorite book."

"What book is that?"

"*The Guernsey Literary and Potato Peel Pie Society.* It's a weird title, and a big story for a little girl, but it was a good one, and it always made me feel better because I remembered my mom smiling *and* crying when she read it. But my father died of a heart attack last year." Her eyes tear up again, her Southern drawl thickening as her emotions take over, turning that tug in my chest to a full-on fissure. "It was completely unexpected. He seemed strong as an ox, and suddenly I was a fallin' star again. Only those lies I told myself didn't come as easily, and I didn't buck up quite as well as I did after I lost my mama." Tears spill down her cheeks, but she's still trying to smile.

I could have sworn I heard her tell her father she loved him on the phone when she answered the door, but I must have misheard. I can't fathom how someone who has suffered so much loss, and in her father's case, so recently, could push through life with such a positive attitude. "Jesus, Destiny, I'm sorry. Do you have other family?"

She shakes her head. "I never met my father's family, so it's just me and, of course, Ruby. She moved here after college but was still there for me. She came back to Georgia and stayed for two weeks, helped me get through the funeral. But I'm not going to lie. I had so much sadness inside me, it felt like it was seeping out my pores and I was leaving a trail of it everywhere I went." She swipes at her tears and looks up at the ceiling. "*Ugh*. Listen to me goin' on about myself." She breathes deeply and wipes her eyes before meeting my gaze. "First you see my lingerie, and now I'm blubberin' about my dead daddy. It's a wonder you're not running out that door."

"Actually, *first* you tried to marry me off to a stalker."

She covers her face. "I can't believe I did that. I'm going to make it up to you. I'll walk Molly every day for a month."

I shake my head, glancing at my beast sleeping by the stairs. "You don't need to do that."

"Yes, I do. It's only proper that I make amends. I love Molly, and she could probably use the exercise while you're teaching. How did we get on the subject of my family anyway?"

"I asked why you got into the proposal business. I'm curious about how you ended up here. Did you move to be closer to Ruby?"

"Yes. The memories in Rosebell were too painful. When I sold my father's auto repair shop, I moved here and started working with Ruby. I don't really need the money, because after my mama died, my daddy bought life insurance, and his business sold for a pretty penny, but I'd go stir crazy sitting around the house all day."

"Didn't you say you were a hairdresser? Did you have any pet grooming experience?"

"No, but it's not so different from making people beautiful," she says cheerily. "Ruby taught me to groom the animals, and I don't work full time. My schedule is flexible, and working part time gave me a chance to settle in and get my website and flyers ready and start collecting supplies for Get the Yes." She motions to the stacks of decorations and other paraphernalia around the room and in the foyer. "Last week

I put out flyers and made my website live." She wrinkles her nose. "And you know the rest."

*I mistakenly thought I did.* "Do you have any experience running a business?"

"No. I just figured I'd learn what I didn't know along the way. But don't worry. I learned my lesson. I'm out a lot of money, and now I know my business is a pipe dream that I should probably let go."

"You're giving up?"

She shrugs one shoulder. "I don't want to. Proposal planning is all I've dreamed about for as long as I can remember, but look at the mess I've already made."

"Can't you ask anyone for help? Or take a few classes on business management?"

"You don't want to know how poorly I did in school. I'm a smart girl, but I can't learn that way. Ruby would help if I let her, but she and her husband are trying to get pregnant, and she likes things done her way. It's best if I just let it go."

*Shit.* The last thing I need is a complication like this whirlwind of a woman in my life, but I'm not an asshole. I can't just walk away and let her give up on her dreams. Especially when teaching is what I do. "I'll help you."

She cocks her head with curiosity. "What do you mean?"

"I'll help you get started and make sure you don't get yourself into any more trouble. I double majored in business and sociology, and I've helped a few friends get their businesses off the ground."

"But you don't even believe in love, and it's a marriage-proposal business."

"I don't need to believe in love to make sure you're crossing your t's and dotting your i's. Even if it's with little hearts."

"How did you know I do that? Have you been spying on me?"

I laugh. "With a name like Destiny Amor, anything else wouldn't be right."

"That's going to be my excuse from now on," she exclaims. "If you were to help me, how much would you charge?"

"I don't want your money."

"Ryan-Fletch, are you insinuating that you want to be paid with sexual favors? Because I'm *not* that kind of girl."

"My name is Ryan Fletch*er*, and I wasn't insinuating anything. I'm definitely *not* looking for sexual favors. Please don't take offense to this, but I'm not interested in you in that way."

"*Whew.*" She sits back, exhaling with relief. "Thank goodness, because nothing about you matches my checklist."

"Your checklist?"

"That's right. You know, the list of things I'm looking for in a guy. But you've got nothing to worry about. I'm not attracted to you *at all.* You're more grumpy Ken doll than can-do G.I. Joe."

*Ouch.* "I'm glad you cleared that up."

"Of course. I wouldn't want any misunderstandings. What should I call you, by the way? I've been calling you Grumpy Gus, but you probably prefer Ryan, or Fletch, like Ruby calls you."

*Grumpy Gus? What the hell?* "Most of my friends call me Fletch."

"Does that mean we're *friends?*" She looks like she just received a sought-after invitation, and she doesn't wait for an answer. "I don't have a lot of friends here yet. *Fletch.* I like that, and I'd truly appreciate your help. I'll walk Molly as often as you'd like to make up for everything that happened today, and please don't tell me no, because I don't take handouts."

I'm about to turn down her offer of walking Molly when another idea comes to mind. "You don't need to pay me back, but if you're dead set on it, I've got a better idea. My family has been all over me about finding a girlfriend, and I'd really like to get them off my back. My brother is getting married at the end of June. Come to the wedding with me and pretend to be my date. That should be enough to shut them up for a while. Unless it's too big of an imposition."

Excitement shimmers in her eyes. "Are you kidding? I *love* weddings. That's what? Six or seven weeks away? That gives us plenty of time to get to know each other. You'll have to let me know when the wedding is so I don't make other plans, and what you're wearing so I can match, and—"

I hold up my hand, silencing her. "We've got time to figure that out. Let's focus on getting your business up and running."

"Okay, but even though I'm going to the wedding, I'm still walking Molly for you. She's my favorite four-legged client, and it looks like she and Clementine have become friends after all." She motions to Molly, sleeping with the cat curled up beneath her chin.

I shake my head. "I will never understand females."

She giggles. "We're not that complicated. But since you're helping me, I'll help you understand women better."

I push to my feet. "No thanks."

"Why not? Because you don't believe in love?"

"Because I'm not looking for a woman, so I don't need to understand them."

She crosses her arms, studying me. "*That's* your real problem, and I'm going to fix it."

"*No*, you're not."

"Yes, I am. I'll help you understand women, and then you'll want a relationship and be open to finding love, and I'll plan your proposal! You can thank me later. Or not. I'm not expecting a thank-you. I don't need one at all. Helping people get to their happily ever after is what I do."

I narrow my eyes in warning. "Not with me it's not."

"We'll see," she says smugly and far too cheerily.

"Don't get your hopes up, sunshine. How about we get started tomorrow? Unless you have other plans."

"I don't. That sounds great."

"I'm playing basketball with some buddies in the park, but I can meet you for coffee at La Love afterward if you're free around one."

"Perfect! I'll be there."

"Okay. Bring your business plan and any other relevant materials."

She wrinkles her nose. "Business plan?"

"You don't have a business plan? An outline of goals and how you're going to get there?"

"I do, but it's not written down. It's super simple. I let people know about my business, and I plan to succeed."

*What have I gotten myself into?*

# Chapter Five

## FLETCH

The sun beats down on my shoulders as I dribble the basketball Sunday afternoon, keeping my back to my older brother, Chuck. Jimmy also showed up, and he's on Chuck's team. I'm partnered with my buddy Marshall Dutch. Marshall grew up in this area, and I met him a few years ago, shortly after he'd moved back, when we were both out for a morning run.

"Should I pick out my tux for your wedding?" Chuck teases.

I made the mistake of telling them about how my stalker took things up a notch yesterday, and they've had far too much fun teasing me about it.

"Maybe you and Jimmy can have a double wedding," Chuck adds. "Right, Jim?"

"Shut the fuck up," I snap.

"Fine," Chuck says. "Did I tell you about the date I went on last night?"

"Only seventeen times." I fake left, then dribble down the court to the right and toss the ball to Marshall, who is standing by the basket.

Jimmy hollers as Marshall jumps up to catch the ball, but Marshall doesn't miss a beat and shoots before his feet even hit the ground. The ball circles the rim, and we all hold our breath until it drops into the basket.

"Yes! Nice shot, dude." I high-five Marshall.

Marshall has an edge to him. He's bearded and tatted from neck to fingers and ankles. He's lived a rougher life than the rest of us. His late wife, Annie, gave birth to a stillborn little girl. Soon after, Annie died by suicide, and he fell down a drug-and-alcohol-induced rabbit hole. He's been clean for several years, and a few years ago he founded Annie's Hope, an emotional wellness center, to honor his late wife.

"That's how it's done," Marshall says cockily. "Even with these idiots trying to distract us."

"Hey, I'm bragging, not distracting," Chuck says with a laugh, and rakes a hand through his thick brown hair. He and Jimmy inherited our mother's dark hair and brown eyes, while I take after our father.

"As a small-town attorney, isn't there some kind of moral code about discretion?" Marshall asks.

Chuck smirks. "I'm talking to you, not my clients, and I never tell you *who* I've been with. For all you know, it could be your sister."

Marshall glares at him.

"Marsh, you and Fletch need some game with the ladies. You could take some pointers from my students," Jimmy says, and passes the ball to Chuck.

I intercept it, dribbling toward the basket with Chuck on my heels. "You teach phys ed to elementary school kids. What're we going to learn? How to pass notes?" I go for the shot, and Chuck knocks the ball out of my hands. "Ass," I say as Jimmy snags it and dribbles toward the basket, but Marshall is all over him.

"Seriously, though," Jimmy says, trying to get around Marshall. "The other day the fifth graders were playing volleyball. This one kid has got a big-time crush on a girl in his class. She was afraid of being hit by the ball, so he kept diving in front of her and batting the ball away from her. The little dude earned my respect."

"The kid's got a lot to learn," Chuck says. "Good dates end with the girl's hand on the ball, not your own."

Jimmy laughs and takes the shot, but Marshall jumps up just before it reaches the net, knocking it across the court. Chuck and I sprint for it, and just as I get my hands on it, Chuck knocks into me, and the ball flies off the court.

"Come on, man," I grit out. "That was a dick move."

"It was an accident," Chuck claims, and we all give him shit, grabbing our water bottles as he retrieves the ball.

A little while—and several points—later, I'm dribbling down the court. The score is tied, and my brothers are being their mouthy selves. Jimmy hollers as I take a shot. We all watch the ball arc through the air. *Go in, go in, go in.* It swishes through the net. Marshall and I cheer and gloat as Jimmy and Chuck bitch and moan, and a cheery feminine voice with a Southern drawl cuts through the air.

"Woo-hoo! Nice shot, Fletch!"

*What the . . . ?* I turn around and see Destiny, wearing pink overall shorts, a white T-shirt, and sneakers, which makes her look awfully young again, and insanely cute. She's carrying an enormous yellow tote bag over her shoulder. Her hair is loose and a little messy, and she's grinning from ear to ear. Those enticingly plump lips send my mind sprinting back to that damn kiss.

She waves. "Hey, Fletch. Hi, y'all."

She's ridiculously happy, but knowing all that she's been through gives me a new appreciation for that cheeriness.

The guys say, "Hi," in unison, looking at me curiously.

"Is that your stage-five clinger?" Chuck asks quietly as she saunters over.

"No. She's the proposal planner . . . and Molly's groomer."

"The bow girl?" Jimmy asks.

"Damn, man," Chuck says. "Set me up."

I feel a niggle of jealousy, and it pisses me off. I glower at him.

"I didn't know you meant you were playing at this park," Destiny says sweetly. "I got to the coffee shop early and thought I'd take a walk before we met up. Imagine my surprise when I saw y'all playing." She sets those expressive hazel eyes on me. "Look at you all buff and jock-ish." She looked at the others. "You boys are *good*." Her gaze lingers on Marshall.

I watch her admiring his tattoos, and her Ken doll / G.I. Joe comment suddenly becomes crystal clear. That niggle of jealousy turns into a spear, and I grit my teeth against it.

"This is the only park in town," Marshall points out.

Her brow furrows. "Really? That's a darn shame. Parks are so pretty. I think towns should have loads of them." She holds out her hand. "I'm Destiny, by the way."

Marshall's jaw tightens. "Did you say Destiny?"

"Sure did. Why? Do I look like someone you know? Everyone says I look like someone they know."

"No. It was my daughter's name," Marshall says.

*Damn it.* I'm about to cut in, when Destiny touches Marshall's arm and says, "Was?"

"She's no longer with us."

Sadness washes over her features. "I am so sorry for your loss. I lost my daddy last year, and I know how cripplin' grief can be. But I'm sure your little angel is smiling down on you."

I notice her drawl thickening, and I have the urge to put my hand on her back and say something to ease that pain. The impulse takes me by surprise, and I try to squash it.

"Thank you. I hope she is." Marshall's voice is thick with emotion.

To give Marshall a minute, I step in. "Destiny, this is my older brother, Chuck, and my younger brother, Jimmy."

"Brothers? Isn't this fun? Which one of you is getting married? I cannot wait to go to the wedding."

*Fuck. I guess we're doing this now.*

The shock on my brothers' faces is inescapable, but their smirks quickly push it away, and I know they're about to give me shit.

"You're coming to my wedding?" Jimmy asks.

"*And* you have a coffee date with Ryry that he failed to mention?" Chuck asks.

His use of my childhood nickname grates on my nerves. "Yes, she's coming to the wedding, and don't make a big thing out of it. Jimmy, please let Beth know Destiny will be my plus-one."

"Is she coming to the rehearsal dinner, too?" Jimmy asks in a way that tells me the answer will signify something bigger than just a plus-one. "Mom will need to know for a head count."

I'm about to shut that shit down, when Destiny gives me an I've-got-your-back glance and says, "Of course I'm going to the rehearsal dinner. I wouldn't miss it! So y'all back off from trying to set him up with your lady friends. I'm sure it seems fast to you boys, but I've been Molly's groomer for three months, and I've had my eye on this handsome guy the whole time." She puts her hand on his shoulder. "Even though we didn't know each other very well until . . . Well, that doesn't matter. When you've found *the one*, you know it. Right, Jimmy?"

*Fuck.* She is laying it on too thick, but my brothers are eating it up. If I'm going to pull this off and get them off my back, I need to keep my mouth shut.

"Yeah, one hundred percent." Jimmy looks at me, baffled.

"You've been holding out on us, huh, bro?" Marshall asks. He looks skeptical. Smart man.

"Hush, Marshall, or he'll get all up in his head again the way he does and scare himself into runnin' away from this magical thing between us. We don't want that now, do we?"

Chuck elbows me. "Dude, she's got your number."

"On that *note*, we're out of here. I'll catch up with you guys later." I toss my empty water bottle in the trash can, put on my shirt, and take Destiny by the arm, leading her away from them.

"Wait! I still have questions," Jimmy calls after us.

I flip him the bird.

"Was that too much too soon?" Destiny asks, walking fast to try to keep up.

"You could say that."

# Chapter Six

## FLETCH

Destiny grabs a table near the back of La Love Café while I order coffee for me and sweet tea for her. As I carry our drinks to the table, I watch her tuck a pen behind her ear and withdraw a few colorful notebooks from that big yellow tote bag, stacking them on the table.

"Here you go." I set her tea on the table and sit across from her.

"Thank you." She takes a drink. "*Mm. So* good." She licks her lips, and the slide of her tongue stirs thoughts I have no business thinking about her. "I'm sorry for taking it too far with your brothers. I was just trying to do you proud."

"It's okay. You sold it well."

She sits up taller. "Thank you. They're really nice, and handsome."

That pang of jealousy returns, and I hate myself for what comes out of my mouth next. "You seemed pretty interested in Marshall."

"He's a little tall for me, but he definitely checks a few of my boxes."

She has a height requirement?

"He's rough around the edges, and I'm not gonna lie. I find all that ink intriguing, and I bet a man like that is good with his hands—"

"Please *don't* go there."

"Why?" She tilts her head, perplexed. "You got something against a man who can fix an engine or build a shelf?"

Now I feel like an ass. "No, I thought you were talking about . . . I misunderstood. Never mind." I take a drink of coffee.

"You thought . . . *Oh.*" She giggles. "Why would I talk about that with *you?*"

"I was wondering the same thing."

"It is sad, though, about his baby. Is he married?"

"He was. His wife died by suicide several years ago. He runs Annie's Hope. It's named after her."

She covers her heart with her hand, sadness rising in her eyes. "It's a wonder how that man's still standin'."

Not wanting to get lost in that tragic topic, I say, "Let's get started. Are these your notes?" I reach for the stack of colorful notebooks, wondering why she didn't pull out her laptop.

"Yes, they are. I know you probably think I'm disorganized after yesterday, but I think you'll be impressed. Everything in them is color coded."

I sift through the notebooks. The one on top is red with CLIENTS written across the front in loopy cursive. Inside, written in red ink, are the headers NAME, DATE, SOURCE, PHONE NUMBER, AND OUTCOME (BOOKED / NO GO). Beneath the headers, Cecilia's information is written in black, with *Flyer* listed under SOURCE, and ~~*Booked*~~ under OUTCOME. Scribbled in red in the margin is *Crazy stalker! Get proof of partner!*

I glance at Destiny.

"That wasn't my finest moment." She sips her tea.

I look at the other notebooks. A blue one is labeled EXPENSES, an orange one is labeled MEETINGS, and a pink notebook is labeled MR. RIGHT CHECKLIST in gold sparkly ink. "Well, well, sunshine, what do we have here?" It appears the coveted list really does exist.

"Those are my questions for clients," she says as I open the notebook and scan the first few items on the list.

1. *Not too tall (big men, big egos!)*
2. *Has moves like Jagger*
3. *Neat feet*
4. *Rough around the edges*
5. *Can fix anything*
6. *Dark hair and eyes like milk chocolate*
7. *Puts love above all else*
8. *Isn't afraid to talk about his feelings*

I turn the page, and I'm shocked to see several more criteria listed. I lift my gaze from the notebook. "How exactly do you ask your clients if they have moves like Jagger, and what the hell are neat feet?"

Her eyes widen, and I see understanding of her mistake taking hold. She gasps and lunges across the table to grab the notebook, but I hold it out of reach, laughing.

She's red faced, eyes shooting daggers. "Ryan Fletcher, you give me that notebook right now, or I'll . . . *I'll* . . ."

"Try to get me to marry a stalker?" I tease, because her feistiness is entertaining.

"No, but I'll do something you won't like!" She struts over and snatches the notebook from my hand, immediately shoving it into her yellow bag. "I can't believe I made that mistake. I guess it is possible to love pink too much. I should've chosen a different color notebook for my business."

"I didn't think you really had a checklist."

She gives me a deadpan look. "Everyone has one, whether they write it down or not."

"Not like that. You must have sixty things listed. How is any man supposed to live up to all that?"

"I know a man won't meet *all* my criteria, but I believe my soulmate is out there, and he'll meet most of them."

"With a list like that, how do you even date? Do you prescreen your guys? Send them a questionnaire? Interview their friends and family?"

"*No.* Do you prescreen the women you go out with?"

I shake my head and turn it back on her. "Tell me something. If you go on a good date, do you come home and doodle your first name with the guy's last name to see how they look together?"

She lifts her chin. "Maybe I do, with stars in my eyes and hope in my heart. Mark my words, *Ryry*, I'll find my Mr. Right, and when I do, you'll be begging me to help you turn all that negative love energy around, so you can find your match, too."

"I've seen your matching skills. They cost me an hour in a police station and made me bother school administrators on a Saturday."

"*I* didn't match you guys. Wackadoodle did."

I can't decide if she's as flighty as the wind or a determined dreamer, but one thing is for sure. There's something enticing about this spunky little Georgia peach, and I have a feeling I've only scratched the surface.

## DESTINY

"Are you going to help me or just tease me all afternoon?"

A slow grin lifts his cheeks. "I'm kind of enjoying teasing you."

I try to give him a serious look, but I'm too amused by this lighter version of him to pull it off. "You might want to be careful. Paybacks could come at awkward times, like rehearsal dinners or weddings."

"A'right. Let's get down to business. Should we start with your man checklist? Because I could show you which items are unreasonable and knock fifty or so off of it."

I'm not happy that he saw my checklist, but it's hard to be mad at a guy who looks hella hot in basketball shorts and a tank top. His muscular thighs are one thing, but I never would have guessed he had sculpted abs under his dress shirts or that he was capable of sharing a warmer smile like the one that's coming out to play right now. "My checklist is none of your business."

"You're right. I don't want any part of that." He takes a drink of his coffee. "I checked out your website last night. It's well done. Inviting and uplifting."

"I'm glad you think so. I hired a friend back home to put it together for me, but I chose all the colors and pictures."

"You did a good job, but I noticed your contact form only asks for a name, email address, and phone number. It might be helpful to ask for specifics, like the location and date for their anticipated proposal, so you can see if they're nearby and can check your calendar before you reach out."

"I don't care if I have to drive two hours to meet them. It's not like I have people beating down my door right now."

"But one day you hope to. You've got big dreams, sunshine. The best way to achieve them is to never doubt it'll happen and pave the path in a way that nothing will slow you down."

I was pretty sure he only offered to help me out of pity because I blubbered about losing my parents, but it doesn't feel like that now. The way he calls me sunshine feels so natural, it's like he really sees *me*, not just my screwup, and genuinely wants to help me. It's been a long time since anyone other than Ruby worried about what I wanted. "I never doubted myself until Cecilia showed me the errors of my ways."

"We'll chalk that up to a learning experience and make sure it never happens again."

"I still can't believe you don't hate me for it."

"I'm a *naysayer*, not a jackass. I have to ask you something before we get down to business. Why are you using notebooks instead of your laptop or an iPad?"

"They're easier for me. I'm not very computer savvy. I used them in high school, but as a hairstylist, I never had use for one beyond the apps for showing clients how different hairstyles might look, and a few other things. I haven't looked at an office program in, *gosh*, nine years." That number hits me hard. "Wow, I can't believe I've been out of high school that long. My mama would say I'm getting long in the tooth."

He chuckled. "If that were true, it'd make me ancient."

"Maybe you are. How old are you?"

"Several years older than you."

"Come on, Ryry. You know my life story."

His brows slant. "I'm going to kill my brothers."

"And I'm going to figure out how old you are." I study him, taking in the tic in his jaw and his narrowing eyes. He clearly doesn't like to be scrutinized. Is that why he seems weirdly oblivious to the women who check him out? I've noticed a few eyeing him since we arrived, but his attention hasn't left me for a minute. I wonder if attention makes him uncomfortable. But he's a teacher, so it can't be that. He said he'd been married and divorced. Did that sour him toward women? Those thoughts won't help me figure out how old he is. "You don't have crow's-feet, so you're probably younger than forty."

*"Forty?"*

"I said *younger than* forty. I'm still figuring you out. You've got wise eyes, but they're way too guarded for you to be younger than thirty. My guess is that you're thirty-five or thirty-six."

"You're better at guessing than at due diligence. Can we focus now, please?"

"I got it right? Go me!" I wiggle my shoulders.

He doesn't even crack a smile. "Back to business. If you're going to succeed, you can't be bringing the wrong notebooks into client meetings or losing them and not having backups. I'll bring you up to speed on documents and spreadsheets and whatever else you need, and we'll organize them with shortcuts so each one is always at your fingertips."

"That would be amazing. I like the idea of keeping records on my laptop, but having a screen between me and a client would feel impersonal. I promise to triple-check my notebooks before each meeting and record all my notes on my laptop, but I think I'll stick to my notebooks for in-person meetings."

"Okay." He pulls out his phone and starts thumbing something out on it. "I'm going to keep a list of what we need to accomplish, and then we'll prioritize and work our way through it." Those light blue eyes find mine. "I assume you have liability insurance."

I wince.

"Are you kidding?" he asks incredulously.

I press my lips together and look around us, up at the ceiling, down at the floor. Anywhere to avoid the look of disbelief in his eyes.

"Destiny, this is serious. Protecting yourself has to be your number one priority, so you don't lose everything you own. If I were anyone else, you could have gotten sued over what happened yesterday. I've got a buddy who sells insurance. I'll hook you up." He thumbs out another note on his phone.

I pull another notebook out of my bag and write *Get insurance!* in it.

He glances at the three notebooks in front of him. "What's wrong with the other notebooks?"

"This one is for our meeting." I show him the front of it, on which I've written *Suggestions from Grumpy Gus*.

The muscles in his jaw twitch again.

Over the next hour, Fletch asks me dozens of questions, and he's all business. He really knows his stuff, and he's incredibly patient as I take detailed notes. I'm starting to see where Ruby was coming from about Fletch being more guarded than grumpy. He definitely has some hang-ups, but he's kind of cute when he takes charge. No wonder his student fell for him. I wonder if he's take-charge in the bedroom, too. That toe-curling kiss comes back to me in delicious detail. If he can make me weak-kneed with an unexpected kiss, I can only imagine what he could do to me if he's intent on pleasure. My mind tiptoes in that direction, and I picture him shirtless, as he was on the basketball court, all those hard muscles and lickable abs on display. I imagine taking off his shorts—

*Nonono. We are not having naked thoughts!*

I try hard to push those naughty thoughts away, but the image of him wearing only those shorts lingers.

"*Destiny*," he says sharply.

"Huh? What? Sorry. I was . . ." *Thinking of you almost naked.* "Thinking about what you said about prospective clients."

"Which thing?"

*Shoot.* "It doesn't matter. I figured it out. Go ahead. Carry on. I'm listening."

"I was just saying that you need rock-solid proof of relationships before you sign any contracts."

I scribble *Get a contract!* in my notebook, thankful for the distraction.

He glances at my note with concern. "You don't have a contract?"

"Not really. It's more of a handshake deal."

"Remember what I said about protecting yourself? Did you set up a business entity? An LLC?"

"I didn't think I needed to."

He curses and messes with his phone again. "What's your phone number?"

I rattle it off. "Why?"

"I'm texting you the number of the insurance guy I mentioned earlier and my brother Chuck's number. He's a lawyer. He specializes in corporate law. I'll give him a call when we're done and set you up with him."

I can't help teasing him. "Wow, you're setting me up with your brother? He's hot, and he seemed fun. Definitely more G.I. Joe than Kenny boy."

His jaw clenches. "Settle down, sunshine. He's not your type."

"You only say that because no one is your type."

"That doesn't even make sense."

"You know it's true." I lower my voice. "Several women have checked you out in here, and you won't even look at them. Nobody is that oblivious."

"What? Who's checking me out?" He looks around. "You're making shit up."

"Oh yeah? Then what's your type? Model perfect? All legs and boobs and flirty as the day is long?"

He grumbles something under his breath.

"What was your ex like? I bet she was beautiful."

"I'm not having this conversation."

"How am I going to find your match if I don't know your type?"

"You're not a matchmaker."

"But I could be, and besides, I need to know those types of things if I'm going to fool your family into thinking we're really a couple. You need to loosen up for this conversation, and I know just how to make that happen. This calls for something sweet." I push to my feet. "I'm going to get a cookie. What would you like?"

He shakes his head. "Nothing."

"You can either tell me what you'd like or leave it up to me to surprise you."

"There you go again, not listening to what I say."

"I listened, but I don't believe you. Everyone loves sweets. I bet you're a scone guy, all hard around the edges, no mushy inside. I'm on it." I can feel his eyes burning a hole in my back as I head up to the counter.

"Hi, Destiny," Heaven, a curvy brunette, says. "I was going to pop over to your table as soon as I got a break. I've got something for you. A guy was in here asking questions about your flyer earlier. He seemed really interested but kind of shy, so I got his number and said I'd pass it on to you." She reaches below the counter and hands me a piece of paper.

"Really?" I look at the paper, which has the name Arjun Patel and a phone number written on it. "*Ar-June?* Did I pronounce that right?"

"Close. It's Ar-jun, and he's super nice."

"Thank you so much! This is awesome. You're the *best*."

"Girl, you know I'm talking you up every chance I get. Maybe karma will come back to me and you'll be planning a proposal for me one day." She leans across the counter with a mischievous spark in her eyes and lowers her voice. "*So*, you and Fletch, huh?"

"Oh gosh, no. He's just helping me get my business organized."

"Mm-hm. *Right.* I see that smile." She winks and whispers, "I'll keep it on the down-low."

"What?" I laugh. "No down-low. I'm just excited about a potential client. Fletch and I are really just friends. Well, kind of friends. Maybe more associates? It's a long story, but I made his life hell yesterday, and he's making sure I never make that mistake again."

"Whatever you say, but just so you know, half the women in this town would love to be sitting at a table with him right now. Not that he gives any of them the time of day, which only makes him mysterious and even more attractive."

I glance over my shoulder at Fletch talking on his phone. *Nope. No butterflies.* But his pinched brows and far-too-serious face do make me smile. I turn back to Heaven. "You see mysterious. I see a tough nut to crack. Do you by chance know what his favorite treat is?"

"I sure do. He goes mad for the lady locks."

"Isn't that ironic? What's a lady lock?"

"You've never had one? They're one of my favorite cookies. They're shaped like cannoli, but the outside is made of a light, flaky pastry, and they're filled with sweet cream."

Boy was I off base about him with a scone. "Great. I'll take two, please."

While she gets the cookies, I look at Arjun's number and feel a rush of excitement. After paying, I bring our treats to the table and set one plate in front of Fletch. "You were holding out on me. You do have a type. It's flaky on the outside, sweet and mushy on the inside."

He looks perplexed. "How does my favorite cookie translate into what I want in a woman? If I wanted that, wouldn't I be with someone like you?"

"Are you calling me flaky? Well, maybe I am a little flaky, but guess who has a potential new client!" I wave the paper and do a little happy dance.

"Where'd you get a new client?"

"Heaven hooked me up!" I do another happy dance.

"Then you'd better get your dancing butt into that chair so we can nail down these interview questions."

"Now? You sure you have time? I don't want to take up your whole Sunday."

"It's either this or I'll worry you'll get your notebooks mixed up and ask him about his feet."

I laugh.

"Seriously, though. I don't mind helping. My only plans are to take Molly for a walk later."

"Thank you!" I lean down and hug him. "I'll walk Molly, just like I said, every day for a month. *Two* months. And don't tell me no. Unless you don't want me in your house because you have something to hide."

"What could I possibly be hiding?"

"That's what I'm wondering. Are you a secret Dexter? Do you have a freezer full of body parts? Or women chained up in your basement? Or a creepy doll collection? *Aw.* Do you collect teddy bears? Now I have to know, and you're not going to change my mind. I'm walking Molly. She loves me, and I have the time, and you're being so helpful and nice, it's only right."

He shakes his head, but a laugh falls from his lips. "Will you take good care of her?"

"Of course."

"You won't let her get hurt or play too rough with other dogs?"

I plant a hand on my hip. "Of course not."

He lets out a long breath. "Fine."

I squeal and hug him again, catching him off guard. As his arms circle me, he says, "I guess we're hugging again," and I feel him tense up. I lean back, still holding on to him. Our eyes connect, and *hold*, causing a flutter in my chest, like a hummingbird taking flight. My pulse quickens, and the din of the café is drowned out by something warm and enticing pulsing between us. *That* startles me out of the moment. "I . . . *Sorry.* I'm a hugger." I plunk down in my seat, scrambling for something to say. "I'll walk Molly every afternoon."

"I'm sure she'll enjoy that."

His brows are knitted, but he says it so casually, I don't think he noticed my foray into Crazy Town.

"But no pressure. If you get busy and can't make it, don't sweat it." He grabs his phone. "I'll text you my address and leave a key under the mat, but *don't* go snooping around my house."

"I can't make any promises," I tease.

His eyes narrow.

"*Fine.* I won't snoop." I make a cross over my heart with my index finger.

"Good. Now back to business. I spoke to Chuck while you were getting the cookies. You can call him when we're done. He said he'll fit you in any day this week if you'd like, even before or after work."

"Really? That's amazing." I can't get over how much he's doing to help me. "I'll call him as soon as we're done. I work until midmorning tomorrow, but then I'm free for the rest of the day."

"Why are you looking at me like that?"

"I was just thinking about how you barely know me, and you're helping me so much. I truly appreciate all the time and guidance you've already given me. I jumped into this business with two feet and I had no idea how many important steps I missed. I might not have realized it until I made even bigger mistakes than I did yesterday. I can't help thinking that maybe you and I were meant to meet. *Fated.*"

"Get your head out of the clouds, sunshine. We met because of my dog and a stalker. Nothing more, nothing less."

"I don't know about that, naysayer. My friends have always come into my life for a reason. I think maybe I am supposed to help you find your match, and you're supposed to keep me out of trouble."

He looks at me like I've lost my mind.

I pick up my cookie and take a bite. The flaky pastry and sweet cream melt on my tongue in a glorious combination of deliciousness. I point what's left of the lady lock at him and say, "Forget all that. My head *was* stuck in the clouds. You obviously came into my life to introduce me to the best darn cookie I've ever had."

That earns a genuine smile.

# Chapter Seven

## Destiny

Monday morning I'm bursting with hope and anticipation. I feel so much better prepared to run Get the Yes now. It's shocking how unprepared I was, but as Fletch suggested, I am chalking that up to a learning experience and looking forward to meeting with his brother Chuck later this morning.

I want to make a good impression, so I wear a cute blue dress and sandals and tuck my sneakers into my bag with the treats I baked last night for Molly. Before heading to work, I leave a message for the insurance rep Fletch referred me to, and my nerves take over as I call Mr. Patel and leave him a message as well.

Fletch warned me not to get my hopes up, but I've never been good at that, and I spend the morning anxiously awaiting Mr. Patel's call. I wish Ruby were working this morning. She would know what to say to calm me down. But she doesn't work until later today, so I channel my nervous energy into talking out my worries with the dogs I groom.

By the time I finish at Perfect Paws and head out to Port Hudson to meet Chuck, I've checked my phone two dozen times. There's still no word from Mr. Patel, and my hopes deflate a notch or two.

Port Hudson is home to Boyer University. It's bigger than Harmony Pointe, and much busier, with several restaurants and bars and interesting-looking shops along the main drag. Chuck works in a brick building not far from the center of town. As I climb out of my car and head across the parking lot, my phone dings with a text. I dig it out of my bag and see Fletch's name on the screen. Happiness bubbles up inside me.

**Fletch:**

Hey, sunshine. How'd it go with Mr. Patel?

**Destiny:**

I left a message before work, but he hasn't called back yet. 😔

**Fletch:**

Remember what I said about managing your expectations?

**Destiny:**

**Fletch:**

Are you sure you still want to walk Molly today?

**Destiny:**

Yes! I'm looking forward to it.

**Fletch:**

I think she is, too. She was pretty excited when I said you were coming over. I left a key under the mat. Keep it for next time. Her leash is hanging by the door. The backyard is fenced, but the front isn't. Please be careful with her. She might chase squirrels or other dogs, and she's strong. You need to show her you're the boss.

**Destiny:**

Like you did at the park? 😅

**Fletch:**

**Fletch:**

Just don't let her off leash. You've seen what she's capable of, and I don't want her or anyone else getting hurt.

**Destiny:**

Do you have liability insurance just in case? A wise man told me it's important to protect yourself. I can give you the number of a guy who can help with that.

**Fletch:**

**Destiny:**

I know better than to let her off
leash. I had a dog named Clifford
when I was growing up, and he was
80 lbs of pure chaos.

**Fletch:**

Was he red?

**Destiny:**

Only when I dyed his fur and
dressed up like Emily Elizabeth for
Halloween.

**Fletch:**

**Fletch:**

How old were you? Six or seven?

**Destiny:**

Fifteen.

Three dots dance on the screen, but they disappear. A jolt of disappointment rattles me, and I try not to overthink it as I walk across the parking lot toward the building, but when I glance at the screen again, the dots reappear, turning my disappointment into anticipation.

I try not to overthink that, either.

**Fletch:**

Please don't dye Molly's fur.

**Destiny:**

I see Grumpy Gus has returned. I've missed him.

**Fletch:**

I'm serious. She could be allergic to dye.

His love for Molly touches me deeply, but it bothers me that he doesn't trust me to know better.

**Destiny:**

Do you really think I'd do that without your permission? And here I thought we were developing some level of trust.

**Fletch:**

Do I need to remind you about the bows?

Shoot. He's got me there.

**Destiny:**

**Fletch:**

Maybe this isn't such a good idea. Molly relies on me to keep her safe,

> and allergic reactions in dogs are no joke.

**Destiny:**

> Careful Gus. I might start thinking there's a warm heart behind all that bossiness. I promise she's in good hands. Take a deep breath. Did you do it? Good! Now stop being a helicopter dad and go smarten up some young minds. I'm meeting your hottie-pants brother in five minutes. Wish me luck!

I silence my phone and put it in my tote as I head into the building. I make my way up to the reception area, and a few minutes later, Chuck's assistant walks me back to his office.

"Destiny, it's nice to see you again." Chuck pushes to his feet and walks around his desk.

He's thicker than I remember, built like a football player, and he looks sharp in a white dress shirt and blue tie. His hair is darker than Fletch's but every bit as thick, and while Fletch's smiles are rare, Chuck's is instantaneous, warm, and inviting.

"It's nice to see you, too." I shake his hand. "Thanks for taking the time to meet with me."

"No problem." He motions to a chair in front of his desk, and as I sit down, he lowers himself to the chair beside it like we're old friends. "My brother said he'd like to help you get things sorted out quickly."

"He probably wants me to get out of his hair." As the words leave my lips, I remember that I'm supposed to be selling myself as Fletch's date for their brother's wedding and try to cover my tracks. "I can be a handful. My daddy used to say I was his little hurricane, whirling through life like I didn't want to miss any of it, and Fletch . . . *Ryan?* I'm sorry, I don't know what you call him."

"I usually call him a jackass," he says with a laugh. "I'm kidding. I call him Ryan, but you can call him Fletch. Everyone else does—well, except our parents—and as far as being a handful goes, there's nothing wrong with a woman who keeps you on your toes, and Ry could use a little shaking up."

"Well, here I am, shaking up his quiet life."

"You must be striking all the right chords, because it's been a long time since he's let a woman get as close as you two seem to be."

I feel a pang of guilt about pretending to be something we're not after how much fun Fletch and I had yesterday—or rather, how much fun I had. I can't speak for him, although he sure joked around a lot, and it felt like we connected—I also feel an unexpected pinch of sadness that we're not easing into something more. That pinch bothers me, because Fletch isn't even in the same realm as my Mr. Right.

Pushing those confusing thoughts aside, I sit up a little taller and say, "Your brother's pretty special. He spent hours teaching me everything I need to know about business yesterday, which is why I'm here. I need to make my marriage-proposal-planning business official."

"Then let's get started."

I'm still flying high when I pull up to Fletch's house to walk Molly later in the afternoon. I change from my sandals to my sneakers, and too excited to hold it in, I text Fletch.

**Destiny:**

> Chuck is amazing! Thank you so much for setting me up with him.

**Destiny:**

> He's filing all of the paperwork
> for Get the Yes, LLC, and writing
> up contracts that I can use, too.
> He said he'll send them over later
> today.

**Destiny:**

> We also went over the questions
> you and I came up with to make
> sure I don't ask anything I shouldn't.
> Don't worry. He said I'm not. 😊

**Destiny:**

> He's going to review my website
> later tonight to make sure there's
> nothing on it that can get me into
> trouble. I can't believe how fast he's
> moving on this!

**Destiny:**

> You Fletcher boys are really
> something. I look forward to
> getting to know him better at the
> wedding. I need to figure out a way
> to thank him.

I slip my phone into my dress pocket, gather my goodies, and head up the walk. The lawn and single line of low, squared-off bushes along the front porch are well manicured, like Fletch. His Cape-style house has a wide front porch, which is pretty but stark. Nothing like my family's front porch back home. We had hanging flower baskets and pastel-colored rocking chairs and tons of colorful flowers out front. I used to spend hours sitting out there in the evenings.

As I step onto Fletch's porch, I look up at the white ceiling. Ours was lavender, my mother's favorite color. "I think Ryry needs a little color in his life, don't you, Daddy?"

I lift the welcome mat, which is boring brown and does not say *welcome*, and find a key with a paper tag hanging from it. On one side of the tag he's written *Fletch's house*, as if I have a stockpile of keys to men's houses. I flip the tag over and read more of his squarish handwriting. *No snooping.*

"I'll try not to," I say as I unlock the door and push it open.

Molly is *right there* to greet me, tail wagging, excitedly sniffing me and my bag of goodies as I close the door. "Hi, Mol. I missed you, too. I know you want a treat, and you probably need to pee. Just give me one sec." I dig out one of the treats I baked for her, and she snags it, bounding into the great room to my left, and jumps onto the couch.

I take a moment to get my bearings and see how the extraordinary kisser lives. I had pictured his home to be all walled-off rooms and muted colors, but I couldn't have been more wrong. An open layout and off-white walls make his home feel airy and bright. The great room is separated from the foyer by only a change in flooring from tile to hardwood, and it feeds into a dining area with a bay window on the side and French doors leading out to a patio. The kitchen is to the right of the dining area, separated from the great room by a bar with high-top stools.

The furnishings, however, are very much like my well-put-together friend. With the exception of a few of Molly's toys on the floor, everything is neat and tidy, including the built-in bookshelves flanking a fireplace on the far wall. A mahogany coffee table matches the wood on the blue and beige upholstered chairs, which complement the beige-and-brown area rug. Molly's lying on a blue throw blanket covered with her fur on the couch as she finishes her treat.

I make my way along the foyer and peer down a hall on my right, where I see a bathroom, a closed door, and what looks like a bedroom and an office, but I don't snoop any further in that direction. Instead, I head over to the bookshelves, skipping the neatly organized books to peruse the family photos, of which there are many. There are several of a couple who can only be Fletch's parents. The man shares the same sharp features, light blue eyes, and dirty-blond hair as Fletch, and although I haven't seen that many of Fletch's smiles, the similarity to the brunette's is unmistakable. Her eyes also give away her love for her sons in every picture. A pang of longing for my own parents washes through me.

I pick up a picture of Fletch as a lanky boy of twelve or thirteen standing on a boat, his red swim trunks hanging low on his slim hips, his mass of longish hair blowing in the wind. He's holding a fish that's longer than his body. Chuck is standing behind him in black swim trunks with his arms up in the air, mouth wide open, like he's photobombing, and Jimmy is lying on a towel beside Chuck, shading his eyes from the sun, looking at the camera. I scan the other photos of Fletch and his brothers at varying ages, playing basketball and sitting by a lake. One picture catches my attention. Fletch looks around twenty years old or so. He and his brothers are standing on a boat, and Chuck and Jimmy are each holding fish. Their heads are tilted back, and Fletch, with those magnificent abs on display, is pouring beer into their mouths. His scruff is unkempt, his skin is bronze, and he's wearing a baseball cap and a huge grin. He looks so different, so *in the moment*. It's hard to imagine the guarded man I know as a carefree kid, much less this partying twentysomething.

I wonder if that's who he is only when he's with his brothers or if that is who he used to be, and something changed him.

Feeling like I'm now full-on snooping, I set the picture down and arrange the goodies I brought in the center of the dining room table, where Molly can't reach them. As if she smells them, she leaps off the couch and barks.

"Perfect timing. Let's get out of here before I accidentally snoop again."

# Chapter Eight

## FLETCH

I walk out of a meeting with university administration and campus security about what happened last weekend and pull out my phone to take it off silent mode. I have voicemail messages from my mother and Chuck, a text from Beth, and several texts from Destiny. As I head out to my car, I scroll through Destiny's texts.

The first few are pictures of Molly walking on the leash at the park. I come to one of both of them. Destiny's brows are lifted, and she's smirking, pointing to the leash, which is wrapped around her hand twice. *Smartass.* I feel myself grinning as I flip through more pictures of them. There's one of Destiny lying in the grass with Molly's big head resting on her arm, one of Molly licking Destiny's cheek, and another of the two of them in the gazebo. Destiny's arm is around my furry monster. That damn dimple taunts me in every picture. The last picture is a close-up of Molly sitting in front of Destiny. Destiny's sunglasses are perched on top of her head, holding her hair away from her face, giving me a better view of her happy eyes and beautiful smile. Her chin is resting on Molly's head, and one arm is wrapped around Molly. Molly's eyes are closed, her expression sheer bliss.

I can't take my eyes off that picture.

Or my mind off the fact that I'm mildly jealous of my dog right now.

Did my beast notice how Destiny's hair smells like strawberries, like I did when she hugged me at the café? My jaw clenches as I remember those hugs and how they got to me. I'm no saint. I don't go without human contact. But even casually dating, I keep my guard up. Destiny makes it impossible to do that. She's not only open with her feelings and opinions, but she invades my personal space, and she's *extra* touchy-feely, and damn it, I didn't want to like the way she felt in my arms.

I force myself to close the picture and read the first message she sent, which is all about how amazing—her word, not mine—Chuck is and how she wants to figure out a way to thank him.

*Great.* Now I'm jealous of my dog and my brother.

I really enjoyed helping her yesterday. I laughed with her more than I have in a long time. She's impulsive and scattered, but she's got the best of intentions. She's driven by her heart to fulfill her dreams. Can't knock that. That checklist of hers is a joke, but Destiny has her own brand of charm, and it's pretty fucking adorable. My mind drifts back to the moment I've been trying to ignore but haven't been able to stop thinking about. The one when our eyes locked and desire crackled in the air between us. I had all but forgotten what that hum of connection, that bone-deep desire to be closer to someone, felt like. I nearly went in for another kiss. I keep wondering if I imagined the longing I saw in her eyes, but hell if I hadn't felt it so strongly, it haunted me all night. I dreamed about stripping off those pink overall shorts to see if the rest of her tasted as good as her mouth did and woke up with my stone-hard dick in my hand.

Images from the dream traipse in, and my dick twitches. In an effort to shut that down before it can take hold, I close Destiny's message and open Beth's. Beth is a surefire boner killer. I love her like a sister, but like a sibling, she can be a pain in my ass.

**Beth:**

Is my future husband on drugs, or do you really have a date for the wedding?

**Fletch:**

Don't make a big deal out of the date, please.

**Beth:**

I won't. I'll just be over here sending notifications to everyone we know. Do you think this will work? FLETCH FINALLY FOUND SOMEONE WHO WILL PUT UP WITH HIS FRIGID ASS.

**Beth:**

I don't bother responding and listen to my mother's voicemail message as I climb into my car.

*Hi, honey, it's Mom. Jimmy told me you're bringing a date to the wedding. I can't wait to hear all about Destiny. Call me when you get a chance. I love you.*

Fucking Jimmy and his big mouth.

I listen to Chuck's message next.

*Hey, Ry. I just met with Destiny. Give me a call.*

I start the car and wait for my phone to sync to Bluetooth before I drive out of the lot, then call Chuck.

"About time you called me back," Chuck says.

"Sorry. I had to teach a class, and then I went directly into a meeting about that student stalker."

"How'd it go?"

"Good, I guess. They expelled her and banned her from campus, and they've got extra security watching out for me, but man, Chuck. She's a twenty-year-old kid. I know I did the right thing, because she took it so far, but it feels shitty."

"That's because you're not the coldhearted bastard you pretend to be. You definitely did the right thing. She crossed a line with that latest stunt. Are you pressing charges?"

"No. I'm hoping the restraining order is enough. The administration seemed to think she'd go back home to Pennsylvania. I'm just glad it's over. How'd it go with Destiny?"

"Ah, yes. Your wedding date."

"*Chuck*," I warn.

"Sorry, man. It's just so easy to rile you up." He laughs. "Destiny and I had a great meeting. I took good care of her. She'll be covered legally. Don't worry."

"Thanks, man," I say as I turn into my neighborhood. "I appreciate your help."

"Anytime. You know that. She's really something, Ry. She's smart, and determined, although it took a few minutes for me to realize she wasn't just flighty as fuck. She's all over the place, but damn. She's a dynamo."

I feel myself smiling. "Yeah, she's something, all right."

"But she's not really your type. I don't normally mix business with pleasure, but if you want to back off and let me give her more than legal advice, I'd be cool with that."

Jealousy sears through me. "What the hell, Chuck?"

"Listen, we both know what you're up to," he says in the serious, big-brother tone he's used my whole life. "You're not really interested in her. You just want to get all of us off your back."

I grit my teeth, partially because I hate that he knows me so well. But mostly because that too-bubbly, too-loud, too-pushy, and too-fucking-adorable chatterbox is *not* my type, and yet here I am, counting down the damn hours until I see her again, and *that* pisses me off.

"You don't know shit, so keep it in your pants." I pull into my driveway and cut the engine. "I appreciate you helping her out, but do me a favor. Send me the bill." She said she's got money, but she also thought she could start a business without ample preparation.

"If you're into her, then this one's on me."

I feel a sliver of guilt at Chuck eating his fees when, despite my loss of perspective, this whole thing is a farce. "You don't have to do that."

"For the first woman you've let into your life in a decade? No worries, bro. I've got you covered. But I have to run. Have a good night."

I pocket my phone and head inside.

Molly greets me at the door, going paws up on my chest. "How's it going, Mol?" I love her up. "Did you have fun with Destiny today?"

She barks and follows me through the great room, tail wagging, nosing my hand for more pets, which I'm happy to give her. My gaze catches on two boxes on the dining room table. A white box with little paw prints drawn on it and a pink bow on top and a pink box from Sweetie Pie bakery in Sweetwater with a blue bow on top.

"What has she done?" I ask Molly, who follows me into the dining room.

I find a thank-you card perched between the boxes and read Destiny's loopy cursive inside.

Dear Fletch,

Thank you for everything you're doing to help me with Get the Yes. The goodies in the white box are for Molly. I baked them myself, and don't worry, I checked the allergy list on file at Perfect Paws first. The goodies in the pink box are for you. Have a good night, and thanks again for all your help and for letting me hang out with Molly!

Destiny

The *i* in her name is dotted with a heart. I open the box from Sweetie Pies, and my mouth waters at the sight of two of my favorite pastries, Loverboys, which are a cross between an éclair and a cupcake, with blue icing on top and thick custard inside.

Molly rubs against my leg.

"You know what's in your box, don't you?" I open the other box and find several bone-shaped dog treats that smell like peanut butter.

Molly barks.

"Don't get used to this. She's not a permanent fixture in our lives." I hold out a treat, and she snatches it. I let her out the back door and can't resist eating one of the Loverboys. I lick the icing from my fingers and pull out my phone to text Destiny.

**Fletch:**

> Thank you for the treats. That was thoughtful and unnecessary. How did you know I liked Loverboys?

**Destiny:**

> Your almost-fiancée told me, remember? They were on the picnic that Molly trampled, and when she said she heard you tell someone that Sweetie Pie was your favorite bakery, you didn't deny it, so I figured she was right.

I wonder how she paid such close attention to that minutia when all hell was breaking loose.

**Fletch:**

> If you keep this up, I won't be able to fit into my basketball shorts.

**Destiny:**

> I've seen your abs. I think you can handle a few treats.

That gives me pause.

**Fletch:**

> Were you checking me out, sunshine?

**Destiny:**

> Does a bird have wings?

Maybe I didn't imagine that moment at the café after all.

**Destiny:**

> There were four shirtless men standing right in front of me. What did you expect me to do? Look away? It's kind of ridiculous how ripped you all are. I mean, what does it take to look like that? Do you guys run fifty miles each week? Starve yourselves? Do a hundred sit-ups every day? I'm tired and hungry just thinking about it.

She has me laughing again, but it doesn't last, because I didn't miss the part about her checking out *all* of us. Molly saunters back inside.

"That's a good thing, right, Mol? It'll help me keep things in perspective when we get together tomorrow night."

**Fletch:**

> I don't run quite that much. I guess abs aren't on your checklist?

**Destiny:**

> There are more important body parts to consider.

I should not be thumbing out my next message, but I can't help myself.

**Fletch:**

> Does Little Miss Sunshine have a dirty mind?

**Destiny:**

> A lady never tells. Now get your mind out of the gutter and go enjoy your creamy treat.

**Destiny:**

>

**Destiny:**

> Excuse me while I pull MY mind out of the gutter.

**Destiny:**

>

I laugh and I look down at my furry beast. "Our new friend is a little nutty, but she sure makes me laugh."

# Chapter Nine

## FLETCH

Destiny sent me a half dozen pictures from her second walk with Molly on Tuesday afternoon. I was surprised at how much they brightened my day. I'm looking forward to seeing her tonight to help her with the computer, but I got held up helping a student after work and head home a little late to let Molly out.

There's a note on the table again in that loopy cursive. I read it as I open the back door and Molly bounds outside.

*Hi! I hope you had an amazing day at work. Please bring Molly tonight. I don't want her to miss out on her daddy time, and Clementine misses her.*

I shake my head. "No way am I bringing my beast to terrorize your cat."

*Stop shaking your head. Molly waits all day to see you, and I bet you miss her as much as she misses you.*

How can she possibly know that?

*I don't care if they race around the house. You saw how close they ended up last time. They're already friends at heart, just like us!*

She signed it with a heart rather than her name, and for some reason, that silly little heart made me happy. I look up as Molly comes in the back door, tail wagging, as if she knows she got an invitation. "I guess you're coming with me." I crouch in front of her, scratching behind her ears. "No chasing the cat this time, okay?" She licks my face, and I imagine she's thinking, *Yeah, right,* and snickering, because my dog is just as smitten with our vivacious new friend as I am.

My phone vibrates with a text.

**Chuck:**

> Your girl is a class act. She brought me a basket of cookies she baked to thank me for my help. When she gets tired of you, send her my way.

She's not my girl. There's no reason for jealousy to be clawing up my spine, but fuck if it isn't. I pocket my phone without replying, trying to break free of that uncomfortable feeling, and head into the kitchen to feed Molly. I drop the note from Destiny in the junk drawer with the one she left yesterday.

After I feed Molly, there's just enough time to get to Destiny's. I snag the second Loverboy Destiny left for me yesterday and polish it off on the way over in lieu of dinner.

I barely finish knocking on the door before it flies open, and Destiny, adorable in a purple scoop-neck T-shirt and cutoffs, exclaims, "I'm so glad you brought Molly!" as my monster bolts past her. "I just got off the phone with Arjun! I'm meeting with him next Thursday at seven." She launches forward, throwing her arms around me.

Destiny's excitement is contagious, and laughter tumbles out. Stifling the urge to go after my dog, I return Destiny's embrace, the strawberry scent of her shampoo infiltrating my senses. I hold her a moment longer than I probably should, enjoying the feel of her in my arms.

"Congratulations, sunshine. That's awesome."

I set her on her feet, and she takes my hand, dragging me inside, talking a mile a minute. "I have so much to tell you!"

Looking past her, I see Molly and Clementine standing on separate couches, staring each other down. Molly's tail is wagging. She's ready to play, but Clementine looks wary. I nod in their direction. "I think I should get Molly."

Destiny waves her hand dismissively. "Don't worry about her. They're *fine*." She reaches up and touches my cheek, drawing my attention back to that winning smile. "I got another email asking for prices, and they want to set up a meeting, but I put them off."

"Why did you delay meeting them?"

"I don't want to meet with anyone until I do my due diligence and check out their socials. *See?* You should be proud of me. You taught me well. I even asked Arjun all the prescreening questions we came up with."

"I am proud of you," I say honestly, knowing how hard she's working and how much this means to her. It dawns on me that without family or many friends in the area, she probably doesn't hear things like that very often. "Your hard work is paying off, and it shows. You should be proud of yourself, too."

"I *am*. I really want Arjun to sign on as a client, and I'm stupidly nervous about meeting with him. I've never been unsure of myself like this before, and I don't like it one bit. That whole fiasco with Cecilia has me second-guessing myself."

The faltering confidence sounds wrong coming from such a vibrant woman, and I can't help but think that I might have something to do with it. I wasn't exactly gentle with my initial criticism. "That incident with Cecilia was a fluke. You have nothing to worry about. You're going to do great. But would it help if I went with you for moral support?"

Her eyes widen. "*Yes!* Will you? Please? I know I'm already taking up oodles of your time, but I'd be so grateful if you would come with me. That way, if I forget to ask something, you can bring it up."

"Okay. I'll be there. Where are you meeting him?" As I say it, Clementine prances across the back of the couch that Molly is standing on, and Molly shoves her nose in the cat's belly. Clementine gives her the equivalent of a deadpan stare and sits on the back of the couch, holding his ground.

"I told you they'd be fine," she says. "We're meeting at La Love. If it's a nice evening, I'm going to walk over and get there fifteen minutes early. The walk will help me calm down. Do you want to meet me at my place at six thirty and walk over with me?"

"Sure, that sounds good."

"Thank you! Come on." She takes my hand again, pulling me through the living room, which I now notice is not as much of a mess as it was the last time I was here, but there are notebooks and magazines strewn about, the blanket from her bedroom is piled on an armchair, and there are several framed photographs on the walls. How did I miss them before?

I wonder about that blanket as she leads me past the dining room table, which is set for two, and into the kitchen. A savory scent hangs in the air. As she heads for a cabinet, I notice two bottles of wine on the counter, along with dirty pots, pans, and other cooking accoutrements.

My gut twists. "Do you have dinner plans, sunshine? We can do this another time."

"No, silly. I'm starved, and I figured you might be hungry after working all day, so I whipped up some fried chicken and mashed potatoes and my daddy's famous Southern fried corn." She turns around with a wineglass in each hand and wrinkles her nose. "*Shoot.* You've got those abs to worry about. I forgot about that, which is weird, because they have been on my mind a lot lately. I probably should have baked the chicken, right?"

I half laugh, half scoff. "*No.* I eat fried chicken, and I'm not obsessed with my abs. I'm a runner. That's all." I hear Molly scamper upstairs and assume she's gone after Clementine.

"Hey, no judgment here. You and your brothers make for nice eye candy."

Never in my life have I been so annoyed by my brothers when they weren't even in the room. She must see something in my expression, because she tilts her head and says, "What?"

"I'm just not used to people saying whatever pops into their heads."

"I've always been this way. My mama taught me to always say what I feel. Heck, my heart gets tangled up with people and things and moments all the time. If I tried to hide it, I'd probably burst." She holds up the wineglasses. "Red or white?"

"White, and thank you for thinking of me. For *dinner*, I mean, not for thinking about my abs."

"I should be thanking *you* for that view." She giggles. "Why don't you take these glasses and grab that bottle of wine and put them on the table while I get some water for Molly and take dinner out of the oven."

A few minutes later, we're sitting at the dining room table. "I don't hear Molly chasing Clementine."

"I told you. They're friends at heart. They're probably up there snuggling."

Holding on to her positivity and hoping she's right, I look at our plates and at the fresh basket of warm biscuits in front of us. I'm floored that with everything else she has going on, she took the time to cook, much less made enough for me. "Other than holidays with my family, I can't remember the last time anyone cooked for me. Thank you. This looks delicious."

"I *love* cooking. It centers me."

"Well, it smells incredible." I pick up the bottle of wine and begin filling her glass.

"That's enough," she says when it's half-full. "I have to keep my wits about me so we can work." She picks up her glass. "To new friends."

"To new friends." We clink glasses and drink, and I start cutting my chicken.

She touches my arm. "What are you doing?"

"Eating . . . ?"

"I guess what Chuck said is true—that you don't like to get your hands dirty?"

My brother is going to pay for that. "No, that's not true."

"Oh. Well, it tastes a whole lot better when you pick it up and eat it."

"That doesn't even make sense."

"Sure it does. Go on and eat that piece you're cutting off."

I eat it, and it's the best damn fried chicken I've ever had. The coating is crisp, tangy, and spicy, and the meat is juicy. "It's perfect."

She picks up a chicken leg from her plate and waves it at me. "Now try it like this." She takes a big bite. "*Mm.* My mama's recipe is the best," she says with a cheek full of chicken. "Go on. Give it a try."

I pick up the chicken leg and take a bite. She's onto something. The tanginess is sharper, the spices more potent, and the meat tastes infused with them. Now I'm shaking my chicken leg at her. "*How* is this possible?"

"I told you! The juices and spices get all up in your gums and teeth and tongue, and it magnifies the flavors. There's nothing better." She takes another bite.

"If you handle your meeting with Arjun as well as you cook, you'll sign him in no time."

"I hope so. He's such a nice guy. He's a computer scientist, and his girlfriend, Maura, is a nurse. They've been dating for four years, and he's so in love with her, I could hear it in his voice."

"That's a good thing, since he's proposing."

"They sound like a great couple. She works long shifts sometimes, and you know what he does? He brings her dinner and eats with her, even if she can only sit down for fifteen minutes, so she doesn't have to eat alone. How romantic is that?"

"Maybe you should add that to your Mr. Right Checklist."

"That's a *great* idea." As we eat, she tells me more about her phone conversation with Arjun. She's animated and enthusiastic and, at times, also a little dreamy eyed. "I checked out his social pages, and there are a million pictures of him and Maura going back several years. I also had my website guy add a place on the contact form for the details you suggested *and* for their social links so I can check them out ahead of time."

"Now you're thinking like a businesswoman."

She beams. "I have a great mentor." She leans against my side. "Don't get upset, but I did a little research on you, too."

"Why would I get upset? Safety first."

"Good." She eats some mashed potatoes. "Your bio on the Beckwith site makes you sound very smart, which I'm sure you are, but you should've smiled in the picture. You have a great smile, and it makes you look less like Grumpy Gus and more like Friendly Fletch. But you have no social pages. What's up with that?"

I don't think anyone would describe me as *Friendly Fletch*. "I'm a private guy. I don't need people like Cecilia stalking me online, too."

"That makes sense. When I couldn't find your socials, I looked for Chuck's and Jimmy's."

*Great . . .*

"Chuck's are private, so I couldn't see them. But Jimmy's accounts are public and loaded with great pictures of him and a gorgeous woman named Beth Peterson. She was tagged in the pictures. I assume she's his fiancée, since they're kissing in most of the pictures."

"She is."

"They look happy together. Do you like her?"

"Yeah. We've known her all our lives. She's great."

"That's good. It would stink if you didn't like her. I went to school with a girl back home whose brother married an awful woman, and now she barely sees him. Anyway, Jimmy had tons of pictures of you and your family. Why didn't you tell me you like to ski and fish?"

"Why would I?"

"Because we're friends, and friends share things. I'm going to a wedding with you, and I feel like I don't even *know* you."

I find myself leaning into her. "We did just meet."

"Yeah, I guess." She sighs, her disappointment palpable.

"What would you like to know?"

Her eyes light up. "Everything. I saw pictures on your bookshelves, so I know you fished when you were younger, but Jimmy's looked more recent."

"Were you snooping, sunshine?"

"Not intentionally. It just kind of happened, and I didn't look at anything but a few pictures. I promise. Do you still fish?"

"Yes. As a matter of fact, I'm going fishing Saturday. We had a boat growing up, and some of my best memories are fishing with my family."

"Where are you from? What are your parents like?"

"I grew up in Sunnyvale, which is about half an hour from here. My parents still live in the house I grew up in, and Jimmy lives a few blocks from them. My parents are steady, you know? My dad is a financial consultant, and my mom works part time as an assistant to a real estate agent. Growing up, they were always there for us, and they still are."

"How often do you see them?"

I shrug. "A couple times a month if our schedules align."

"If my parents were still alive, I'd visit them all the time."

She glances behind us, and I follow her gaze to a framed photograph on a hutch of a man with black hair, bushy brows, dark, happy eyes, and weathered skin and a blond woman with a mile-wide smile and a deep dimple in her left cheek.

I put my hand on Destiny's, giving it a reassuring squeeze. "I'm sorry. Are they your parents?"

"Yeah," she says softly.

"They're a nice-looking couple. Do you mind if I ask how you lost your mother?"

She shakes her head, and her eyes tear up, gutting me.

How did that happen so fast? "I didn't mean to upset you."

"You didn't. These are happy tears." She blinked them away. "I warned you it happens when I think of them sometimes, didn't I?"

I can't remember if she warned me or not, but if she did, it wouldn't have prepared me anyway. I'm not sure anything could. I don't like seeing tears in her eyes. "Would you rather not talk about it?"

"No, I like talking about them, and you should know the hard stuff since I'm meeting your family. As I told you, my mom was fearless. She could do and fix anything. My dad told me that when he moved to the States and got a job as a mechanic, she'd go down to his shop at night and on the weekends, and beg him to show her what he was doing. She loved tinkering and gardening, and she built these little wooden wheelbarrows that she'd plant flowers in. I was at school the day she died. She was in the backyard, and as best my dad could tell, she was searching through an old woodpile or cleaning it up, and she jostled a bees' nest. She was stung thirty-seven times, and she went into anaphylactic shock. He found her when he came home to have lunch with her, which he did all the time. They didn't even know she was allergic." A tear slips down her cheek. "My father had me tested right away, and I'm not allergic. I'd give anything if she hadn't been."

My heart cracks open, and even though she told me so much about herself the other day, I feel like I'm seeing *her* for the first time. Not her personality or her enthusiasm, but the incredibly strong, positive woman who has been a falling star two times too many and has somehow managed to pick herself back up to not only tread on but to flourish and live out her dreams. I want to know more. I want to know *everything* about her, to understand how she overcame so much. I want to know all her secrets and fears.

I wipe her tears with the pads of my thumbs and take her hand between both of mine. "Your father must have been beside himself with grief. Don't take this wrong, but you were so young, I'm glad he found her before you did."

A pained smile curves her lips. "My dad said the same thing. But I wish I had gotten there first to save him from having that be his last memory of her."

I wipe more of her tears. "Has anyone ever told you that you have a boundless heart?"

She shakes her head.

I feel something at my feet and glance beneath the table, surprised to see Molly lying with her paw over Clementine. I was so caught up in Destiny, I didn't even notice they'd come downstairs. How did Destiny know they'd be good friends? I lift my gaze to her sweet hazel eyes and realize there must be a hint of magic in that boundless heart of hers.

I hold her hand a little tighter. "I think you do, sunshine, and that's a beautiful thing."

# Chapter Ten

## DESTINY

"I don't get why you're so nervous," Ruby says over video call the following Thursday evening as I pull on another dress option for my meeting with Arjun. "You're great with people, and you've been working with Fletch every day. You said you did great when you practiced last night. I bet you could sell this guy on your business in your sleep."

Other than Saturday night, when Fletch hung out with his brothers after playing basketball, he and I have spent every evening together for the past week and a half. He's taught me a lot, and it's been wonderful getting to know him and exchanging fun texts throughout the day. I'm enjoying walking Molly and leaving them both little goodies, like the socks I left for Fletch with basketballs on them. He wore them over the next night and said he wasn't as boring as I thought he was. *Spoiler alert: I don't think he's boring at all.* Then he handed me a pair of plain white socks, in case I wanted to see how the other half lives. I love our friendship, and he's incredibly supportive. He texted yesterday afternoon asking if I wanted to get together and role-play to prepare for the meeting, and I jumped on the offer.

"I did do well, but I was with Fletch, and he makes me feel like I can do anything." I take a quick look in the mirror at my short-sleeved, flowy pink-and-white floral dress, slip my feet into nude block-heel sandals, and turn toward the iPad so Ruby can see me. "What do you think?"

"I think you look as pretty as you did in the last three outfits. *Why* are you so nervous? Did you call your dad? That always calms you down."

"You know what? I *didn't* call him. I was going to first thing this morning, but then Fletch texted and said I was going to nail the meeting tonight. We got to texting back and forth, and I guess I forgot."

"Is there something more between you and Fletch that you're not telling me?"

"No. Why?"

"Because even *I* can't do for you what calling your dad does for you."

That gives me pause. "I . . . He just sidetracked me, that's all. You know how my mind works."

"Uh-huh. Are you sure you're not into him for more than business tutoring?"

"*Please.* He only ticks off two things on my checklist."

Ruby's brows lift. "So you've checked?"

"*No.*"

"Then how do you know he only checks off two things?"

"Because I have my list memorized. It's always in my head, and he was my inspiration to add one of them—"

"Which was . . . ?"

"A guy who isn't afraid to tell me I'm wrong and help me be the best I can be."

"Okay. I approve. What's the second thing he checks off?"

I look away, mumbling, "*He'sagoodkisser.*"

"What?"

"He's a good kisser, okay?" I don't tell her that while *good kisser* was already on my list, I changed it to *Gives me unforgettable kisses.*

"You kissed him?"

"*No.* He kissed me. I just kissed him back. I told you about it when all that stuff went down at the park with that stalker girl."

"You definitely did *not* tell me that. I'd remember if you said you kissed Fletch! Have you kissed him since?"

"No." *But I think about it all the time.*

"Is that why you're so nervous? Do you want there to be more between you two?"

"*No.* I'm nervous because he's helping me so much. I don't want to disappoint him."

"Oh. *Oh.* That's big."

It is big, and I didn't mean to blurt it out.

A knock sounds at the front door. "He's here! I've got to go. Wish me luck."

"I wish you all the luck in the world, but tomorrow you and I are going to talk about that kiss and—"

"Goodbye, Rubes." I end the call, hurry downstairs, and answer the door. Fletch looks as handsome as ever in a blue button-down that makes his eyes appear even bluer and dark slacks. A dusting of chest hair peeks out from his open collar, his sleeves are rolled up to his elbows, and his smile sets my heart aflutter. "Hi."

"Hey, sunshine." His gaze takes a slow stroll down my body, and my temperature rises. "You look beautiful. Ready for your big night?"

I take a deep breath. "I think so. I'm nervous. Come in. I just need to get my things."

"Nervous, huh?" He follows me in.

"Yeah." I close the door, and when I turn around, he's *right there,* serious eyes studying me.

He places his hands on my shoulders and gazes deeply into my eyes. "You're Destiny Amor. You were born to do this, and there's nothing you can't do if you put your heart into it. You're going to win this man over and walk out of that café with a new client. I believe in you, and

I know your parents are cheering you on tonight, so no more doubts, sunshine. Okay?"

His support tugs at my heartstrings almost as much as the mention of my parents does. I nod, my emotions too raw to speak.

"I brought you something to mark your big day." He reaches into his pocket and pulls out a slim black box.

My pulse quickens. "You didn't have to get me anything."

"It's not a big deal, but I think you'll like it."

"I already do, because it's from you." I open the box, and nestled among black silk is a gold pen with GET THE YES! engraved in pink. "*Oh, Fletch*" falls from my lips with disbelief. This isn't the kind of gift he could walk in off the street and buy at any gift shop. This took forethought and planning, and the fact that he did that for me makes it feel like much more than just a pretty pen.

"They don't normally engrave with pink lettering, but I wanted it to be as unique as you are, so I might have bribed the guy with the promise of a perfect proposal event at some point in his future."

I laugh. "I couldn't love it more. Thank you!" I throw my arms around him, and my heart races as his arms circle me, holding me tight, the way he's been doing lately when I go in for a hug.

"I'm glad you like it."

His voice is low and husky, sending a shiver of heat through me. I want to stay right there in his arms. But I know he's just being nice, and I'm being weird, so I step back, admiring the gift *and* the thoughtful man who gave it to me.

"We'd better get a move on," he reminds me.

I grab my bag and tuck my beautiful new personalized pen into the interior pocket. As I head out the door with this incredible, supportive man by my side, I swear I feel my parents smiling down on me brighter than ever.

◆ ◆ ◆

# FLETCH

Watching Destiny with Arjun, a kind, dark-haired man with glasses and a careful demeanor, further convinces me that proposal planning is exactly what she was meant to do. I don't know why she was so nervous. Over the course of the last hour, she's connected with him in a way that makes them seem like old friends, just like she's done with me. She's funny, confident, professional, and passionate, and her love of *love* radiates in everything she says and does. She answers each of his questions thoroughly and thoughtfully and listens intently as he tells stories about how he and Maura met, what his favorite things about her are, his favorite moments in their relationship, their favorite hiking spots and pastimes, and a dozen others. It's easy to see that Destiny is genuinely invested in their story, and she's included me in the entire conversation, asking for my opinion, touching my arm or leg as she comments on this or that, and making correlations to our friendship. This whirlwind woman is a rare force of nature, and it's that warmth and enthusiasm that has me equally as invested. I *want* this man to give Maura the proposal of her dreams, and I want Destiny to be the one to help him get his *yes*. I believe Arjun wants her to be that person, too.

"What's the one dream you and Maura share that is out of reach right now?" she asks.

"That's easy," Arjun says. "Going to Paris. We both feel like it's calling us. We've even learned to speak French, but between my deadlines and the hospital being short-staffed, we haven't been able to coordinate enough time off to go."

"Even the thought of Paris is romantic," Destiny says dreamily. She gasps. "I have a great idea! How would you feel about bringing Paris to Maura for the proposal? I see a magical setting, a Parisian café, a replica of the Eiffel Tower. It could be the proposal of a *lifetime*."

She's brilliant.

Hope glimmers in Arjun's eyes. "How would we do that?"

"If you're open to the idea and decide to book with my company, just leave it to me. I'll put together an outline of the event and a budget for your approval, of course, and if you don't like something, we can tweak it or move on to a different idea. I'm never short on ideas."

"I want everything to be perfect for Maura, and she'll never expect a Parisian-themed proposal," Arjun says. "I've been so stressed about how I could possibly make the proposal as special as she deserves, but I feel better now. I know I'll be in good hands with you. Let's do it."

"That's wonderful!" she exclaims, and turns that megawatt smile at me.

I stifle the urge to tell her how great she is and how proud of her I am, turning instead to Arjun. "You're making the right choice. Destiny has a magic touch."

"I can see that," he says.

Destiny touches my arm, her joyous eyes flicking briefly and appreciatively to mine, before she returns her full attention to her new client.

As they go over the contract and sign it, I notice Destiny taking an extra moment to look at her new pen. She's done it a few times while taking notes, and each time brings the sweetest slightly bashful smile I've ever seen. I bury the warmth it stirs as she explains to Arjun that she'll send an invoice for the deposit, along with a copy of the contract by email.

"I'm excited to get started." She tucks her pen into a pocket in her bag and puts the contract and her notebooks away. "This proposal is going to be everything you and Maura dream of and more. I work part time at Perfect Paws, and I'm booked tomorrow morning, so I'll start scouting locations Saturday." Her hand lands on my leg, and she beams at me. "I know you have plans, so I won't ask you to come, but I promise to send pictures."

"I'll change my plans to Sunday and scout locations with you."

"You will?"

"Absolutely. I can't have you picking the wrong location," I tease, earning a chuckle from Arjun.

"You're the *best*." She leans over and hugs me.

"You two make a great team," Arjun says. "How long have you been together?"

"*Oh*, we're not . . . We're just . . ." She looks at me and laughs softly. "We're friends . . . and *business associates*?"

I put my hand over hers, squeezing it reassuringly. "Thank you, Arjun. We do make a good team. We haven't known each other that long, but Destiny has a way of making you feel like you're supposed to be in each other's lives." *How true is that? Now I even sound like her.*

Destiny's smile chases her unsurety away.

"She definitely does. I'm sorry, but I have to run. I look forward to hearing from you." Arjun pushes to his feet, and Destiny and I rise to ours.

She takes Arjun's hand. "Thank you for trusting me with your special moment. I'll send the documents over tomorrow and will get started right away."

"I'll be on the lookout for them." He extends his hand to me. "It was nice to meet you, Fletch."

"You as well. Have a great night."

After he leaves the café, Destiny lets out a cheer and throws her arms around me. "We did it!"

I embrace her. "*You* did it. Congratulations, sunshine. Get the Yes is officially in business."

"Are we pretending the picnic fiasco didn't happen?"

I pick up her bag and hand it to her. "You weren't even an LLC back then. It doesn't count." She couldn't look happier, and I don't think I could, either. I drape an arm over her shoulder as we head for the door. "What do you say we celebrate?"

"You lead, I'll follow."

# Chapter Eleven

## DESTINY

"I want to start by looking at the places where they like to hike. The overlook he mentioned sounded beautiful . . ." I'm on cloud nine, chattering away about my ideas for a Parisian-themed proposal as we walk to a pub around the corner from the café. I'm glad I get to share this epic moment with Fletch. When I think about how close we've gotten, the thoughtful gift he gave me, and what he said when he arrived at my place, about my being born to do proposal planning and my parents smiling down on me, I really do feel like we were fated to meet.

"You've got some great ideas, sunshine. I look forward to watching you put it together."

He holds the door to the pub open for me and puts a hand on my back as we walk inside. It's crowded and noisy, with enormous paintings of wild animals wearing colorful glasses on the dark wood walls. People are gathered around a couple singing karaoke on a small stage, and I'm immediately enamored with the funky pub.

I take Fletch's arm, leaning closer so he can hear me over the music. "I love karaoke!"

"Of course you do." He shakes his head, but he's grinning.

We spot two high-back stools at the bar and head that way. As we weave through the crowd, Fletch puts his arm protectively around me, pulling me close. I try not to dwell on how nice it is to be taken care of like that and focus instead on the bright green floor, pink tabletops, and eclectic mix of wooden and leather chairs around us.

"This place is fantastic," I say, dropping my bag to the floor by the bar. I climb onto a barstool, checking out the crowd. Fletch moves my bag from the floor to the back of my chair, just as he did in the café, because *You never know what kind of filth you're setting it in.* I've never worried about things like that, but I like that he does.

I lean in so he can hear me, resting my hand on his leg. "What's the name of this place?"

"The Lucky Lizard."

"That sounds dirty."

He chuckles. "I'm sure it's meant to."

"I didn't take you as the noisy bar type."

"I come here with my brothers to grab a beer every once in a while, but it's not usually this crowded or loud."

"I guess you don't come on Thursday nights." I point to a chalkboard hanging behind the bar announcing Thursday-night karaoke. The way he's watching the people around us, I wonder if he's uncomfortable. "Do you want to go someplace quieter?"

He arches a brow. "And feed into your Grumpy Gus image of me? I don't think so. We're here to celebrate your success, and you love karaoke."

"Does that mean you'll sing with me?" I ask hopefully.

"Not in this lifetime, but I look forward to hearing you sing," he says as the bartender, a rugged-looking Black man, comes to take our order.

The bartender gives me an appreciative glance and lifts his chin to Fletch. "How're you two doing tonight?" His baritone voice cuts through the noise.

"Great! We're celebrating. I just got my first client for my proposal-planning business." I catch Fletch's amused expression.

"Congratulations," the bartender says. "The first round is on the house. What'll it be?"

"Aren't you the sweetest? What do you recommend? Is there a house drink?"

"Yeah, the Lusty Lizard. It's great if you like sweet drinks, and it's strong."

"Now, that's a great name for a drink. I'll take it! I *love* sweet drinks, and it *is* a celebration." I lean into Fletch again. "Have one with me?"

"Sorry, sunshine, but I think I'll stick to beer." He orders and asks, "How can we get her name on the karaoke list?"

I'm surprised, and pleased, that he thought to ask.

The bartender points across the bar. "Go see Mac, the bearded guy at that table by the stage. He'll put her on the list."

"Great, man. Thanks. Can you run a tab for us?"

I slide off my stool. "I'll go see Mac."

Fletch grabs my hand. "Want me to go?"

"No. I'm good, thanks." I'm touched by his offer, but I want to look over the song list.

It takes a few minutes to get signed up, and I talk to a guy who's also waiting to sign up, and we share a laugh when Mac asks if we want to sing as a duo. As I make my way back through the crowd, I notice two women standing near the bar checking out Fletch, but Fletch is watching me. Our eyes connect, and I swear that hummingbird takes flight in my chest again. I don't know what that's all about. It's not like he's my type. He doesn't even believe in love, and putting love above all else is definitely high on my checklist. So is singing karaoke with a guy who loves it as much as I do, and that's definitely not Fletch.

But I *am* happy when I'm with him, and I love working side by side with him, sharing a common goal, and teasing each other. It feels good when we're together. But too often during the last week or so, it's felt *too* good, and I've found myself wishing he'd kiss me again. I've been trying not to make too much of the way his texts make my pulse dance, and when he calls me sunshine? *Whew.* I really like that. I've also been trying not to snoop when I pick up Molly for our walks. But I did look at more of the pictures on his bookshelf, and my heart warmed at each one. I like seeing the carefree pictures of him with his family and wish I knew how to make him smile that way, too.

I'm sure I feel so close to him because we're spending so much time together. It probably doesn't help that I miss my family and haven't gone on a date in . . . *Let's not go there.* I need to get myself under control. Fletch is too good to me to mess up our friendship because of my silly, confused emotions.

When I reach the bar, he steps off his stool and pulls out mine. "Everything go okay?"

"Yup. All signed up." As we climb onto our seats, I see a bright green drink waiting for me. The joined stems of two cherries are perched on the rim of the glass, one cherry hanging on either side. I've never been more thankful for alcohol in my life. I reach for my drink. "I hope this is as good as it looks."

He puts his hand on mine, stopping me from putting the straw in my mouth, and picks up his glass. "Here's to you, sunshine, and your bright new future with Get the Yes."

"I couldn't have done it without you."

"You could have. You just might have been sued a few times first."

I laugh as we clink glasses, then take a sip of my drink. "*Mm.* You have to taste this. It's zingy and fruity, like liqueur-infused melon." I move the straw to his side and hold out my glass.

He waves me off. "It's okay. I'm good."

"Come on, Ryry. Live a little." I hold it up again.

He takes a sip and draws back, brows slanting. "*Damn,* that is sweet, and he wasn't kidding about it being strong. What's in it? Vodka, tequila, rum?"

He licks his lips, and I go right back to wanting to kiss him, remembering the hard press of his lips, the hungry swipe of his tongue. I don't stop there. Suddenly I'm seeing him as he's been in my dreams all week. Gloriously naked and—

"I think there's gin in there, too," he says, jerking me from my fantasy as he sets the glass down in front of me.

"Gin. Uh-huh." I take a big gulp of the green goodness, trying to chase my lustful thoughts away. I should *not* be thinking about him naked.

"Better be careful, sunshine, or I'll be carrying you to bed."

I choke on his words, spewing my drink onto the front of his shirt and slacks, and cough as what's left in my mouth goes down the wrong tube.

"Are you okay?"

Coughing and nodding, I manage, "Sorry . . ." I clear my throat, grab a napkin, and start wiping his shirt and slacks. "It went down the wrong tube. I'm sorry about your clothes."

"It's okay." He grabs my wrist, stilling my hand.

"I'm trying to help." I look up, and his tight expression has me glancing down at my hand, which is dangerously close to the bulge behind his zipper. "Oh, um . . . *sorry?*" I pull my hand back. "I wasn't trying to . . . I was just . . ." I toss the napkin onto the bar and cover my face with my hands. "You can take me out back and shoot me now."

He pulls my hands down, laughing softly. "Would you stop? That's the most action I've gotten in six months."

My jaw drops. "No way. Six months?"

He takes a drink without responding.

"You can't just drop something like that and clam up. Don't you date?"

His eyes narrow in that way that tells me he's not going to answer.

"Please tell me you're not the kind of guy who sleeps with women once and ghosts them."

"I have more class than that."

"Aha! Then you *do* date?"

"Casually. Nothing with any permanence."

"Has it really been six months?"

"Maybe not that long, but probably close."

"You should do a video on social media about that. It proves men's *you-know-whats* don't really fall off if you don't use them. You'd probably go viral and save thousands of teenage girls from feeling anything but proud of themselves when boys use that line on them and they turn them down. Women all over the world would be thanking you, *and* lining up to go out with you. Not that you need more women after you."

His brows lift with amusement. "That mind of yours is something, sunshine."

"I don't know about that, but I know there are several women in here who look like they would be happy to rectify your dry spell." *Including me, which is a problem.*

"No thanks."

"Come on, Fletch. You're a great guy and good-looking for a blond."

*"Ouch."* He bumps me with his shoulder.

We both laugh, and I realize it's things like that little shoulder bump that make me like him even more. But I know what I have to do to stop thinking about him that way. Fletch needs a girlfriend, because I'd never have dirty thoughts about another woman's man.

I drink more liquid courage, preparing for my mission, even if the thought of setting him up with a woman makes me feel a little queasy. "I'm serious, Fletch. You need more than casual dating. You need to connect. To find that spark that makes your heart race with the person who invades your every thought."

"Sounds painful."

"It does *not*." I swat his arm. "Trust me. You need some love in your heart, and I'm just the girl to help you find it."

"Let it go, sunshine."

"Nope." *I need you to be taken, so I don't ruin our friendship.* "I need to narrow down your type, and right now all I know for sure is that it's not a chatty, impulsive girl from the South. What was your ex like?"

He gives me the side-eye and takes another drink.

I turn in my seat, scoping out the women around us.

Fletch turns around, too. "What are you doing?"

I nod in the direction of the brunette. "She's cute, and she was watching you when I was signing up for karaoke."

"I'm not looking for a lady friend."

"You're bullheaded for such a laid-back guy."

I spend the next ten minutes trying to pry his type out of him, but he's locked up tighter than a girdle. We finish our drinks and order another round, with a basket of fries for him and mozzarella sticks for me. I'm halfway through my second drink and feeling good all over when I decide to try to pry information out of him from another angle.

"How long have you been divorced?"

He eats a fry without answering.

"More than five years?" I push.

"Twice that."

"Really?" I take a bite of a mozzarella stick. "Have you had any long-term relationships since then?"

He arches a brow. "Have you?"

"Since I was seventeen? Let's see. I dated one guy in high school for about six months. Jackson Robby. I *really* liked him. He was great with his hands. A real rough-and-tumble kind of guy. But when he went away to college, he wanted the full college experience, which didn't include being tied down to a girl back home."

"That must have sucked."

"It was hard, but it was for the best. I found out two months later that before he left for school, he was seeing another girl who went to a different school, and she ended up pregnant."

"So he was a cheating asshole."

"I know how to pick 'em." I take another drink. "I always seem to be attracted to guys who aren't great for me. I've dated a few guys since then, but none that feel like Mr. Right. What about you? It sounds like you got married young."

"Married at twenty-four, divorced at twenty-six."

"Wow. It only lasted two years? What happened?"

He stares into his drink for a minute, and I can tell he's contemplating his answer. He looks at me, his serious, slightly pained eyes tugging at me. "I don't think it was any one thing."

He says it so low, I have to lean closer to hear him. "What do you mean?"

He sets down his glass, giving me his full attention, and studies me for a beat. "Are you sure you want to hear this?"

It feels like there's more to his question, but I can't put my finger on what that *more* is. "You're helping me every day, and I want to do the same for you. I'd like to know why you've closed yourself off to the best, most magical feeling in the world, but if you'd rather not tell me, it's okay."

◆ ◆ ◆

## FLETCH

Rather not tell her? She's the only person I've wanted to open up to since my divorce. Nothing about our situation makes sense. I haven't spent this much time with a woman since I was married, much less wanted to. I like quiet, and her mouth moves faster than the Energizer Bunny. *Still*, there's something about the sweet, sensitive, over-the-top beauty that reels me in and makes me want to do a hell of a lot more than talk.

But she thinks I'm some sort of grumpy Ken doll who's good-looking for a blond, for fuck's sake, and she's trying to set me up with random women, so I know I'm alone in this.

She's sucking down that cavity-sweet drink through a straw, wiggling her shoulders to the beat of the music as some guy sings off pitch. She's masking her disappointment in my reluctance to spill my past well, which isn't like her. But there's no escaping it. It's like a wall between us, and that breaks my restraint. I lean closer so she can hear me and say, "I've never felt that magical feeling you talk about."

She sets down her drink, brows knitted. "You mean love?"

"Yeah. I thought I loved Elaina, but it never felt the way you describe it."

"Not even at first?"

"We were twenty when we first started seeing each other. At that age, I don't think I'd know something magical if it bit me in the ass."

"Yes, you would." She picks up a mozzarella stick and takes a bite, pointing the remainder at me. "It's unavoidable, like that itch you get in the middle of your back and can't scratch, but in the very best way." She pops the rest of the cheese into her mouth and leans closer, adorably tipsy. "I guess there were no fireworks when you . . . *you know.*"

"You mean orgasms?"

"*No.* Fireworks, with lights and sounds and overwhelming sensations."

I scoff.

"You act like you don't believe it can happen." She waggles her finger at me. "I'll have you know that when you get down and dirty with your forever love, it's unlike anything you've ever felt before. There are definitely fireworks."

"I thought you've never been in love."

"I haven't."

"Then you know this because . . . ?"

"Ruby told me," she says with a lift of her chin.

God, she's cute. "Is that on your checklist, too?"

"Of course! I don't want to miss out on good lovin'. Honestly, Ruby and I both thought sex was *way* overhyped. I mean, it doesn't even last that long, and from what I've experienced, guys can't help but get the good stuff, while I'm always left feeling like . . . *Really? That's it, then?*"

I grit my teeth, wishing she hadn't put the image of her with other guys in my head. "Sounds like you've been doing it with the wrong guys."

"You've got that right. But let's get back to *you.* There were no fireworks, and you *still* married her?"

"In all fairness, I didn't know there could be fireworks, or I might have held out."

"Now you know." She pats my cheek. "But I don't know if you'd've held out. I think you're like a golden retriever. You know, loyal, *golden*." She runs her fingers through the side of my hair.

"Did you just compare me to a *dog*?"

"Yup. But don't fret," she says, petting my scruff. "Lots of women love golden retrievers. I like pups like Molly."

"Disobedient?"

"*Rascally.* But I do like the feel of your scruff." She pulls me closer and rubs her cheek along mine, humming. "*Mm. That's nice.*"

What did I do to deserve this torture?

She sits back, blinking at me expectantly. "So? Were you happy?"

My brain is busy conjuring the sexy hums and moans she'd make if she felt my scruff on her inner thighs. I clear my throat and take a drink, silently berating myself. "Happy enough. We were just kids, going to school and having fun in the Big Apple. We'd go out after studying, and stay up half the night having sex. What more could we want?"

She whispers, "*Fireworks.*" Then louder, "Did you live together before you got married?"

"Yes, while I worked and went to graduate school and she started her career. After we got married, I had my nose to the grindstone with school, work, research, and trying to get published. I thought things were good."

"But she wasn't happy?"

"I guess not. She was a buyer for a high-end retail chain of department stores, and she traveled a lot for work. She met someone while she was traveling and had an affair."

"Oh, *Fletch.*" She puts her hand on my leg for the millionth time. "That's so hard."

*If your hand moves any higher, I will be, too.*

I down my drink, hoping to drown out the desires she's stirring. "It stung, but looking back, it's clear we wanted different things all along."

She steals a fry off my plate and takes a bite. "Like what?"

"Everything. I didn't love living in the city, but she did, so we stayed, and on holidays she wanted to go on vacations, while I wanted to see my family. It was easier to do what she wanted than to fight, so . . ."

"You gave up holidays with your family?" She looks appalled. "What did they think about that?"

"They weren't thrilled that I married her in the first place, so that just added to their concerns."

"Whoa, slow down, Casanova. Did they tell you that?"

"My father tried, and Chuck came right out and said he thought I was making a mistake. But I thought I loved her, so they backed off. I should have listened."

She sips her drink, brows knitted. "You said you'd never choose a woman over family, but you did?"

"Right, and I learned my lesson. I think I was just comfortable and happy *enough* that I didn't need to go looking for more."

"*Golden retriever,*" she says in a singsong voice, stirring her drink with her straw.

"Sure, okay. Maybe. But sometimes you don't realize how wrong something is until you're in too deep."

"Or how *right* it is. It happens both ways." She picks the cherries off the side of her glass and lowers one into her mouth. *"Mm."*

That sound is just as torturous as it was the first time around.

She holds the other cherry out for me. "Want my cherry?"

A slow grin crawls across my face.

"*Ryan Fletcher*, you have a dirty mind."

"Hey, you offered, but since we're talking about *fruit*, I'd much rather watch you eat it."

She flashes a sassy smile, holding my gaze as she places the cherry on her tongue, and then eats it with another alluring moan. Her hand lands on my thigh again, and she says, "Want to know a secret?"

Hell yeah, I want to know a secret, and even though I know I shouldn't, I hope that secret is that she'd rather I eat *her*. "What do you think?"

She crooks her finger for me to come closer. I lean in, and her cheek brushes mine as she says, "Jackson Robby got *my* cherry."

My protective urges claw at me. I put my hand over hers on my thigh, keeping her close, my eyes on hers. "Lucky bastard didn't deserve it."

She inhales raggedly and grips my thigh tighter, just as her name rings through the bar, announcing her turn at karaoke. For a second neither of us moves, but I'm not going to be the dick that steals her chance at doing something she loves on her big night. I force myself to let go of her hand. "That's you, sunshine."

"Yeah. Me. Okay." She blinks several times without moving, and then, as if infused with energy, she jumps off her stool and says, "Wish me luck!" and rushes toward the stage.

Several guys turn to check her out in that sexy pink-and-white dress. I fight the urge to follow her to stake my claim and shut them down. But she's a forever girl with a list a mile long of things she wants in a man, and I'm not that guy, so I shove that urge down deep and order another drink as she gets situated onstage.

Several guys whistle and clap, earning a smile that lights up the room as "I Love It" by Icona Pop comes on, blaring through the bar. The crowd cheers as Destiny struts across the stage like she owns it, scream-singing horribly off-key about crashing her car, watching it burn, and loving it. Every time she belts out that she doesn't care, she faces the crowd and smacks her chest with her fist like the lyrics are torn from her heart. She has the audience eating out of the palm of her hand, clapping to the beat. She motions for everyone to sing with her, and they join in. As she sings about being on different roads, one grounded, one high in the sky, her beautiful eyes find mine, and her grin grows impossibly wider.

I thought she was a force of nature before, but *damn*. She doesn't seem to notice or care that her voice could shatter glass, and that energy and confidence are two of the sexiest things I've ever seen. Second only to the hint of sweet vulnerability in those shimmering eyes that I'm sure nobody else can see as she struts across the stage. I'm so drawn to everything about her, by the time she sings the last words, she couldn't sound more beautiful to me.

The crowd goes wild, whistling and applauding, and Destiny looks bashfully from the audience to the floor and back again. Fidgeting with the mic, she puts one foot behind the other and does a half curtsy. She hands the mic to Mac and hurries off the stage.

I push to my feet as she rushes over, and that bashfulness gives way to a beaming grin. I take her hand, pulling her closer. "You must have been a pop star in a previous life, sunshine. That was awesome."

"Thanks. I know I can't hold a tune, but I *love* singing."

"Don't give me that nonsense." I pull her stool out for her. "You sounded great. Everyone loved it."

As we sit, she exclaims, "Oh *good*. I still have some of my drink left." She puts the straw to her lips, glancing at me with a sexy glint in her eyes.

She is going to be the death of me. I can feel it in my bones.

I also feel like the luckiest guy in the place to have her all to myself.

When we finally leave the bar, she's giddily tipsy and I'm fighting a losing battle to keep my distance. She puts her arms out to her sides and looks up at the clear night sky.

"I did it, Daddy. I'm officially in business with my first client. I hope I make you and Mama proud."

The reminder that she has no family guts me anew, but her unabashed love for them speaks to that organ in my chest that I've spent the last ten years coating in steel. Wanting to be closer to her, to let her know she's not alone, I drape an arm over her shoulder as we walk down the sidewalk. "Do you talk to him often?"

*"Yes."* She presses herself against my side. "I picture him and my mama as stars watching over me. Wanna hear something kind of silly?"

*"You,* say something silly?"

She swats my stomach.

I laugh. "Tell me your silliness."

"I still pay for his cell phone so I can call and hear his voice. I leave him messages, too. I know it sounds a little wackadoo, but it makes me feel closer to him."

I hold her tighter, wishing I could bring her family back, and press a kiss to the top of her head. "It's not silly, and you don't sound crazy. Do you ever talk to your mom?"

"Sometimes, but not like my dad. I was so young when she died, I didn't get a chance to know her as an adult, like I did with my dad. He and I used to talk a lot. He was my best friend other than Ruby."

"Does he ever answer you?"

"In my heart he does, and sometimes he sends me signs." She looks up at me. "Like the day of the fiasco. Before you came over, I was ready to give up on Get the Yes, and I asked him to give me a sign so I would know if I should or not." We turn the corner, heading for her place. "Then you knocked on my door and told me not to give up."

"You think your father sent me, and it had nothing to do with returning the wallet you dropped at the park?"

She shrugs. "I think he did, but it's okay if you don't. All I know is that you've gotten into my head, Ryan Fletcher, and I can't stop thinking about you."

I want to grab hold of those words and take them at face value, but I have a feeling this is just the alcohol talking. "Maybe that's because we're working together every day."

"Nope. I work with Ruby almost every day, and she's not in my head. I was talking to her today and realized I didn't even talk to my dad this morning when I was so nervous about meeting with Arjun.

I usually talk to him about all the big things in my life. But I talked to *you* instead, and you made me feel better." We turn onto her street. "Even Ruby can't make me feel better the way talking to my dad does."

"I'm glad I helped, but I don't want to take your father's place, sunshine." *My thoughts about you are definitely not paternal.*

She snuggles into my side, and man, she feels good. "Nobody could take his place. Besides, there's the whole *kiss* thing, and my thoughts on that are definitely not father-daughterly. I don't know where you learned to kiss like that, but I can't stop thinking about kissin' you."

This was *not* helping me keep my distance. "Is that right?"

"Yes, sir. Your kisses are hotter than Betty Jean's barbecue back home, and that stuff is flamin' hot. I swear I think about kissing you a dozen times every day. A dozen times every *hour*," she says as we ascend her porch steps. "Then there's the dirty thoughts I keep having about you. I imagine your face, and *so* much more. I should be *ashamed* they're so dirty."

Was she trying to shred my restraint one confession at a time? Because she was doing a damn good job of it, and now I wanted to make those thoughts a reality.

"Listen to me going on like a giddy girl. Did I say too much?" She blinks up at me innocently and somehow also seductively, her hazel eyes brimming with so much desire, something inside me snaps.

*"Fuck it."* I sweep my arm around her and seal my mouth over hers the way I've wanted to all night. I tell myself to go slow, so I don't overwhelm her, but she's right there with me, greedily returning my efforts as I devour her. Her mouth feels impossibly familiar. I revel in the sweetness of it and in the feel of her hands on my chest as she goes up on her toes, seeking more. *That's it, sunshine. Take what you want.* I push a hand into her hair, getting a whiff of strawberry as I tangle it around my fingers at the base of her skull. Angling her mouth beneath mine, I take the kiss deeper. She moans, and my body flames at the sound that has fueled my fantasies all week. I've never been so turned on by kissing before, and I can't get enough of her. I grab her ass, holding

her tight against me, knowing she'll feel what she's doing to me. Earning more sexy sounds, I tighten my hold on her hair, kissing her more possessively. She makes a sound between a whimper and a moan, and I reluctantly pull back. "Too hard?"

"No." She tugs my mouth back to hers.

We feast like starving animals, groping and grinding like we may never get another chance. It's been so long since I've felt this type of primal passion, I had wondered if it even existed inside me anymore. I want to take her inside, strip her down, and devour every inch of her. To give her what no man has been able to. To show her that fireworks can come without everlasting love. But that thought reminds me of the inescapable fact that she's *all* about love, and I'm on the opposite end of that spectrum. She's also tipsy, and both of those things give me pause. I respect her too much to do something she might regret, so I ease my efforts, kissing her softer, savoring every press of our lips, every sensual sound she makes. As I draw back, she says, "*More.*"

I'll probably go straight to hell for it, but the plea reels me in for one last, sensual, lingering kiss. The thought of ending the kiss and walking away is agonizing, but I know I have to. I pull away slowly, brushing my lips over hers as I whisper, "I should go, sunshine."

"*Oh* . . . You don't want to come in?"

The disappointment—or hurt?—in her voice slays me. "I want to come in more than I've wanted anything in a very long time, but you're tanked up on Lusty Lizards, and we've got a great friendship. I don't want to screw that up by doing something you'll regret when your head is clearer."

She frowns and runs her hands over my chest. "Why do you have to be such a good guy?"

"Because if I let my G.I. Joe side come out and you wake up tomorrow wondering what the hell you did last night, you'll probably scurry back to Georgia, and poor Arjun will never get his once-in-a-lifetime Parisian-themed proposal."

She laughs. "I won't regret it."

"Let's not test that theory. I'm a casual dater at best, and you're a forever girl. For what it's worth, you weren't the only one who couldn't stop thinking about that first kiss." I press a kiss to her forehead. "Now go inside and lock up so I know you're safe, and drink some water before you go to bed. I'll see you Saturday."

# Chapter Twelve

## Destiny

"You left me hanging last night. Why didn't you text me back? I'm dying to know what happened at your business meeting," Ruby asks too fast and too loud for my throbbing head, when she walks into the grooming room Friday morning, causing the adorable poodle I'm grooming to bark.

The sound echoes in my head. I groan and whisper, "*Shh*, Barley."

"You look awful," Ruby says. "Are you sick?"

"No. I drank two Lusty Lizards last night and woke up feeling like someone used my head as a punching bag."

She laughs. "Congratulations."

"For the hangover?"

"No, for getting the client!"

"*Shh.* How'd you know?"

She deadpans. "Whenever you go out celebrating, you somehow forget that you're a lightweight and you end up looking like this the next morning. Remember the night you moved here?"

"Don't remind me." We celebrated by going out for Italian food and I had several glasses of sangria despite Ruby's warnings about regretting it in the morning. Fletch's similar warning comes back to me for the millionth time, bringing memories of the toe-curling kisses we shared and the embarrassing secrets I spewed.

"I think I need to give you a shock collar, or maybe you need a tattoo across your forehead that says CAN'T HANDLE MORE THAN ONE DRINK, so whoever you're with can try to stop you."

"A shock collar might work, but I think I need two. One for drinking, and one for kissing Fletch." I groan and rest my forehead on the pooch's furry back.

"You kissed him again?" she exclaims.

"*Shh!*"

She hurries over, talking just above a whisper. "Tell me everything."

Slowly and quietly, I tell her everything, from the thoughtful gift and pep talk he gave me, to the way the conversation flowed easily between me, Fletch, and Arjun, and how Fletch had jumped in with input and opinions and compliments about me, to how much fun I had with him at the bar and how the night ended. "I can't believe I basically told him I dream about him *naked.*"

"So what? Lusty Lizards give everyone loose lips."

"*Ugh.*"

"I don't understand why you're not happy about it. You guys obviously have some kind of connection, and you were having fun and you kissed. Why is that a big deal?"

"We also groped. Ohmygod, Rubes. His hands are so big and so much stronger than I imagined. I can still feel them on me, and the way he tugged on my hair? *Mm.*" I lower my voice to a whisper. "I didn't even know I'd like that."

"I don't know much about hair pulling." She touches her buzz cut. "But I know how good big, strong hands can be, and I know that look, Destiny Amor. *Now* I see the problem. You want more than just a little front porch action from Fletchy, don't you?"

"I can't believe I'm saying this about Grumpy Gus, but . . . *who wouldn't?* He's gotten to me, but you know I don't do casual sex, and he's not my Mr. Right. I can't even pretend he could be. He doesn't believe in love. He doesn't even date with an intention for more. He only casually dates. But when we kiss, it feels so good, I don't care about any of that. I turn into a shameless harlot. I want to tear off his clothes with my teeth and let him ravage me. Not that there's anything wrong with that, but I've never been that girl."

"You know what your dad would say?"

"I try not to allow thoughts of my father and sex to commingle."

"As good a point as that is, he'd say if you don't try new things, after a while you'll start moving backward."

"I'm pretty sure he wasn't talking about sex."

"But the logic still applies. It's been a long time since you've been with a guy, and you obviously like Fletch. I think you should go for it. Satisfy your lust and enjoy every second of it. Just make sure you're up front with Fletch, and keep that dreamy heart of yours at bay."

"My heart is *not* a problem where Fletch is concerned. He doesn't even sing karaoke," I say, trying to convince myself as much as Ruby.

Laura walks in with a King Charles spaniel, and having already been shushed by me, she hands Ruby the leash, speaking in a hushed voice. "This is Spencer. He's here for the full spa treatment." Ruby kneels to greet the pup, and Laura looks at me with curiosity. "Flowers just arrived for you. I'll go get them."

My pulse quickens.

Ruby waits for Laura to leave the room before she says, "Sounds like Fletchy's not done, either."

Laura walks back in with a vase of pink carnations. A lump lodges in my throat as she hands it to me. "Open the card. Let's see who they're from."

As I open the card, I half expect to see my dad's horrible handwriting on it, which sounds stupid even in my own head. I don't, of course.

It's Fletch's blocky letters that bring tears to my eyes, which I quickly blink dry so the others don't notice.

CONGRATULATIONS, SUNSHINE.
I HOPE YOU DON'T THINK THIS IS WEIRD. I DON'T WANT TO FILL YOUR DAD'S SHOES, BUT I DON'T WANT YOU TO LOSE THAT WON-DROUS LOOK IN YOUR EYES WHEN YOU TALK ABOUT HIM, EITHER. I KNOW HE AND YOUR MOM ARE PROUD OF YOU, AND I'M SURE HE'D WANT YOU TO HAVE THESE.
YOUR NOT-BAD-FOR-A-BLOND FRIEND,
FLETCH

I'm speechless, unable to believe he remembered what I'd said about the carnations.

"Well? Who are they from?" Laura asks.

I know how Laura looks at Fletch, and I don't want her to get the wrong impression, so I say, "Just a friend congratulating me on my first client."

"That's so sweet," Laura says. "I'll be at my desk if you need me."

Ruby pins me with a worried stare as Laura leaves the room. I show her the note, and her brows knit as she reads it. When she hands it back, her tone is careful. "So much for keeping your heart at bay."

I lift my chin, and for the first time in my life, I flat-out lie to my bestie . . . and *not* for the first time, I lie to myself, too. "My heart is *fine*. He's just being kind because I told him that I talk with my dad sometimes."

"Are you sure he's not looking for more than a casual thing with you?"

This time I don't have to lie. "Yes, I'm sure. He was very clear about that."

# FLETCH

I've been in a shitty mood all day and cannot wait to leave work. As I gather my things, my mind drifts back to Destiny. It hasn't strayed far since we started hanging out. I didn't text her this morning, because I didn't want her to feel pressured or get the wrong impression and think there was more between us after last night. I'm definitely into her, but not with strings that lead to rings.

I figured she'd text me after she got the flowers, but I haven't heard from her. I thought maybe the flowers hadn't been delivered, but I called the florist and confirmed that they had. I wonder if she thought I'd overstepped by sending them, or maybe she hadn't gone into work. Hell, I don't know what to think. I must've picked up my phone to text her about a dozen times today, but that felt weird, too. I'm not a needy guy. I didn't send her flowers to be thanked. I did it to brighten her day. But this silence is gnawing away at me. I'm used to getting texts with her rambling thoughts throughout the day and pictures from her walk with Molly.

That gives me pause.

Maybe she decided not to walk her. That shouldn't bum me out, but it does. If she didn't walk Molly, there'll be no note in that loopy handwriting left for me with a silly heart over the *i* in her name. Yes, I realize I'm a selfish bastard for even thinking that way when there are more important factors at play, but it's been a long time since I've felt anything, and even her notes make me feel a hell of a lot.

"Hey," Talia says as she pops into my office. "Derek and I are meeting Ben and Aurelia at Bridgette's for dinner. Want to come?" Ben and Bridgette are two of Talia's siblings, and Aurelia is Ben's wife.

"No thanks," I say tightly.

"Bad day?"

I don't respond.

"You're usually in celebration mode at the end of finals week."

"Let me ask you something" comes out before I can stop it. "Let's say you go out and have a great time with a friend, and things get a little hot. The next day he does something nice, and you go radio silent. Would you want that friend to reach out, or . . . ?" Am I really asking Talia for dating advice? "*Fuck.* Never mind."

"Is this the same friend you've been helping every night?"

"Yes." We leave my office and head down the hall.

"Okay, and how hot did it get?"

"I'm not in the mood for an inquisition, but not *that* hot."

She grins. "You *like* her."

"As a friend, yes."

"Uh-huh," she says with amusement. "You don't get *hot* with friends."

"Cut the shit, Tal. She's sweet, and cute, and we have fun together. It's nothing more than that. I just hope I didn't make her uncomfortable."

"Did you try to take advantage of her?" she asks as we walk out the doors to the parking lot.

"You know me better than that."

"Exactly. So what are you worried about? She's probably busy. You said she just started a new business."

"Yeah, maybe."

"This isn't like you." Her tone turns serious. "What did you do for her today?"

"She got her first client, so I sent her some flowers that her dad used to send her. He passed away last year."

"I thought you said you two weren't serious."

"We're not."

"A thoughtful gift like that says otherwise."

I curse.

"You're not a stupid man, Fletch. You know a gift like that sends a message."

"I didn't think about it that way." I stop by the row of cars where Talia's vehicle is parked. "I didn't really think about it much at all. I was happy for her, and I wanted to do something that would make her happy."

"Better be careful around this one. When a man like you stops thinking with his head, there's no telling what's next."

I exhale frustratedly and head for my Range Rover.

"If you change your mind, dinner is at seven."

"I won't, but tell everyone I said hello," I call over my shoulder. I'm not fit to be around people right now. I don't even want to be around myself.

When I get home, Molly's all sloppy kisses and tail-wagging joy. It's hard to be in a shitty mood when I'm greeted like that, but I manage to hold on to it. That is, until I spot a card on the dining room table, and my fucking heart hammers in my chest. I snag it on my way to let Molly out.

*Dear Fletch,*
*Thank you for the lovely flowers. Molly and I had a great walk today.*
*Let me know if you still want to scout locations with me tomorrow. No*
*pressure.*
*Destiny*

*PS: I hope you still want to come with me.*
*PPS: But again, no pressure.*

*Damn.* I obviously made her uncomfortable. There are no exclamation points like in the other notes she's left me this week, and she didn't dot the *i* in her name with a heart.

I head into the kitchen and put the card in my junk drawer with the others she's left over the last couple of weeks. Needing air, I walk out back and sit on a chair on the patio. Molly bounds over with her ball, and I toss it into the yard for her. She runs after it, and I take out my phone to text Destiny.

**Fletch:**

I'm glad you liked the flowers. I hope sending them didn't make things awkward between us.

Dots dance across the screen like she's typing, but they quickly disappear. *Shit.*

**Fletch:**

Sorry if I overstepped last night. I thought we were on the same page when we kissed.

Those dots dance again and then disappear. This is another kind of torture I've never experienced before. The dots reappear, and I grip the phone so tight, my knuckles blanch.

**Destiny:**

You didn't overstep! We WERE on the same page!

"Then why does this feel off?" Molly brings me the ball, and I throw it across the yard again.

**Destiny:**

You did the right thing by leaving.

I breathe a little easier, but it only lasts a second as I realize she's drawn a line in the sand and we're on opposite sides.

**Destiny:**

You were right. I am a forever girl.

**Destiny:**

**Destiny:**

And you're definitely not my forever guy.

**Destiny:**

Yup, the line has been drawn, and I fucking hate it, even if she's not wrong.

**Destiny:**

But I wouldn't have regretted doing more.

**Destiny:**

Even forever girls like to have fun.

**Destiny:**

**Destiny:**

We can leave all that behind us and move on. Thanks again for watching out for me. I'm glad we understand each other now.

Yeah, I understand. Last night would have been fun, but the opportunity has passed. Got it. As I begin thumbing out a response, another message pops up.

**Destiny:**

> I love our friendship!

**Destiny:**

>

**Destiny:**

> Please tell me you'll still scout locations with me tomorrow. 🙏 We make such a great team!

I hate the opposite sides of the line deal, but I'm not about to turn down spending more time with her.

**Fletch:**

> I'll be there. Let me know what time to pick you up.

**Destiny:**

> Yay! I ended up taking a couple of grooming clients for tomorrow morning, and I'm sure you'll want to walk Molly since we'll be out for a while. Want to go after lunch? 2:00?

**Destiny:**

> If that's too late and you have other plans, I understand.

**Fletch:**

> Why would I make other plans
> when I already committed to going
> with you?

**Destiny:**

**Fletch:**

> See you at 2, sunshine. Have a good
> night.

**Destiny:**

> It's already much better than my
> day was. I was nursing a major
> headache all day. I'm finally feeling
> better.

A hangover? And she still went to work and walked Molly? That's impressive, and it might explain her earlier radio silence and the lack of enthusiasm in the card. I should have reached out to check on her today.

**Fletch:**

> Those Lusty Lizards were potent.
> Sorry about your headache. I hope
> you're able to get some rest.

**Destiny:**

> Clementine and I are going to bed
> early.

That's one lucky cat.

**Destiny:**

I'm sure I'll see you in my dreams.

**Destiny:**

*Fuck.* How did we graduate from friends to friends who torture each other but must keep their lips to themselves?

**Destiny:**

Sweet dreams, Ryry!

I scoff.

And women think *men* are complicated?

# Chapter Thirteen

## DESTINY

"I had high hopes for this site, but I don't know, Fletch." I plant my hands on my hips, taking in the view of sprawling hills and dusty valleys from a rocky overlook at the end of a trail where Arjun and Maura like to hike. It's almost six o'clock, and the sun hovers low in the sky, perfect for a coming sunset. I take a few pictures of the view to look over later and maybe post on social media, but something is missing. This is the fourth site we've checked out today. We looked at a park two towns over, at another trail Arjun and Maura frequent, and at the outdoor café where they had their first date, which is about an hour from Harmony Pointe. But like this overlook, each spot has left me feeling flat.

"The view is beautiful," he says matter-of-factly.

Fletch has been acting *flat*, too. Maybe that's impacting how I'm seeing things. He's guarded again. Keeping his distance. It's not like he's being mean or even curt. He's not even back to being Grumpy Gus. He's giving me *just enough* friendliness that anyone else might not notice the difference. But I *feel* it in the lack of friendly touches and knowing jokes, and I don't understand it. It's like he's an imposter, and he's getting it all wrong. The few times I tried to ask if something was wrong, he brushed me off. I thought we cleared the air last night, but he must have changed his mind about me. I know I'm not a beauty queen, but I'm cute, and sure, I'm a handful. But I thought he liked who I am. After our front-porch make-out session, I want him more than ever. I was all revved up to throw caution to the wind and take the plunge into a casual tryst with him. But now there's awkwardness and tension between us that wasn't there before, and I don't know what to do about it.

Trying to bury that frustration for the hundredth time since he picked me up, I pull up my big-girl panties and hold my head up high. "It is pretty, but it doesn't scream *Paris* to me."

"Because we're in New York."

*Flat, flat, flat.* I try to lighten the air. "Do you think I don't know that, naysayer?"

The edges of his lips twitch like he's stopping himself from smiling.

"That's why Arjun hired *me* to bring the magic," I remind him too sharply, but I can't help it. "And that's exactly what I'm going to do. I just have to find the right location. I want it to be so romantic and breathtaking that even the air Maura breathes feels infused with love. I thought doing it outside would be perfect. In my head, I see a sunset proposal, with a table for two, a violinist, decorations that make it look like a Parisian café, and a replica of the Eiffel Tower draped in greenery and flowers and lights." I sigh. "I can see it all so clearly. But Arjun seems like a private person. The park and the café are too public, and I didn't realize how long the hikes were. By the time Maura got here, she'd be dusty and dirty. That type of romance has its place, but not for a grand *Pah-ree* proposal."

Fletch is watching me like he's trying to figure me out.

Today is *not* the day for *that.* "Do you think you can build a tower like that for me?"

"No. I'd definitely screw it up. But I know someone who can."

His guarded tone is driving me nuts. I want my friendlier friend back. "You do? Who?"

"My friend Talia's sister Piper. She owns a contracting company, and she does excellent work."

"Do you think she'd be interested in doing it?"

"I can ask. I know she likes unique jobs."

"That would be great. If you're sure you don't mind."

"I'll take care of it." He pulls out his phone, thumbing out a text.

"Thanks." As we head down the trail, he walks behind me, and I try to work out my thoughts. "Now I just need to figure out a better location. I want something with a great view, but I don't think I can pull off Paris with Upstate New York landscape. They should be looking out at the lights of a city, but it still needs to be someplace private. I wish I knew of a restaurant with a great view and rooftop dining. I wonder if Arjun would mind going into the city. But that's not private."

"I know of a place."

"Hm?" I didn't think he was listening.

"My buddy Rich owns an Italian restaurant on the outskirts of Sunnyvale. The dining room has a great view, so I'd imagine the view from the roof is even better. There's no rooftop dining. You'd probably be looking at a dirty old roof."

"I can work with that. Think he'd let me see it?"

He pulls out his phone. "I'll give him a call and see if we can stop by."

My efforts at small talk fall short on the forty-minute ride to the restaurant, and my frustration amplifies. I've gone over everything we've said to each other, and I can't think of a darn thing that would have rubbed him the wrong way. I climb out of the car feeling like a guitar string strung so tight, I'm ready to snap, and force myself to focus on the restaurant. It's impressive, all stone and dark glass, sitting majestically on the top of a hill, which reminds me of a certain walled-off man at the moment.

Said man keeps his distance as we head inside. There's no friendly hand on my back or arm around my shoulder, and I yearn for those simple touches that showed how our friendship had blossomed.

I tuck that away as he informs the hostess we're there to see Rich. When she goes to get him, I take a moment to admire the dark wood, plush leather, and crystal chandeliers. "I like the atmosphere. It's romantic and luxurious without being overdone or intimidating."

He nods. "It's a nice place."

I open my mouth to ask him if I've done something to upset him, but a deep voice booms through the silence. *"Fletch."*

I turn to see a dark-haired, thick-chested, and equally thick-waisted man approaching.

"It's great to see you." He embraces Fletch and claps him on the back. "It's been too long."

"Yes, it has. Rich, this is my friend Destiny, the proposal planner I mentioned. Destiny, my buddy Rich Capella."

Fletch's tone is lighter than he's used with me all afternoon, and that stings, amping up my irritation. But I manage to keep a lid on it *for now* and offer my hand to his friend. "Hi, Rich. It's a pleasure to meet you."

"You as well." Rich shakes my hand. "I can't imagine my roof is what you're looking for, but let's head up and you can check it out."

As we follow him through the restaurant, I ask the question I would have asked Fletch on the way over, had I felt he was open to conversation. "How do you and Fletch know each other?"

"We grew up together and played basketball and baseball on the same teams from the time we were yay high." He holds his hand about three feet off the floor.

"I bet you have some fun stories to share."

"We got into some trouble, but not as much as Jimmy did." Rich opens a door, and we follow him down a hall. "How'd you two meet?"

"I groom his dog, and I tried to marry him off to his stalker." I tell him about the proposal fiasco as we ascend a staircase.

His deep laughter rings out as he opens another door and we step onto the roof. "That's a great story. I'd give anything to have seen your face, Fletch . . ."

Their conversation is drowned out by the magnificent view unfolding before me as I walk to the middle of the roof, taking in the lights of the town against the backdrop of the setting sun. It's exactly what I had hoped to find. I can picture it as clear as day. The decorated tower, café-like setup, and violinist set against the backdrop of a starry sky and twinkling lights of the town. I take out my phone, snapping pictures from every angle, mentally planning out the event. I'd cover the roof with fake grass and add a red carpet lined with gorgeous planters overflowing with red roses. *No. Not red carpet. Cobblestones.* They might have to be fake cobblestones, but they'd be the perfect entrance to Arjun and Maura's magical night.

I turn around to tell Rich and Fletch as much and catch Fletch watching me, jaw tight, eyes hooded. My stomach sinks, but I won't let that steal my joy.

"This is *perfect.*" I head over to them. "What would it cost to rent the roof for a night?"

"I'm sure you know what you're doing, but have you *looked* at the roof?" Rich asks. "It's going to take a crew to clean this mess up, and I don't know how clean it'll get."

I haven't looked beyond the view, and I take a moment to assess the grungy rooftop. "I don't know much about cleaning roofs, but my father power washed the outside of his auto shop, and it looked like a whole new building when he got done. I have a picture in my mind of what this proposal should look like, and this fits it to a T. Rich, if you're willing to rent it out for a night and you give me a ballpark price, I'll run it by my client. If we move forward, I promise you won't have to do a thing, and I'll do my best not to disrupt your restaurant business."

He looks between me and Fletch. "Are you sure about this?"

I press my hand to my chest. "I've already got my heart set on it. I don't know if my client will feel the same until I put together my vision board and lay it out for him, but I have a good feeling about it."

"Did you have a good feeling about the woman who wanted to propose to Fletch?" he asks with amusement.

"That's a fair question," I say at the same time Fletch says, "That wasn't the same."

Shocked that he came to my defense, and with such a stern voice, my thoughts stumble.

"She's far more prepared now than she was at that time," Fletch adds. "If this fits her vision, I'd appreciate you considering renting it to her for the event."

"I was joking. I'm happy to let her use it." Rich looks at me. "But I'm not going to charge you to use it. It's going to cost you a pretty penny to get this place cleaned up."

"You're sweet to worry about that, and I appreciate the offer, but I can't take a handout."

"It's not a handout. Consider it a test run. I've been overlooking the best view in all of Sunnyvale. If your event goes well, I might consider finishing this space off and holding my own events up here."

I pat his arm. "Look at you, thinking outside the box! I love that idea, and I'm thrilled to be your inspiration." I move to hug him, then stop short, remembering I'm supposed to be a professional. I offer my hand instead. "Thank you, Rich."

"Put that hand away. I'm a hugger, too." He wraps me in his beefy arms, and I beam at Fletch, who's finally showing a fissure in his frustrating facade and is *almost* smiling.

I tell Rich about my vision for the proposal, and he seems excited, though wary about whether I can really pull it off. We talk about bringing in safety barriers to make sure nobody gets too close to the edge, and after exchanging contact information, I promise to be in touch soon.

I'm flying high as we head to the car. "Thank you for taking me here. This is where it's meant to happen. I can feel it."

He opens my car door. "I'm glad you're happy, sunshine."

That's the first time he's called me that all day. I didn't realize how much I'd missed it. I climb into my seat and watch him walk around to the driver's side. I wish I knew why he's been acting so standoffish. As he settles behind the wheel, I try again to ease the tension.

"Rich is a peach. I bet you two had a lot of fun when you were kids."

"We had a good time."

His bland tone doesn't improve on the drive home as I ask him questions about him and Rich and try to lighten the mood. When we reach Main Street, I'm a breath away from losing my mind. "Just drive to your house. I'll walk from there. I need some fresh air."

He eyes me disapprovingly.

"Don't look at me like that. I'm a big girl. I can walk around the block without a chaperone."

"I'll walk you home." He grits his teeth and turns down his street.

He sounds so annoyed, I can't take another second of it. "*What* is wrong with you?"

"Nothing." He turns into his driveway and cuts the engine.

"Don't give me that nonsense. You know darn well you're not acting like yourself. Are you upset with me? Did I say or do something to bother you? I've been thinking about it all day, and I can't think of a time I was rude or anything. Unless . . ." *The flowers.* My stomach sinks. "I should've texted or called to thank you right away when you sent me those flowers. That was rude of me, and I know better. But they meant a *lot* to me, and I was afraid I'd come across like a buffoon or a clingy girl trying to snatch you up, and I didn't want to make you feel like I was getting that way toward you."

"I didn't expect a thank-you," he grits out. "And I know you're not looking at me that way."

"Then *why* are you keepin' your distance from me? I thought we had a connection. A meaningful friendship. But you're treating me like you don't even want to be here."

"I *do* want to be here. I'm just trying not to step over the line," he says tightly.

"Have you lost your mind? *What* line?"

"The one you drew in the sand yesterday."

"What in farm hill are you talkin' about?" I don't mean to raise my voice, but I can't stop. "I wasn't anywhere near sand yesterday!"

"It's a *metaphor*," he practically growls.

I throw my hands up. "For *what*?"

"*Jesus.* You were damn clear yesterday about *not* wanting me to kiss you again, which is fine. That's your choice. But you've gotten under my skin with your sweet Southern accent and over-the-top exuberance, and I'm so damn attracted to you, I can't turn it off." His voice escalates, his words dripping with frustration. "So am I keeping my distance? You bet your ass I am, because if I get too close, I'm afraid I'll cross that line, and I don't want to disrespect you."

"I still don't know what sandy line you're talking about, but *I* didn't draw it!" I shout. "Are you saying you *want* to kiss me?"

"Fuck yes, I *want* to kiss you."

"Then stop looking for lines and get over here!" I reach across the console and grab his shirt, tugging his mouth to mine. Our kisses are feverish and hungry, awakening desire so greedy and hot, I feel feral. His hands are in my hair, on my breasts. The sounds of my moans mixing with his guttural growls make my entire body flame. He tears his mouth away, and I long for its return, but his teeth are on my jaw, sending wicked sensations searing through my core. I arch into him, gripping his arms as he lowers his mouth, biting my neck and lingering with open-mouthed kisses. Heat gathers between my legs.

"*Fletch*," I pant out. "Let's go inside."

He frames my face with his hands, his blue eyes pinning me in place. "I like spending time with you, and I'd like nothing more than to take you inside and make you come until you can't see straight. But I'm not looking for a relationship, sunshine, and I'm definitely not looking for love. So let's be damn sure we're on the same page this time, because I do *not* want to hurt you with another misunderstanding."

My heart is racing, and I don't really want to face this, but I think we both need to hear the truth. "Then let me be very clear. I like you a lot, Fletch, but I know we're not a match made in heaven. This combustible thing between us? That's lust in its rawest and rarest form. There might be a fine line between lust and love to most people, but to me it's a ravine, and it isn't drawn in the sand. It's drawn in blood straight from my heart. That's a ravine not easily crossed and certainly not by a man who doesn't nail nearly every item on my checklist. But since we're fake dating for Jimmy's wedding, we might as well enjoy the real benefits, right? After the wedding we'll go back to being just friends. I'll restart my quest to find Mr. Right, and you'll go back to being Grumpy *No-Love* Gus."

"I don't know if I should be bothered by that or relieved."

"I vote for relieved and thanking me with a kiss."

"I'll thank you all night long." He crushes his mouth to mine in a greedy, passionate kiss that has me squeezing my thighs together to quell the urge to climb over that console and straddle him.

# Chapter Fourteen

## FLETCH

Time moves in a blur of lustful kisses and greedy gropes as we make our way into my house. Molly is all over us, jumping up excitedly. It takes everything I have to tear myself away from Destiny, and she just laughs, petting Molly with one hand, as we kiss and stumble toward the patio door. Molly bolts outside, and I leave the door open for her.

As I turn back to Destiny, she reaches for me. I fucking love her eagerness. Our mouths fuse together, and I box her in against the dining room table. *Fuuck.* Her mouth drives me up the wall, so sweet and willing, but I'm not going to rush to the finish line. I lift her onto the table, and she lets out an adorable, surprised squeak. I haul her to the edge and pull her shirt over her head, slowing us down as I drink in the sight of her lust-brimmed eyes, pinking-up cheeks, and pert breasts peeking out through a sexy yellow lace bra. She reaches for me again, and I catch her hand, holding it as I run the fingers of my other hand over her breast. Her nipple tightens against my touch. "We're not rushing, sunshine." I brush my lips over hers. "I'm not going to be one of your disappointments." I take her in a slow, sensual kiss that burns through me. "I'm going to find all the places that bring you pleasure." She inhales sharply, and I trail kisses down her neck, slowing to lick the pulse point at the base. Her breathing hitches. I linger there, licking and kissing, giving it a moan-inducing suck.

"*Fletch*," she pleads breathily, clinging to my arms.

I close my eyes, hoping she isn't having second thoughts. "Want me to stop?"

"*God no.* I just . . . *More.*"

Music to my ears. I run my tongue along her lower lip. "I promise to give you everything you want and more than you think you need, but I told you, I'm not rushing." I kiss her softly. "By the time we're done, you're not going to be able to stop thinking about the pleasure I brought you. Starting *here.*"

I lower my mouth to that pulse point again, lavishing the tender spot until she's squirming, begging for more again. Only then do I kiss my way across her collarbone, ridding her of her bra, and kiss the swell of her breasts. "You're so sexy, sunshine," I murmur against her heated flesh. Her breasts barely fill my palms, but no one has ever felt so perfect. I brush my thumbs over her nipples, loving the way she closes her eyes, and her breath falls from her lips, like she's been waiting forever for this. I rise to kiss her again as Molly bounds inside and shoves her big head between us.

I grit my teeth at my obliviously happy dog. "You're killing my groove, Mol."

Destiny laughs and pets her as I close the door. "I missed you, too, Molly."

Her sweetness toward Molly tweaks something inside me. Annoyed with myself for letting that get to me, I throw some food in Molly's bowl and say, "We're going upstairs."

I help Destiny to her feet and take her hand, heading for the stairs. When Molly follows, I glower at her. "*Stay.*"

Molly cocks her head, panting. I kick the guilt she stirs to the curb and lead Destiny upstairs. Molly follows. Destiny giggles, but I'm not amused. There's no way I'm letting my furry, slobbery beast into the bedroom with us. When we reach the master suite, I let Destiny enter first, and I block Molly's way. My dog looks at me expectantly, as if to tell me to move my ass. I don't blame her. It's her room, too.

I crouch beside her, giving her a scratch behind her ears. "Sorry, girl, but you're staying out here. I'll make it up to you another time." I give her a pet, shoving that guilt deeper as I close the door behind me. One look at Destiny, blushing, bare chested, and reaching for me obliterates that discomfort. "Where were we?" I close the distance between us and wrap her in my arms. "Oh yes, I was about to make you come."

She bites her lower lip, cheeks flaming.

"Change your mind, sunshine?" *Please say no.*

"*No.* I just . . . Don't be disappointed if I can't get there."

"I'd only be disappointed for you, but I don't think you have to worry about that." I kiss her tenderly.

"Yes, I do," she whispers, lowering her gaze. "It's not easy for me."

My chest aches at that, and I wonder if other guys have caused her to feel bad about it. Even the idea of that pisses me off. I lift her chin, holding her gaze, and take a giant leap of faith, hoping I don't offend her. "Is it easy for you when you're thinking of me and you touch yourself?"

"I don't . . . I . . ."

"You know you can trust me, sunshine, or you wouldn't be here. Can you make yourself come?"

She breathes harder, brows knitting as she nods.

"Then I promise you, I'll get you there." I kiss her then, deep and slow, tangling my hands in her hair the way I've already learned she likes. I kiss her until she goes soft and trusting in my arms, and then I slide one hand down her back, crushing her to me, kissing her longer and deeper, wanting to make up for all the assholes who ever made her feel like she wasn't enough.

When our lips finally part, I tug off my T-shirt and kneel to take off her sneakers and blue polka-dot socks, which for some reason make me smile. I remove my sneakers and socks and rise to my feet, kissing her again as I unbutton her jeans. I strip them off, leaving on her yellow lace panties, giving her time to get used to being undressed with me. She's all sleek, gentle curves and flushed skin, like a stunning, delicate bird. But the only thing delicate about this strong, feminine beauty is her tender heart, which, as I trail my hand along her waist, I vow to protect.

She watches me strip down to my boxer briefs and reaches for me. Our mouths come together in a soul-searing kiss that has us both moaning. I rain kisses along her jaw, down her neck, and across her shoulder, intent on finding the pleasure points I'm sure have been overlooked. I caress her breast and trail kisses down her arm, slowing to kiss the sensitive skin along the crook of her elbow. I'm rewarded with a hitch in her breathing. I continue kissing down to her wrist, earning more sensual noises. Clutching her hip with my other hand, I kiss her palm and draw her closer.

"*Fletch*," she pants out.

"Pleasure points, baby." I lower her hand and slide my fingers along the top of her thigh and the edge of her panties. She moans, breathing harder as I move behind her and gather her hair over one shoulder. I graze my teeth over the back of her neck, rubbing my cock against her ass. She whimpers needily. "Like feeling what you do to me, sunshine?" I kiss down her spine and nip at her ass cheek. She jerks, gasping, but it isn't a scared gasp. And the way she pushes her ass back into my hands as I glide my tongue along her inner thighs shows me how much she likes it. She trembles, heat radiating from her pussy through the damp material. "I cannot wait to get my mouth on you." I run my hands down her outer thighs and kiss my way lower, slowing to love the backs of her knees. Her breath rushes from her lungs, and her knees buckle. I put my arm around her, rising up along her back. "I've got you."

"I can't take it."

"Yes you can. It'll make everything better." I kiss just below her ear. "Easier for you." I slide one hand around her, rubbing her through her panties, and press my cock against her ass. She holds her breath. "Breathe, baby." When she does, I slide my finger beneath her panties, teasing without entering her. "You're so wet for me, so ready to come."

"Yes, *please*."

"Soon." I move around to her front, holding her gaze as I slide my fingers between her legs, rubbing there, over her panties, and slick my tongue over her nipple.

She grabs my arms, panting out, "You're making me crazy."

"Good." I suck her nipple to the roof of my mouth, and she cries out, fingernails digging into my arms. I slide my tongue over the taut peak again.

"Suck it again," she begs.

"That's it. Tell me what you like." I fulfill her desire.

*"Fletch—"*

She's so close to coming, but I want her wild with it, unable to hold back, so I rise up, taking her in a rough, passionate kiss, and hook my fingers into the hips of her panties. "I've fantasized about taking these off you since I first saw them hanging by your window."

I drag them lower, kissing the apex of her sex, the tops of her thighs, and her knees, every touch of my lips causing a sharp inhalation as I slip them off. Taking my time, driving us both out of our minds, I kiss my way back up her legs and grab her ass as I slide my tongue along the sensitive skin of her inner thighs, so close to her pussy, my scruff brushes it. Her breath rushes from her lungs, and I continue taunting her until she's begging for more, her arousal wetting my cheek and her inner thighs. I lick those thighs clean and skip over where she needs me most, pressing a kiss beneath her belly button. I want to throw her on the bed and feast on her until she begs me to fuck her, but our time for that will come.

Just like she will.

Right now she needs me to go slow and show her that I'm a man of my word, so I fight the urge and appreciate the beauty before me as I rise to my full height and brush the backs of my fingers along her cheek. "You're gorgeous, sunshine, so fucking beautiful."

I take her hand, leading her to the bed, and pull back the blanket. She climbs onto the bed, and I follow, lying beside her, and run my hand along her side. "You okay? You're awfully quiet."

"I feel like I'm going to combust."

*"Good."* I kiss her.

"I've been thinking about us . . . doing *this* . . . all week," she confesses. "I'm afraid I'll wake up and realize it's just a dream."

She's so damn cute. "Does this feel like a dream?" I lower my mouth to her breast, caressing it with my hand, and tease her nipple with my tongue.

"*No,*" she says in one long breath.

I intensify my efforts, using my teeth and tongue, until she's writhing beneath me. When I suck her nipple to the roof of my mouth, she bows off the mattress and grabs my head, keeping my mouth on her. *"Don't stop."*

I continue teasing with my mouth and hand, earning one sensual sound after another, and slide my hand down her stomach, my fingertips grazing her clit. She rocks her hips, and I lower my hand, sliding through her wetness. She inhales a jagged breath, and *fuck*. She feels so good, and the little noises she's making have my cock throbbing. I can't hold back a growl as I work her clit slowly, reading her body, sliding lower every few strokes, then back up again. She fists her hands in the sheets. "Like that, baby?"

She makes a little noise but doesn't answer.

I move my mouth to her other breast, gradually increasing the speed and intensity of my fingers, and suck her nipple harder, grazing my teeth over the taut peak. She whimpers and moans, digging her heels into the mattress, knees rising. "That's it, baby, chase your pleasure." I *feel* her orgasm building, hear it in her hampered breathing, see it in her thighs flexing. "Tell me what you need, sunshine. *Faster? Slower? Harder?*"

She makes a sinful noise, but my little chatterbox doesn't say a word.

Determined to deliver on my promise, I blaze a path down her body and slick my tongue along her pussy, taking my first real taste of her. Her fists tighten in the sheets. "So damn sweet." I go back for more, quickening my pace, and a pleasure-drenched sound sails from her lips, spurring me on. Sliding two fingers inside her, I move my mouth to her clit, flicking it faster and harder, and crook my fingers inside her, pumping slowly, seeking the spot that will take her higher. "*Oh my,*" she pants out. I return my fingers to the spot where they were and wiggle the tips. "*Ohgod. That feels good. Don't stop.*"

*Thank you, sunshine.*

Zeroing in on that magical spot inside her, I bring my other hand into play, my fingers joining my mouth on her clit. She moves with me, and when she rocks along my fingers, riding them faster, I quicken my efforts.

Her moans grow louder, heels digging deeper into the mattress. I quicken my fingers on her clit, and it doesn't take long before she's writhing and "*Yesyesyes—*" shoots from her lips. Her body pulses tight and hot around my fingers, her loud, sensual cries rocketing off the walls. I stay with her, fucking her with my fingers, lapping up every drop of her arousal. When I feel her coming down from the high, I find that hidden spot like a heat-seeking missile, sending her right up to the peak of another climax.

When she collapses to the mattress, breathless and sated, her body jerks with aftershocks, and I kiss my way up her stomach, to her gorgeous breasts, where I linger, earning sharp inhalations with every slick of my tongue, every press of my lips. I perch above her, drinking in her beautiful, sated smile and closed eyes, and brush a kiss to her lips.

"That was . . . Wow." Her eyes flutter open. "Do I have to call you Orgasm King now? Because I don't think I can do that in public."

I dip my head beside hers, kissing her neck. "Then you can call me *OK* for short. It'll be our little secret." I kiss her again, and she winds her arms around me, pushing her hands into my hair. I have a fleeting thought about how much I like the feel of it, but my cock demands something that will feel much better. I rub the shaft against her entrance.

She grinds against it. "*Mm.* Are you as good with your scepter as you are with your hands and mouth?"

"My scepter?" I laugh again.

"Well, you *are* the king. Or maybe you're so good with your hands and mouth to make up for your lack of scepter skills."

I scoff, kiss her hard, and move to the edge of the bed. She goes up on one elbow, watching as I stand to take off my boxer briefs. "You should do a striptease for me."

"And you should call me Orgasm King in public, but neither one is going to happen."

Her eyes light up as I free my cock and step out of my boxer briefs. "Now, *that's* a mighty scepter."

God, she makes me laugh. I snag a condom from my nightstand and press my lips to hers as I roll her onto her back and follow her down. "Do you want to talk about scepters all night? Because I'm dying to feel you wrapped around me and hear you cry out my name so loud, the neighbors hear it."

She blinks up at me, whispering, "Option two, please."

"So fucking cute." I kiss her again and rise up on my knees. Tearing open the condom packet with my teeth, I give my cock a tight stroke.

"Again," she says huskily.

*My sunshine has a naughty side.* "Nobody likes a dry hand." I reach between her legs, but she snags my hand, pulling it to her mouth. I catch myself with my other hand beside her head, balancing as she drags her tongue over my palm several times, licks along each finger, and sucks my index finger into her mouth with a look of pure seduction in her eyes.

"*Careful,* sunshine. I'm already obsessed with your mouth, and seeing it wrapped around my cock is my favorite fantasy."

"Maybe if you're still the reigning king after this, you'll get to live out that fantasy."

"You know I'm an overachiever."

"I'm counting on it," she says sassily. "Now, how about putting that hand to good use and giving *me* something to fantasize about."

*Jesus, talk about fantasies.* I go back on my knees and fist my cock, giving her the show she craves, and use my other hand to tease between her legs. Her eyes remain trained on my hand sliding along my dick. I can't resist seeing how far she'll go, and I stop touching her. "Touch yourself, beautiful."

Her cheeks flame and her eyes find mine, the vulnerability in them enchantingly seductive.

"Come on, baby, give *me* something to fantasize about." I say it as if I haven't been cataloging her every gasp, moan, and quiver.

Her hand slides down her stomach, stopping short of her pussy, and she bites her lower lip. She was so bold in relaying what she wanted from me, her hesitation is unexpected, and surprisingly alluring. I have a visceral ache, a bone-deep desire to be the one to help her cross this bridge. "Don't be nervous, sunshine. It's just you and me." I stroke myself, and her eyes shift to watch. "Like what you see? Show me how much. Let me see what it does to you. Show me what you wish I was doing to you."

Her chest rises with her heavier breaths as her fingers slide through her slick, swollen sex. "That's it, baby. *So* damn sexy." I stroke myself faster, and her fingers match my pace. "Rub your clit, baby. I want to see you come."

Her gaze flicks to mine, cheeks burning again. "You want me to . . . ?"

"More than I want my next breath. Make yourself come, and I promise, when I get inside you, I'll make you come twice as hard."

Her eyes widen, then narrow. "Then you'd better not make yourself come, which might be difficult, because I want to keep watching you do that."

*There's my bold girl.* "Have you not noticed that I have supreme control?" I drip spit into my palm and fist my cock, giving her some incentive. She licks her lips, her fingers quickening. "That's it, baby."

God, she's so fucking sexy, watching me stroke myself, and teasing her clit. Her legs flex, and her breathing turns ragged. "Good girl. Almost there." I reach down, pushing my fingers into her slick heat, quickly finding the spot that makes her toes curl under and her eyes flutter closed. Her hips rise off the mattress, and a loud, surrendering moan flies from her lips. Consumed with her pleasure, I release my cock and go down on her, feasting and fucking her with my fingers, sending her right back up to the peak of ecstasy.

As she comes down from the high, she sinks into the mattress, breathing hard. "I can't believe you got me to do that."

"That was one of the most beautiful things I've ever seen." I come down over her and kiss her softly. "Thank you for trusting me enough to do that."

Embarrassment colors her cheeks, but a challenge rises in her eyes. "You'd better live up to that promise you made."

"I won't let you down, sunshine." I kiss her again and roll on the condom.

Her arms circle me as I lower myself down and kiss her. Pushing my arms beneath her, I cradle her against me, thrusting slowly, savoring every sensation as her tight body stretches to swallow inch after inch, until I'm buried deep. Heat flares in my chest. *Holy hell.* It's like her body was made for mine. "*Fletch*" falls desperately from her lips as "*Des*" spills from mine. She folds her arms over the back of my neck, whispering, "Don't move. Just kiss me."

*Fuck.* She feels too good not to move, but I seal my mouth over hers, trying to redirect my carnal urges. My tongue plunges deep and demanding. She tastes of lust and need and something deep and soft and *new.* I want to chase that taste like an addiction. Her sinful noises claw at me as we devour each other. My cock throbs inside her, making it even harder to hold back. "I've got to move, baby," I grit out.

"*'Kay.*"

She tugs my mouth to hers, and we lose ourselves in another passionate kiss as we find our rhythm. We pump and grind, every thrust taking me higher, closer to the edge. Her body's tight as a vise, and I can't get enough of her. I push my hands beneath her hips, angling them, taking her deeper. "*Yes,*" she cries out, and grabs my ass, her fingernails digging into my flesh. "*Harder.*" I hike her legs over the backs of mine, driving into her with everything I have. She's as feverish as I am, groping, clawing, clutching, touching, *biting*. I feel her tension mounting in the press of her nails into my flesh, in the flexing of her thighs, and I know she's close, but I also know she might have trouble getting there. As much as I love being in control and want to go wild until I'm blinded by the need to come, I crave her pleasure more than my own. That realization startles me, but as our mouths come together in a feast of fervor, it's the only thought that matters. And I want to *see* her passion playing out.

"I want you to ride me." I cradle her in my arms and roll beneath her, making her giggle as she straddles me. Her thick blond hair tumbles around her beautiful face, white-hot desire flaming in her eyes. She runs her hands over my pecs and plants them just below my shoulders as she begins to move, perky tits bouncing, hips gyrating. She leans forward, her hair falling into our faces as we kiss, and her fucking mouth casts its spell. I lose myself in her, possessing and consuming her mouth, until she breaks away with a needy sound and rides me harder.

I grip her hip in one hand, helping her move faster, using my other hand between her legs as she rides my cock. I grit my teeth against the need to come as her eyes close and her head falls back. I quicken my efforts and reach up with my other hand, squeezing her nipple just hard enough to send her orgasm crashing over her. She cries out, loud and unencumbered, as her inner muscles clamp tight and perfect around me, severing my control. Heat sears down my spine, and my release barrels into me like a bullet train. "*Destiny*—" flies from my lungs like a curse, and I ride out our passion in a hailstorm of fractured thoughts and scintillating sensations.

When she collapses over me, sated and trusting, I wrap her in my arms and kiss her, trying to outrun the depth of emotions I saw brimming in her eyes and the ones she's stirring in me.

# Chapter Fifteen

## Destiny

I lie in Fletch's arms in a blissful state of disbelief as we try to catch our breath and the last of the tremors moves through me. I've never been touched so thoroughly or experienced so much pleasure. He was so intent on making me feel good, it made me want it that much more.

"You're awfully quiet, sunshine. What's going on in that head of yours?"

"*Fireworks.* No wonder Barbie stuck with Ken for so long."

His body tenses up around me. "I'm not your forever guy, Destiny."

"I know you're . . ." Our fireworks conversation comes back to me like a slap in the face. "*Oh. Nonono.* I didn't mean I saw fireworks because I'm in love with you. Ruby was *wrong*. You don't have to be in *love* to see fireworks. You just need to be with someone you trust. Someone who's patient and determined and talented. I swear you made the earth shake. I felt explosions and saw lights. I didn't even know my body was capable of feeling that good, and for your information, I like you a lot, Fletch, but being the orgasm king does not wipe out all the other items on my checklist."

"That's a relief." His head falls back, and he closes his eyes like he's dodged a bullet.

"Hey." I swat him, and he catches my hand, pressing it against his chest with amusement in his eyes. He's so freaking cute with his hair all messy and a goofy smile. "I'll have you know, there are plenty of guys who would like for me to fall in love with them and be proud to be my Checklist Guy. I don't know who they are, but I'm sure they're out there somewhere waiting for a girl that's chatty and creative, and maybe a little disorganized and impulsive, who has love for all kinds of things."

He pulls me into a kiss. "Can we *not* bring other guys into bed with us?"

"I'm just making a point."

"Point taken, sunshine." He rolls onto his side, pulling me against him. "I'm sorry for acting off today."

"You should be. Why didn't you just say something?"

"What could I say that wouldn't make me sound like a dick?"

"The truth usually works."

His brows slant. "Not in my experience."

"That's because you haven't been with a super-awesome girl like me. If the women you've been hanging out with don't appreciate honesty, it's no wonder you don't want love in your life. But I can assure you, honesty always works for me, and if we're going to be the kind of friends who sleep together, I need honesty across the board."

He tucks my hair behind my ear, kissing me softly. "You may say that, but I don't think you mean it."

"Yes, I do. When I hugged you hello, you could have said you'd been thinking about kissing me all night, and I would've done a happy dance and told you to kiss me right then. You could've saved me hours of overthinking and saved yourself hours of acting guarded again."

"In what world do friends greet each other by revealing something like that?"

"I don't *know*. It sounded good in my head."

"I bet it did," he says playfully. "But let's take that Destiny Amor greeting one step further and assume my interpretation of your texts was correct. If that were the case, and I'd said what you just suggested, you would've felt like I was pushing for something you didn't want. See the issue?"

"*Hm.* That does make sense, but I still think talking about things is better than not."

"I'll try to work on that." He kisses me again. "I'll be right back."

He climbs from the bed gloriously naked. He has a ridiculously fine ass, and each cheek is marred with my scratches. "Thanks for the inspiration," I call out as he saunters toward the bathroom.

He looks back at me and lifts his chin in question.

"I'm adding MUST HAVE SQUEEZABLE PEACH to my checklist."

He grins and shakes his head as he disappears into the bathroom.

I flop onto my back, giddily happy, and roll onto my side before slipping off the bed. I pull his T-shirt over my head, getting a whiff of his spicy scent, and those hummingbirds take flight in my chest again. I'm picking up my panties when he comes out of the bathroom, his formidable cock hanging between his muscular thighs.

"You look cute in my shirt." He pulls me into his arms and kisses me. "Shirt Thief."

"Do you mind? Mine's downstairs."

"Not at all."

"Good, because it's soft and I like that it smells like you. I'll be right back." I turn toward the bathroom and he smacks my ass. I squeal and try to glower at him, but it's kind of hard when he looks so relaxed and happy.

After using the bathroom and washing up, I take a good look at myself in the mirror. I feel so light inside, I expect to look different, but the only difference I see is an unstoppable smile. When I come out of the bathroom, he's wearing shorts, but he's still shirtless. *Thank you, Lord.* I do have a thing for his chest. It's broad and strong, but not too muscular, and that dusting of chest hair is irresistible.

I go to him and run my fingers through it. "Thanks for showing me what I've been missing."

"My pleasure." He lowers his lips to mine in a deep, delicious kiss. "Are you hungry?"

"*Starved.* Want me to whip something up?"

With a wolfish grin, he tugs me closer. "The only thing I want your hands busy with is me." I'm gifted another toe-curling kiss.

"You won't hear me complaining."

"How about we order a pizza?" He fishes his cell phone out of his jeans.

"*Yum.* My favorite feel-good dinner. Pineapple and steak, please."

"Is that even a combination option?"

"If you ask nice enough it is." As we head for the stairs, he puts a hand on my back. You'd think after having his hands all over me that touch wouldn't feel so intimate, but it does, and I revel in it.

"Please tell me you don't greet your pizza delivery guys the way you suggested I greet you."

"Only the cute ones." He smacks my butt again, and I run down the last few stairs, only to be met with sloppy doggy kisses. I giggle and crouch to love Molly up.

"What the *hell?*"

"She's just happy to see . . ." My voice trails off as I push to my feet and see shreds of my shirt and bra strewn across the living room.

"Shit." Fletch heads for Molly, and I frantically start picking up the pieces of fabric.

"It's not her fault. She's just mad that I took you away from her." I turn around, and my heart stutters.

He's crouched next to Molly with his arm around her, speaking quietly. "I'm sorry, Mol. I shouldn't have locked you out of the room, but you know better than to eat clothes." His gaze moves to me, and his voice grows thick with concern. "I've got to take her to the emergency vet before it gets into her intestines."

"I'll go with you." I head for the stairs, and he stays where he is.

"Would you mind getting me a shirt so she doesn't run up there? They're in the second drawer in my dresser, and grab my socks and sneakers, please."

"Okay." I take the steps two at a time, hoping Molly is okay.

Half an hour later we're waiting in the emergency veterinary clinic while they x-ray Molly. Fletch finally stops pacing and sits beside me, worrying with his hands, his leg bouncing nervously. I put my hand on his leg. He covers it with his own, interlacing our fingers and holding tight.

"I'm sorry. I should've brought my things upstairs."

"It's not the first time she's eaten something she shouldn't, but usually it's socks." He bumps my shoulder. "Or *bows.*"

I wince. "I'm *sorry.*"

"It's not your fault. I know better than to leave clothing where she can get to it, and you were right. She was jealous. My room is her room, too. She sleeps with me every night, and I never shut her out."

"Ever? Not even . . ." I can't bring myself to finish the sentence and ask about the other women he's casually dated. It's none of my business.

He shakes his head. "I don't bring women back to my place. It's not fair to Molly."

That might be one of the most telling things I've learned about him yet. "Then why did you bring me inside? I would've understood if you said you wanted to go to my place or if you left the bedroom door open."

He leans closer, speaking gruff and low. "Because I couldn't have waited another second to get my hands on you, and I love my dog, but I didn't want her anywhere near your naked body."

The vehemence in his voice makes me feel warm and squishy inside. I tuck that away along with the other special things about Fletch I've learned, like how good he made me feel, and how deeply he loves Molly.

"Next time we'll go to your place."

I love that he wants a next time, but I keep that to myself. "We can't do that to Molly. She spends all day without you, and you're her person.

She'll miss you too much. What if we give her some of her favorite treats or a special antler to chew on and leave the bedroom door open? Do you think that will help?"

He shakes his head. "You're really something, sunshine. Most people would say she's a dog. Put her outside." He lifts our joined hands and presses a kiss to the back of mine. "We'll figure it out."

"I feel bad for her. I hope she's okay."

"She will be, one way or another. I'm glad you're here. Thanks for sticking around."

"Do you really think I'd let you go through this by yourself or leave without knowing if Molly was okay? What kind of friend would that make me?"

He kisses my temple, and I lean against his side, tossing up more silent prayers for Molly.

A while later, Dr. Wilkinson, the veterinarian, comes into the waiting area with Molly trotting beside him. We push to our feet, and Fletch tightens his hold on my hand.

"Molly did great," Dr. Wilkinson assures us. "She swallowed one fairly good-size piece of fabric, but it was still in her stomach. We induced vomiting, and she threw it right up."

"Thank goodness," I say.

"There's nothing in her intestines?" Fletch asks.

"No. She should be good to go." He pets Molly. "Her stomach will be a little irritated, so take her food and water away overnight. If she seems fine in the morning, you can give her small amounts of water and some bland food, and take your cues from her. She shouldn't have any issues, but if you notice anything, give us a call."

"Thank you." Fletch shakes his hand and takes Molly's leash.

As Dr. Wilkinson walks away, we love up Molly. "You gave us quite a scare, Mol. How about we don't do that again?" Fletch drops a kiss on her forehead.

"I won't come between you and your daddy again," I whisper, petting her. I'm not ready to leave them yet, but I'm sure Fletch wants to decompress and spend time alone with Molly. Besides, it was my clothes she ate, which makes me a reminder of what she's just been through. "Do you want to drop me off on the way home?"

As we head out the door, he drapes his arm over my shoulder. "Are you sick of us, sunshine?"

"Not at all."

"In that case, how about we get that pizza and chill for a while with Molly?"

Happiness skips through me. "I'd like that."

## FLETCH

We're four episodes into *The Office* when Destiny snuggles deeper into my side on the couch, moving her hand from my leg to pet Molly, who's lying on my other side with her head on my lap. What a turn today has taken. I feel like a boomerang. This morning I was reluctantly heading in one direction, putting space between me and Destiny. Now I'm nestled between my favorite four-legged girl and the woman who's quickly becoming my favorite two-legged girl, with my feet up on the coffee table beside an empty pint of Cherry Garcia ice cream and two spoons in an empty pizza box.

I didn't even realize how badly I wanted to be here. I could have done without the incident with Molly, of course, but that's my own damn fault. I wasn't thinking. Well, I *was*, but not about anything other than getting Destiny naked. And *Jesus*. Sex with Destiny is out of this fucking world. I don't know if it's because of how close we've gotten at breakneck speed, or her sexy mix of innocence and seductiveness, or something else altogether, but sex has never felt so intense.

As the episode comes to an end, I reach beside my leg for the controller, and Destiny puts her hand over mine, wide eyes gazing hopefully at me. "Just one more episode? I love the scenes with Pam and Jim, and I really want to see if they get toge—" A yawn swallows her voice.

She's so damn cute. That's exactly what she said after each of the last two episodes. I've seen the whole series before, but this is her first time watching it. I don't dare tell her she has to watch a few more seasons before she gets her answer. I'd be happy to sit here all night playing with the ends of her hair while she binges the show, just so I can hear her giggles, *aw*s, and ongoing commentary. She talks to the characters like they might actually listen to her. I have a feeling that as much as she likes the idea of all-consuming death-till-you-part love, she's enjoying the anticipation of hoping Pam and Jim come together, too.

The next episode starts, and she snuggles in again. "Thanks for watching another one with me. I promise to leave right after it's over." She made the same promise after the two previous episodes.

I had forgotten how nice it is to enjoy the company of a woman like this. I'm not ready for our night to end, but the angel on my shoulder reminds me that I don't want to give Destiny the wrong impression. The less angelic creature on my other shoulder says it's just one night and reminds me that we've more than cleared the air about where we stand. Destiny's voice whispers through my mind, underscoring that reminder. *That's a ravine not easily crossed and certainly not by a man who doesn't nail nearly every item on my checklist . . . Being the orgasm king does not wipe out all the other items on my checklist.* My competitive side hates that I could fall short in anything, but that's just my ego talking. The man behind the ego would much rather have the title Orgasm King than Forever Guy.

Having convinced myself that one night together is safe, I press a kiss to her head. "I think Molly wants you to stay."

She glances up at me. "You think *Molly* does, huh?"

"Look at her." I nod at Molly, who looks perfectly content with my arm over her back and Destiny's hand resting beside her head. "She's had a rough night. She deserves a little extra attention."

"Mm-hm. Okay. I'll stay."

We settle in to watch the show. When her hand slips off Molly's head to my leg, I cover it with my own, holding her a little closer. *I'm glad you're staying* is on the tip of my tongue, but when I speak, "Thanks for staying for Molly" whispers out.

# Chapter Sixteen

## Destiny

I wake to the tickle of dog fur on one cheek and Fletch's breath warming my other. I'm trapped between them. *Literally.* Molly's lying on top of the covers, her big body pressed against my side. I'm beneath the covers from chest to toes, but Fletch has somehow managed to bunch up the covers between us around my legs. His upper body is under the covers, his arm resting on my stomach, his hand cupping my boob, and his leg is bent at the knee, trapping both of mine beneath it.

I don't move, for fear of waking them. We stayed up late watching *The Office*, and after finally coming upstairs, we fooled around again with Molly sleeping across the bottom of the bed. I've never laughed so much during sex. Or, rather, had the urge to laugh and tried to silence it. We were trying not to move too much or make too much noise, so as not to wake Molly. But Fletch is over six feet tall, and sharing a bed with an eighty-five-pound dog means far less foot room. Just thinking about how hard we tried not to laugh, shushing each other and covering our mouths, makes me laugh—and it bubbles out too fast to stop it.

I clamp my mouth shut, but it's too late. Molly rolls over, and her front legs land on my stomach and Fletch's arm, earning an "*Oomph*" from me and startling Fletch awake.

He groans, trying to push her away as she covers our faces in slobbery kisses. Now I'm even more trapped, and all I can do is crack up.

"Come on, Molly. That's enough." Fletch lovingly pushes her off my chest, and she plops down beside me. He leans over me and pets her. "Good girl."

I love that he's such a softie for her. Those amused baby blues find me, and my stomach flip-flops. I tell myself it has nothing to do with the way he's exuding some new, disarming charm or the incredibly fun, sexy times we shared last night and that it's only happening because I'm seeing him in a different light than the usual perfectly put-together Fletch. His hair is sticking up all over, his sleepy expression is devastatingly sexy, and his scruff has thickened, giving him an edgier vibe. But I know it's a mirage. He'll shower and shave, and an hour from now he'll be back to normal, my stomach will settle, and the vibration in my chest will stop.

"Sorry about Molly." He leans in and kisses me.

"She's fine. I'm in her bed, not the other way around. What time are you leaving to go fishing?"

"I'm usually gone by now."

"*Oops.* Sorry."

"I'm not. It was worth it. I'll just get a late start."

"Do you want me to take care of Molly for the day?"

"Thanks, but I'm taking her with me. She's my fishing buddy."

"Lucky Molly. Where do you go? Sugar Lake?" Sugar Lake is in Sweetwater.

"No. Too close to civilization for us. We like peace and quiet. We're going to Lake Whatchacallit."

"Did you say *Whatchacallit*? That can't be real."

"It's a real lake, but it's a fake name. When we were younger my brothers and I couldn't remember the name of it, so it became Lake Whatchacallit."

"That's adorable. I love that you still call it that. My dad used to take me fishing. We never caught much, but we had fun."

His brows slant. "Do you want to tag along? It's an hour's drive, and it'll be a long day in the sun, baiting hooks and entertaining Molly. It might not be your cup of tea. It can be buggy, and there aren't any public restrooms, but there are plenty of woods."

If I've learned one thing about Fletch, it's that he's as much of a realist as I am a dreamer. I'm fairly certain he's trying to prepare me, not dissuade me, but I can't help teasing him. "Wow, you really know how to make a girl feel wanted."

"You know I wouldn't invite you if I didn't want you to go with us."

"*Do I*, though?"

"Who knew you were so high maintenance?" He gives me a quick kiss and clears his throat. "Miss Amor, Molly and I would be honored if you'd join us for a day of fishing."

I lift my chin. "I don't know if I should. You didn't warn me that you were part octopus, and that makes me wonder what else I'll find out about you if I let you take me to a remote location."

"Part octopus? What are you talking about?"

"Don't play coy with me, Ryan Fletcher. Do you usually glom all over Molly the way you glommed on me?"

"I didn't *glom* on you."

"What would you call it?"

"Not *that*. I was . . ."

"Don't even try to pretend you were spooning me, because you have way too many prongs to be a spoon."

He plops onto his back. "*Shit. I was* glomming, wasn't I?" He gives me a stern look. "What the hell, sunshine? What'd you do to me?"

"Me? *Fess up*. You usually sleep with a big teddy bear, don't you? Where's it hiding? Under your bed? In your closet?"

He laughs, and as he drapes his leg over me again, I catch sight of his feet. His second toe is bigger than his first, and it has a bulbous tip. "Uh-oh. Ken is defective. He needs to go back to the factory."

"What? Why?" He follows my gaze, and I quickly look away from his foot.

"Nothing. Never mind." I press my lips together.

He tickles my ribs, making me laugh. "Spit it out, sunshine."

"It's your toes! You've got a long second toe with a big ball at the end. I want to clip it off at the last knuckle."

"Clip it *off*?" He lifts his foot and looks at it. "What's wrong with having a longer second toe?"

"Look at it! It looks like it doesn't belong with the others. Don't you want me to . . . ?" I make scissor motions with two fingers.

"*No.* In fact, from here on out, you're not going anywhere near me with scissors. Or knives. Or metal nail files."

We both laugh.

I pull my foot out from beneath the covers, showing him my toes. "See how mine are angled in height, with the big toe being the longest? You have to admit my toes make much more sense."

"Mine make perfect sense."

"Oh, *please.* Look how cute my toes are." I wiggle them.

"Are you toe-shaming me? Because for a girl who claims to have love for all kinds of things, you don't seem to have any love for long second toes."

I lower my foot, feigning a pout. "Now you're just making me feel bad."

"I'm making *you* feel bad? I'm not the one with the *neat feet* requirement."

"I told you to forget what's on my checklist, didn't I?"

"I only wish I could."

"Not that it matters since you're *you*, but with the exception of those two shameful toes, you do have neat feet."

"Don't try to backpedal," he teases.

"I'm *not.* They're clean, your nails are clipped, and the tops aren't all hairy, which is good."

"You're totally backpedaling." He moves over me, pinning my hands beside my head. "Now you're in trouble." He kisses my neck.

Molly shoves her big head between us, trying to lick my cheek. I close my eyes and mouth, turning away, trying not to laugh.

"All right, you big cockblocker. *Off.*" He points to the floor, and Molly leaps off the bed.

He takes a quick visual sweep of the floor, but we were careful to ensure nothing was left out last night. When he gazes down at me, his eyes smolder. "That's better." His voice is liquid heat, and my body floods with awareness. He presses his lips to mine, light as a feather, and trails kisses to my ear, whispering, "I finally have you all to myself," sending rivers of heat slithering through my core. He nips at my earlobe, and I inhale sharply. Before I catch my breath, he seals his mouth over my neck, sucking, licking, and nipping, until my entire body is on fire, and I'm a writhing, moaning, needy mess of desire.

"You're driving me *crazy. Kiss me—*"

He crushes his mouth to mine, rough and urgent, grinding his hard length against my panties, and I know they're going to melt off. I'm right there with him, clutching his arms, his back, his incredibly firm butt. I spread my legs wider, wanting so much more. He makes a guttural, lustful noise. "I'm obsessed with your mouth," he growls, and as our mouths fuse together, I think I'm worse off than he is. I can't get enough of *any* part of him. He slows us down, grinding against that sensitive bundle of nerves, kissing me deep and sensually. I feel like I'm going to come, but I know that's impossible. I chase the sensations, rocking against him, kissing him harder, until I can't stand it anymore, and I tear my mouth away, begging with everything I have, "I need you inside me."

He moves faster than lightning, stripping off our clothes and sheathing his length, and enters into me in one hard thrust. I cry out a loud, indiscernible sound, and Molly barks, but Fletch doesn't miss a beat. He captures my moans and gasps as we pound out a frantic rhythm. I'm swept up in him. In his demanding kisses, his strong hands gripping, clutching, lifting, angling, and his talented cock stroking over that magical spot inside me that has my toes curling under and my insides drawing up tight. When he pushes his hand between us, working my clit to perfection, the rest of the world falls away and I *detonate*, surrendering to erotic bursts and explosions that rival the Fourth of July as Fletch gives in to his own powerful release, gritting out "*Sunshine, sunshine, sunshine—*" like a mantra. And then I'm floating through a gust of erotic sensations, my body prickling and shuddering as I come down from the clouds, and he groans through the last of his release, collapsing over me.

He gathers me in his arms, lavishing me with kisses, and my heart soaks up every one of them as he murmurs against my cheeks and lips, "God, sunshine . . . so good . . ."

I don't want to let go. Don't want to miss a second of this feeling, but my arms are so tired from clinging to him so tightly, they flop to my sides like wet noodles, and I pant out, "You're ruining me."

"For . . . ?"

"I don't know." The truth brings a heaviness to my chest. "Whoever comes after you."

His brows knit, and an incredulous chuckle falls from his lips as he dips his head beside mine and sinks his teeth into my neck.

I gasp. "*Hey.* What was that for?"

He looks at me with a cross between a serious and amused expression. "What'd I tell you about bringing other guys into bed with us?"

His words ease the weight of the truth, drawing a smile. "I meant it as a compliment."

"I can see I'm going to need to keep your mouth *much* busier."

## FLETCH

To say we got a late start would be an understatement. We didn't end up leaving Harmony Pointe until after eleven. Destiny had to go home to get ready and to feed and give attention to Clementine, since she worried her cat had missed her last night. While she was there, she insisted on packing a picnic lunch, snacks for us and Molly, blankets, towels, and who knows what else she has in her bag. For a woman who was flying by the seat of her pants in business, she has outing organization down pat.

Although, I have to admit, she's done an impressive one-eighty with her business. She spent the hour's drive to the lake making a list of all the places she wanted to call to price out the event for Arjun and mapping out her week, which included a follow-up call with the potential client she picked up last week. She is definitely more focused and determined to do it right.

But fishing? *Not so much.*

I glance at her, a good distance downstream from me, in her skimpy cutoffs and white bikini top with green polka dots, wading through knee-high water, using her fishing rod like a maestro's baton as she sings Taylor Swift's "the 1." I can't be sure if it's her traipsing through the water or her singing that's scaring the fish away, but I don't think she knows how to be still unless she's exhausted. In the couple of hours since we arrived at the lake, Destiny has eaten lunch while walking along the rocky shoreline with Molly on her heels, thrown a ball with Molly, sung "Heart Attack," "Girl on Fire," and about fifty other off-key pop songs, and a few country songs, too. I caught myself humming along to some of them, and Molly looked at me like she didn't recognize me.

*Join the club.*

I don't recognize myself most of the time when I'm around Destiny, either. She's cast some sort of spell over me. I haven't woken up next to a woman in a decade. Last night, after she fell asleep, I lay awake for a while wondering what the hell I was doing and worrying I'd be a dick to her in the morning. Not that I wanted to, but I'm not used to having someone in my space, much less in my bed. Sharing a bed during sex is one thing, but I had all sorts of scenarios in my head about waking up feeling suffocated and wanting her to leave. I was surprised this morning when I woke up happy she was there. Then again, I don't know how anyone could wake up to that smile and her sweet demeanor and not be in a good mood.

I keep waiting for that *oh shit* moment to hit, but she's dangerously fun to be with.

Destiny spins around, flashing her pearly whites as she pushes her oversized sunglasses to the bridge of her nose, and Molly pops to her feet. Destiny's skin is sun-kissed. The lighter blond streaks in her hair shimmer in the afternoon sun, making her eyebrows look even darker. It's mind-boggling how much more beautiful she gets each day. She starts singing a slower song. I feel like I've heard it before, but other than a line about buying dirt, the lyrics don't ring a bell.

"Sing with me," she urges.

"Not gonna happen, sunshine."

"Party pooper." She begins singing again. *"Find a honey you can't breathe without. Buy her a diamond and drop to your knee. Hm-hm-hm-hm-hm. Something about pencil marks and growing grass and guys who have a great ass."*

I laugh. "You should go on tour."

"They'll call me Off-Key Destiny, and people will come from miles around to hear me sing."

"I'd buy a front-row ticket."

"You'd better buy two. One for you and one for Molly. She loves my singing. Right, Mol?"

Molly barks and bounds into the water, splashing Destiny, who simply tucks the fishing rod under her arm and showers her with attention. "That's my good girl. You're going to need to come see me at work after this."

They both look so happy, I take out my phone and snap a picture of them. Destiny notices and bends down, wrapping her arm around Molly's neck and grinning as I take another. Then she kisses Molly's head, says, "Come on, Mol!" and runs through the shallow water chased by my pooch.

My phone vibrates with a text from Piper.

**Piper:**

> Sorry I didn't get back to you
> yesterday. Frankie threw my phone
> and it landed in Jiggs's water bowl.
> Don't ask.

Frankie is Piper and her husband Harley's almost one-year-old daughter, and Jiggs is their very spoiled dog.

**Fletch:**

> She's got your temper.

**Piper:**

> And Harley's love for Jiggs. She
> wasn't mad. She was throwing it
> to Jiggs so he could use it. Is your
> friend still looking for someone to
> build that tower?

**Fletch:**

> Yes.

**Piper:**

> I have a crazy week. Is it urgent?

**Fletch:**

> Sort of. She needs to get a price
> so she can get budget approval
> from her client. If you don't have
> time, do you think Kase would be
> interested?

Kase Force is a contractor who works for Piper.

**Piper:**

> I'll make it happen. Is she around today?

**Fletch:**

> Yes. We're out now, but we'll be heading back that way later.

**Piper:**

> Can you bring her by my house? Anytime after 4 is good.

**Fletch:**

> Absolutely. I'll text when we're on our way. Thanks. I appreciate it.

**Piper:**

> 👍
>
> And don't think I didn't notice the WE.

As I pocket my phone, Destiny parks a hand on her hip, a mannerism I've already come to associate with her, and looks out at the lake. "What is going on with the fish? We've been here for hours and haven't caught a darn thing." She glances back at me. "Know what my daddy would say?"

*That you're scaring them off?* "What?"

"Fish don't get to grow big by being stupid."

I chuckle and reel in my line.

"My mama used to say, that's why they call it fishin' and not catchin'."

"Smart woman. Hey, Piper finally texted back. We can stop by and see her on the way back into town."

"She did? *Yay!*" She walks out of the water with Molly, and as Destiny sets down her rod, Molly shakes off the water, splattering her.

"*Molly*," I holler, but Destiny's carefree laughter drowns me out.

"It's fine. Did you know dogs shake off like that near us because they love us?"

I set down my fishing rod and grab a towel for her. "Who told you that lie?" As I hand her the towel, I lean in and kiss her. As soon as our lips touch, I realize I probably shouldn't've done it.

"It's not a lie. It's a doggy-love ritual."

Why does she have to find love in everything? I grit my teeth.

She tosses the towel onto one of the chairs I brought and goes up on her toes, winding her arms around my neck. "You can relax, *No-Love Gus.* Kisses between friends who are enjoying the benefits of fake dating aren't going to make me dream of walking down an aisle to you." She presses her lips to mine, as if to emphasize her point.

I'm relieved, but now I feel like an asshole. Partly because I hate that she noticed a reaction from me and partly because apparently my ego has decided to be a dick where she's concerned and it wants to claim all the titles even if I don't want them. I'm well versed in shutting down emotions, so I kick my ego to the curb, and then I tie the fucker up so he can no longer annoy me.

I put my arms around Destiny and touch my forehead to hers. "Sorry for acting like an ass." I gaze down at her. "I'm afraid I don't know where to draw the line. I don't spend time like this with women I casually date."

"You *don't?*" she asks incredulously.

I shake my head. "I might take them to dinner or out for drinks, but that's about it."

"Then it's a good thing I'm your friend, because according to my dating handbook, you've got casual dating all wrong. But don't worry. I'll make it my mission to train you properly."

I cock a brow. "Train me?"

"You know. Show you the ropes."

"Wait, are you telling me Little Miss All About Love has experience with casual dating?"

"*Well . . .*" Her eyes spark with mischief. "It's *recent* and more along the lines of fake dating a friend, but I think it's similar enough that the rules can be the same."

"No, they can't. I'm not as good of friends with the women I casually date as I am with you. You don't have a hidden agenda, and in my experience, most women go into casual dating hoping for more, even when they deny it, so I don't want them hanging out at night with me and Molly or fishing with us."

"You know you have major trust issues toward women, don't you?"

"Yup."

Her eyes narrow, and she lowers her hands from around my neck. "And I'm not good at hiding things, which is why you're okay with our arrangement, isn't it?"

"I hadn't put the two together, but it probably has something to do with why I originally spent so much time helping you. But now that I know you better, I like you and I trust you."

"Good, because you should, so you can stop worrying. The way I see it, we already set up guidelines about the future, so we can do anything we want without worrying it'll be taken wrong, including kissing in public if we feel like it." Her brow wrinkles. "Unless you don't want that?"

"What I want is not to worry about every little thing we say and do, so as long as we're on the same page with this thing not leading to more . . ." I tug her back into my arms and lower my lips to hers, giving us both my answer. My cell rings, and I groan. "What is this? Grand Central?"

She giggles and heads over to the picnic basket, while I answer the call. Molly follows her like she's the Pied Piper.

"Hi, Mom."

"Hi, honey. How are you?"

"Good. How are you?" I watch Destiny open a bag of chips and walk back into the water as she eats them. Molly lies down at the water's edge, watching her.

"I'm fine. Your father and I just got back from a nice walk. What are you up to today?"

"I'm fishing."

Destiny drops a chip into the water, and she bends at the waist like she's studying it.

"How *nice*. I'm glad you're taking a break. You work so hard. Are you at your cabin or at Lake Whatchacallit?"

"Lake Whatchacallit." Destiny purposefully drops another chip into the water.

"Ohmygosh! The fish like chips! Fletch!" She spins around, sees I'm still on the phone, and covers her mouth as Molly bolts into the water, splashing her, and we both laugh, the sound ringing out.

"Who's with you?" my mother asks. "Is that Destiny?"

"Yes. She came fishing with us." Destiny looks over and points at Molly, then at the potato chips. She steeples her hands, mouthing, *Please? Just one?* I nod, silently reiterating, *One*. She wiggles her shoulders and gives Molly a chip.

"How wonderful that she likes fishing, too. Chuck said she's quite an impressive young lady, and from what he and Jimmy have said, she seems like a bundle of Southern sass and charm. Did you know she baked him cookies to thank him for helping her?"

"Yeah, I know. She's a sweet one."

"It's been a long time since I've heard you sound this relaxed and happy. I don't want to keep you from her. I just called to give you the date for your father's birthday dinner. We're thinking of doing it next Friday at six, at Rich's restaurant. Do you think you and Destiny can make it? We're anxious to meet her."

"I don't know what her schedule is, but I'll be there."

"Okay, sweetheart. Let me know this week if you can, so I can make reservations. Tell Destiny I look forward to meeting her whenever she has the time. Have fun today. Love you."

"Love you, too, Mom." I end the call and glance at Destiny eating chips as she walks through ankle-deep water with Molly, singing about someone bringing her coffee in the morning and bringing them inner peace. I realize with surprise that I wouldn't mind if she came with me to dinner with my family, but I'm not about to commit to that.

# Chapter Seventeen

## DESTINY

Fletch offers me his hand as I climb out of his Range Rover at Piper's house in Sweetwater. He looks handsome and comfortable in a gray T-shirt and navy shorts. He's sporting a tan that makes his eyes *pop*, and he didn't shave or trim his scruff this morning after all, making him even more irresistible.

"You sure it's okay to show up like this?" I look down at my white T-shirt, which has a giant sunflower on it but isn't so white anymore. "We should've stopped to get a bottle of wine or something to thank her for seeing us on a Sunday."

"You look beautiful, and there's no need for a gift. She's a friend." He opens the back door, and Molly jumps out.

"All the more reason to be grateful."

"If you really feel the need to give her something, my brother loved the cookies you gave him. Maybe you can bake some for Piper at some point. She's a real sugar fiend."

"Perfect!"

He puts his hand on my back, and we head up the walk with Molly. "Don't be surprised if she gives me a hard time."

I stop cold. "Why? Did you pressure her into meeting me today? I don't want to bother her if she's busy or doesn't want to help. I can find someone else to build the tower."

"It's not that, sunshine. Piper is *Piper*. I don't make a habit of bringing women around, and she's nosy and sarcastic and unfiltered."

"*Oh*, you meant that kind of hard time? Then what are you worried about? We should get along just fine."

"Yeah, you're probably right." We head up to the door. "By the way, her husband, Harley, is Marshall's older brother."

"He is? Do they know we're going to the wedding together?"

His jaw ticks. "I doubt it. Marshall's not one to gossip."

"Want me to play up the wedding date?"

"How about you just be yourself?" He knocks, and a dog barks inside.

Molly whines excitedly, tail wagging, as the door opens. We're greeted by a petite woman with straight shoulder-length blond hair and a cute baby bump, holding an adorable little girl with wispy golden-brown hair and big blue eyes. A pit bull barrels past her onto the porch. I stumble backward, and Fletch sweeps his arm around my waist, pulling me away from the dogs and holding me against him as they bark and jump on each other, causing the baby girl to squeal with delight.

"Should we have left Molly in the SUV?" I ask frantically.

"No. She's fine," he says in my ear, and presses a kiss beside it as the woman yells, "Harley, call Jiggs." A loud whistle comes from within the house, and Jiggs and Molly bolt inside.

"*Go on out back, you rascals*," a deep voice booms from within the house.

"Sorry about that." She looks curiously at Fletch, whose arm is still belted around me. "You must be Destiny. I'm Piper, and this is Frankie. Welcome to our madhouse."

"It's nice to meet you both." I look at Frankie, who is wearing a cute yellow romper. "Aren't you precious." I tickle her bare foot, and she giggles. "I hope I don't smell like the lake. We were fishing, and I didn't have time to clean up."

"Fishing, huh? Isn't that interesting?" She glances at Fletch, who shakes his head. "We're a household full of dog hair and diapers with a boat out back, so if you do smell like the lake, you'll fit right in." She steps aside. "Come on in."

Fletch's hand moves to my back again as he follows me in.

"Your *friend*, huh?" Piper says with a snort-laugh as he walks by.

"Let it go, Pipe," he warns.

*"Eh, eh, eh!"* The baby rocks forward and back, reaching two grabby hands toward Fletch.

"Give me that little nugget." The second Frankie is in Fletch's arms, everything about him softens, from his jaw and his gaze to the set of his shoulders and even the way he breathes. He nuzzles against her cheek as he carries her into the living room. "How's my princess? Did you miss Uncle Fletch?"

I'm fairly certain my ovaries are going to explode.

"You okay, blondie?" Piper asks.

I realize I'm still in the entryway, staring at Fletch, and try to shake it off. "Uh-huh. Yeah. Fine."

Piper smirks. "Would you believe that when Frankie was born, he wouldn't even hold her?"

"That doesn't surprise me as much as seeing him morph into a marshmallow right before my eyes. What changed?"

"My family had a baby boom, and Fletch had to sink or swim. Now he's Uncle Fletch, and all the kids adore him, but he still claims not to want a family of his own."

"Don't be spilling my secrets, Pipe," Fletch says earnestly, then turns a sweeter tone on Frankie. "Your mother has a big yapper."

His gaze flicks to me for only a heart-stopping second, but it's long enough for me to see the truth in them. He doesn't want a family. That's one more item on my checklist he fails to meet. I tell myself it's a good thing and use it to fuel the perspective that has been slipping through my fingers like sand all day.

A burly brown-haired man comes in through a sliding glass door on the other side of the room. He looks at Piper adoringly, and I know he's Harley. His hair is darker than Marshall's, but they're both bearded. Harley is beefier than Marshall, and he has no visible tattoos, but those aren't the things that set the brothers apart in my mind. It's that Harley doesn't immediately give off as much of a don't-mess-with-me vibe as Marshall does. I know how loss can change a person, and I wonder if it changed Marshall or if he was always like that.

*"Dadada."* Frankie lunges toward Harley.

"Whoa, careful, princess," Fletch says, handing her over to Harley.

"That's my baby girl." Harley kisses her cheek. "Good to see you, Fletch."

"You too." Fletch motions to me. "Harley, this is my friend Destiny."

"Hi." I wave. "Thanks for letting us interrupt your evening."

"No worries. Fletch is family, and we always have time for family." He claps Fletch on the back. "Can you guys stick around for dinner? The dogs are having a blast, the grill is ready, and we've got plenty of food."

Fletch glances at me. "What do you think, sunshine?"

I notice Piper and Harley exchanging a curious glance, which I assume is because of the endearment, and I wonder what they're thinking.

"That sounds great to me." I look at Piper. "If you're sure it's not too much trouble."

"We wouldn't have it any other way," she says.

While Harley and Fletch get dinner ready and take care of Frankie, I fill Piper in on my business and describe the event for

Arjun and the tower I'd like to have built. She shows me a sketch of a miniature Eiffel Tower she put together after getting Fletch's text yesterday and explains how she'd build it and roughly what it will cost. It's more than I thought it would be, but I think Arjun will love the idea.

"That's exactly what I had in mind," I say. "I have to finish the budget for my client and get his approval before I can give you the green light, and I still have to get prices from the roof cleaners, and the florist, and, well, basically *everything* at this point. But assuming my client loves the idea and approves the budget, how long do you need to build it, and how will we get it up on the roof of the restaurant?"

"I can build it in a week. Less if you're on a tight timeline, and as far as getting it onto the roof, leave that to me. I've already got some ideas."

"That's wonderful. You don't happen to know anyone who can make a cobblestone path on the roof that can be deconstructed after the event and who might have access to turf, do you?"

"Sure do. But cobblestones are expensive. If you go with stone pavers, or even fake stone, it'll be much cheaper. The guy I'm thinking of often has extra stone from projects that he unloads cheap. I'll see if I can swing a deal for you."

"Are you sure you don't mind?"

"Not at all. He owes me a favor. Did Fletch tell you that my sister Bridgette owns a floral shop? I bet she'd give you a great deal."

"He didn't mention her, but I'd love to talk with her."

Piper writes down Bridgette's phone number. "Her shop is called The Secret Garden, and you can't miss it. It's in the center of town, and it adjoins our sister Willow's bakery, Sweetie Pies."

"I was just there getting Loverboys to surprise Fletch. Is your sister also blond and pregnant and a real talker?"

"Yes, that would be Willow."

"I loved her, and those Loverboys are delicious."

"Everything she makes is insanely good. You'll like Bridgette, too. She's more low-key than Willow but not as low-key as Talia."

"*Talia*. She's the one who's close to Fletch, right?"

"Yeah. They both teach at Beckwith. They're two peas in a pod. Very cerebral."

I get a twinge of jealousy, wondering if she's one of the women he has casually dated.

"Everyone thought they'd end up together," Piper says, turning that twinge into an uncomfortable knot. "But then she fell in love with Derek, and now they're married with a family of their own, and Fletch has you. How long have you guys been seeing each other?"

"Not that long. He's been helping me get organized with my business, and we hit it off."

Piper's brow furrows. "Let me get this straight. The guy who doesn't believe in love is helping you with your *marriage-proposal* business? How did that happen?"

"It's an embarrassing story . . ."

I tell her about the picnic-proposal fiasco, which seems like it was ages ago. It's easier to laugh about it now and to admit how naive I was.

The guys find us in stitches when they finish grilling, and as we sit down to eat, Piper relays the story to Harley. He teases us relentlessly. Fletch takes the opportunity to make fun of Piper and Harley's engagement, and I learn that when Harley proposed, Piper was so freaked out, she ran away and tried to bury her love for him in doughnuts. Clearly it didn't work, because there's so much love between them, it fills the room.

Fletch puts his hand on my leg, leaning closer to say, "Maybe we should give them a do-over proposal."

His use of *we* burrows into my heart, and my perspective takes on that sand-like quality again, leaving me futilely trying to stop it from slipping through my fingers.

◆ ◆ ◆

When we leave Piper's, we chat the whole way back to my place, and as he pulls into my driveway, I'm not ready to say goodbye. That feeling has become a broken record when it comes to him, and I know I need to get my arms around it.

He gathers my picnic blanket, towels, and the other things I brought with us and walks me to the door. I fish out my key. "Thanks for letting me crash your fishing-buddy time with Molly and for arranging for me to meet with Piper."

"I'm glad you came with us."

"I had the best time." I turn to unlock the door, and he slides an arm around me from behind. My pulse quickens.

"I did, too. I've been thinking about kissing you all night."

His warm lips trail over my neck, sending heat slithering through me. I fumble with the key and close my eyes, trying to center my thoughts.

"Having trouble, sunshine?"

"It's a little hard to concentrate when you're doing that."

"If my good night kisses only affect you a little, I'm doing something wrong. Is this better?" Those tender neck kisses turn to enticingly sensual open-mouthed kisses. My breath rushes from my lungs. "Let me help you." He sets my things on the porch and reaches around me from behind again. His chest presses against my back as he takes the key from my hand and unlocks the door.

I turn in his arms, the desire in his eyes wrapping around me like a ring of fire as our mouths come together, and we devour each other. A voice whispers through my mind, telling me to protect my heart, but Ruby's voice barges in—*Go for it. Satisfy your lust, and enjoy every second of it*—giving me the reinforcements I crave.

"Come inside," I say between fervent kisses.

"That's probably not a good idea," he rasps against my lips. "Two nights with you could become a habit."

"No, it can't," I say, desperate for more. "We have an expiration date. We're like a coupon that won't be valid after the wedding."

He presses his smiling lips to mine. "And I won't stay the night."

"Perfe—" He recaptures my mouth and pushes the door open, kissing me as we stumble inside. We both break the kiss, saying "Molly" in unison. He curses, and I laugh as he runs outside to get her.

# Chapter Eighteen

## FLETCH

As Molly and I set out for an early run, it feels like it's been a month since our last morning run. I do a quick calculation and realize it's been that long since Destiny blew into our lives. Time has passed in an enjoyable blur of activities and accomplishments and unstoppable heat. I swore I wasn't going to stay at her place last Sunday night after we got back from Piper's, and one way or another, we've ended up hanging out together in the evenings and have woken tangled up in each other every morning for the past week.

*That's* the spell my new sassy friend and enticing lover casts on me, with her tangential talks and guileless smiles. When I'm with her, time ceases to exist. She's seeped into my world like water, filling every crevice, bringing something into my life that I didn't even know I was missing. Like sunshine to a freaking flower.

Getting Molly out of Destiny's bed this morning was *not* an easy task. I swear Clementine gave me the stink eye for taking his bestie away when he'd been cozily curled up beside her. I glance at Molly running begrudgingly beside me as we turn into the park. While I'm trying to figure out how this thing with Destiny has progressed so fast, Molly's probably wondering why she's missing out on her morning snuggles.

Destiny has been working like a fiend, making calls, collecting estimates for Arjun's proposal, and setting up meetings with potential clients, while still working part time at Perfect Paws and walking Molly in the afternoons. I don't know how she keeps it all straight and manages to maintain a positive attitude. That's why I offered to cook her dinner Monday night when she texted to tell me she spoke to Bridgette and set up a meeting with her. She brought work with her to my place, and after dinner we went over the budgets she's putting together and discussed ideas for the new inquiries she'd gotten. One thing led to another, and we ended up talking until almost midnight. There was no sense in her leaving that late. She joined me and Molly for an evening walk Tuesday, and we watched *The Office*, playing the one-more-episode game until after eleven, when one kiss led to another, and a wild night of passion ensued. That's how naturally it happened, every single night.

Last night she showed up to surprise me with a peach pie she'd baked and vanilla ice cream. I forwent the pie, preferring Destiny à la mode instead.

*Sweetest dessert ever.*

I woke up this morning sprawled over her like the octopus she claims I am. I didn't want to get out of bed, and it had nothing to do with the fact that my semester has ended and I didn't need to be at work—and *everything* to do with the sleeping beauty I had trapped beneath me. That's why I gave Destiny a kiss goodbye, told her to sleep in since she didn't have to go into Perfect Paws today, and got my ass out of there to try to clear those all-too-comfortable thoughts from my head.

I haven't spent an evening alone for weeks, and I love my alone time. How could I let it slip away? Maybe that's what I need. A night alone to get my head on straight.

Yes. That's *exactly* what I need.

I look down at Molly. "Tonight it's just you and me, girl."

I swear she gives me the side-eye. As we come over the crest of the hill, the oak tree where my unlikely friendship with Destiny began comes into focus, and just like that, I wish she were by my side, chatting up a storm.

"Hey, Fletcher!"

I turn at the sound of Marshall's voice and see him running up the path behind me. "Hey, Marsh, how's it going?"

"I should be asking you that. Where have you been? I haven't seen you running lately, and you blew off basketball this weekend."

"I've been busy." Suddenly I understand Jimmy a little better. Not that I'm in love with Destiny, but given the option of playing basketball with the guys or a sexy morning with her, the guys will lose every time. *Therein lies the problem.*

"I thought school was done for the summer."

"It is." My workload is lighter over the summer, and my days start later, since I'm only teaching two classes, but there are still meetings to attend and students to meet with. "I've been hanging out with Destiny. Late nights, early mornings, you know how that goes."

"Dude, that's great. You must really be into her to spend that much time together."

"She's fun to be with, but don't make a thing out of it."

"Are you kidding me? Why not?"

I give him a look that should shut that down, but Marshall's not one to be silenced.

"I think she's great. Did she tell you she dropped off a basket at Annie's Hope for the reception area? It was loaded with cookies and books on recovery and pocket-sized cards with positive affirmations on them. She also wrote me the sweetest note about how she thinks about my little girl often and wishes me well and all that."

"She didn't mention it, but I'm not surprised. She didn't tell me when she gave Chuck cookies to thank him or that she put together a thank-you basket for Dr. Wilkinson and his staff." The only reason I know about that basket is because I saw it on her counter when I was at her place. "She's not looking for a pat on the back. She's just incredibly thoughtful." That boundless heart of hers is just one of the things about her that makes it so hard for me to keep my distance.

"You mean Wilkinson, the vet?"

"Yeah. Molly . . . *uh* . . . ate some clothing, and we ended up there two weekends ago."

Marshall chuckles. "What kind of clothing?"

I don't answer, but there's no stopping my grin as memories of that night come rushing back.

"Damn, Fletch. You're a lucky bastard. I'm glad you found each other. You deserve to be with a special person."

Reality wipes the grin off my face, and I know I have to come clean to Marshall. He's a good friend, and I trust him not to rat me out to my brothers. "Don't get too excited. This thing between me and Destiny has an expiration date." The words cut like glass.

"A *what?*"

"You know, like a coupon that's only good for a certain amount of time." *Fuck.* Now I'm using her analogies?

"Are you seriously comparing your relationship to a coupon? What the hell, man?"

As we run down a hill past the kiddie play area, I remind him of how she and I met and tell him the truth about our relationship. "She was determined to pay me back for my help with her business, and I was sick of my family giving me a hard time about dating again, so I asked her to go to the wedding with me. One thing led to another, and I guess we've evolved from fake dating to friends with benefits." That doesn't sound right, either. She's more than a friend. "Hell, I don't know what to call us, but after the wedding, we're done."

"Then I'd call you a fucking idiot if you're willing to let her go."

"I just told you it's not real," I bite out. "I really like her, but you know I'm not looking to walk down any aisles. I like my life the way it is. It's comfortable."

"I think you mean *safe*," he says as we pass the basketball courts.

He's not wrong. The last thing I want is to get in too deep and go through another painful breakup, which is exactly why I needed to get out and clear my head.

"You're spending a lot of time together. Don't you feel a connection to her?"

Molly veers into the grass, and I stop to let her pee. "I didn't expect to, but I do."

"It's no wonder you're confused. It sounds like you're in a situationship."

"What is that?"

"It means you have a deeper connection than friends with benefits, but you're not in a full-on relationship. I'm sure it's confusing, but I'd do anything to be in your shoes even for a little while. After I lost Annie, I didn't think I'd ever want to be in another relationship, but it's been years, and lately I've been missing that special connection, you know? That feeling that when you see your person, even the bad shit doesn't seem so bad. I miss how rejuvenating it was."

"Like sunshine to a fucking flower," I grumble.

"Exactly," he says, and we start walking again.

"Whatever, man. The bottom line is, I'm not sold on love being the end-all, and Destiny is all about finding true love and marrying Mr. Right."

"She's all about love and she's cool with this being temporary? She doesn't think you could be the right guy for her?"

"No way." The truth stings, and I have to work too fucking hard to shove it down deep. "She has a checklist two pages long of things she's looking for in a man, and I'm not anywhere close to being that guy."

"Damn. Delaney and her girlfriends think you're a catch." Delaney is Marshall's sister. "What's Destiny looking for? A billionaire? A prince?"

"I don't think she cares about any of that, but I only saw part of her list, so your guess is as good as mine. From what I saw, she wants someone like her dad. A guy who's rough around the edges and can fix anything, who puts love above all else. She's got stars in her eyes and a hungry heart."

Marshall scoffs. "I think you're a great guy, but if that's what she's looking for, what's she doing hanging out with you? You can barely change a light bulb, you've got cynicism in your eyes, and then there's that stone-cold heart of yours."

"Dick." I shove him off the path.

"All right, maybe not stone cold, but you definitely keep your heart on lockdown, and don't even try to deny it."

I don't say shit, but the truth is, she's already chipped away at those walls quite a bit.

"I, on the other hand," Marshall says with a smirk, "take pride in being rough around the edges, and not only can I fix just about anything, but I was also a firefighter. I made it all the way to a hotshot crew out West."

I shoot him a narrow-eyed stare. "What's your point?"

"I'm just saying, when that expiration date hits, I'll be there waiting to rescue her loving heart and fill the shoes that are too uncomfortable for you to walk in."

*"Asshole."*

Later that evening, after my class prep and errands are done and I'm driving home, I'm still thinking about the things Marshall said about having a connection with Destiny. I downplayed our connection with him, but I'm not a fool. I know what I'm feeling for Destiny is bigger than anything I've felt in years.

Maybe even *ever.*

It's hard to remember what I felt at the beginning with Elaina, but I know I never felt the same visceral desire to be with her that I do with Destiny. There isn't just *something* about Destiny that draws me in and makes me want to be closer to her. It's *everything* about her, from the way she wrinkles her nose when she thinks I don't get her jokes or won't agree with what she says to the way she finds love in everything.

Gripping the steering wheel tighter, I try to remember any of those nuances about Elaina, but I was too young and too focused on school to notice the smaller things. Or bigger things, like what I wanted in a relationship and a partner. If I had only taken the time to think it through, I could have saved us both the heartache of a failed marriage. I know she felt horrible about her infidelity, but she wasn't a bad person. She just made bad choices.

We both did.

It took me a long time to get past the hurt and allow myself to see my own failings. But I always try to learn from hindsight, and my biggest takeaway from that time in my life is that Elaina trusted me when she fell in love with me, which was well before we got married. She trusted that I'd watch out for her emotional and physical well-being, as partners should. I was at fault for not giving that trust the attention it deserved. I'm not talking about praise or time spent together. I'm talking about putting my contentment in the relationship aside and taking the time to really think about *her* needs before we got married. To figure out if I would be able to be the man she needed in the long run. I've tried over the years to write that off by blaming my age at the time, but I'm too smart for that.

I fucked up all those years ago, and I'll never make that mistake again.

As I turn off the main drag, Destiny's smiling eyes appear in my mind, and my chest constricts. I saw enough of her checklist to know I'm not the forever guy she's looking for. I can tell myself I'm the guy she needs, but that's not fair to her, and I'm not even sure it's true, because *want* and *need* are tangled together like Twizzlers.

My thoughts reaffirm my need to take a break from seeing her tonight. When she texted pictures of her walk with Molly earlier and asked what I was doing this evening, I told her I was lying low to prepare for my classes. She asked if I wanted company, and I responded honestly, saying I *wanted* company but needed to focus and it would be better if I was alone. I fucking hated shutting her down like that, and I loathed it even more when she responded with a sad-face emoji and immediately followed it with Good luck prepping! 😔

I pull into my driveway and have to pry my knuckles from the steering wheel. I reach for my laptop and see the gift bag with the shirt I bought for Destiny this morning to replace the one Molly ate and a smaller bag with a gift card to a lingerie shop to replace her bra. Yeah, we need a break, but that doesn't mean I have to be an asshole and let her go without the things my dog ruined.

As I head up to the front door, I stop cold at the sight of planters hanging over the porch railing on either side of the steps. One is over-flowing with yellow and purple flowers, the other with pink and purple flowers, and hell if they don't make the house look more inviting.

*Fucking Destiny.* An incredulous laugh falls from my lips as I step onto the porch and see they're hanging from hooks, but there's a three-inch hole in the ceiling. I shake my head and turn to go inside, nearly tripping over a rock with a pink envelope tucked beneath it.

I move the rock to the side and pick up the card on my way inside.

Molly ambushes me.

"Hey, girl. I missed you." After giving her lots of love, I let Molly out back, and as I set my things on the table, I notice one of the chairs is pulled out, and there's a faint stain in the middle of the cushion. Molly. I look outside and see her rolling in the grass. I head into the kitchen and grab a beer from the fridge, then open Destiny's card, hearing each word in her sweet Southern drawl.

*Fletch,*

*Molly said you sometimes forget she's female and likes to be surrounded by pretty things. She wanted bows, but I held firm and let her pick out the flowers instead. I didn't tell you this, but last Monday when I groomed her, she begged for bows and I felt like a meanie telling her no.*

*I owed her something, and the flowers were perfect! Well ... almost perfect. I promise to repair the hole in the porch ceiling. Please don't hate me for that! I asked my dad what to do about it, and he gave me a hard time. Then he told me to blame it on Molly! Ha! I told you he answers me! But he did remind me that we once fixed our back porch roof together, so I can definitely fix yours with help from YouTube! I couldn't find your ladder. Do you have one? I thought you had a shed, but nope! Where do you keep your lawn mower and your other tools? I had to stand on one of your chairs, and it got a little dirty, but I cleaned it. I couldn't find a hammer, either, but Molly and I found a rock out back and I used that (hence the hole!). I hope the flowers make you smile enough to make up for the bad stuff!*
*XO, Sunshine*

I imagined her reading it the same way she talks, barely taking a breath between excited sentences. I have no idea how she made a hole in the ceiling, but the idea of her hunting for a hammer and dragging a chair out front to bang a hook with a rock has me grinning like a fool.

*Sunshine to a fucking flower, indeed.*

I take a pull on my beer as Molly runs inside and glance at the chair as I close the door. The stain makes sense now. *Why am I still smiling?*

That's why I need to take a break tonight. I'm getting too damn close.

I stalk into the kitchen to feed Molly and tug the handle on the junk drawer. There are so many cards stuffed in it, it won't open. I stick my hand in and hold them down, forcing the drawer open. I cannot fit another card in that drawer.

Gathering the pile of cards, I head into the living room, looking for a place to put them. The green blanket Destiny cuddled beneath the other night is on the floor beside the couch with one of Molly's elk antlers on top of it. I could have sworn I put the blanket away in the guest room. I open a drawer in the end table by the couch and drop the cards in. *Out of sight, out of mind.* I fold the blanket and put it away in the guest bedroom.

The fewer reminders of Destiny tonight, the less I'll miss her.

As I head back down the hall, I realize I should thank her for the flowers.

*No. I can thank her tomorrow. I'm taking a break tonight.*

That makes me feel like an ungrateful dick. I'll just keep it short so I can get on with my night.

**Fletch:**

> Hey, sunshine. Thanks for the beautiful flowers. Molly definitely seems happier now that we have them.

**Destiny:**

> I'm so glad! Sorry about the chair and the hole in the porch ceiling.

**Destiny:**

**Fletch:**

> No worries. I'll get the cushion cover dry-cleaned, and I know a guy who can fix the porch.

**Destiny:**

> You know a guy? Is that your cute way of saying you can fix the porch?

**Fletch:**

> I don't do cute. That's your
> department.

**Destiny:**

> You do cute all the time! You just
> don't know it. Like right now, I bet
> you're frowning and your eyebrows
> are pinched together.

**Destiny:**

How can she possibly know?

**Destiny:**

The damn hearts force my scowl into a smile. I imagine the tease in
her eyes, the dimple in her cheek, and that sassy smile, so different from
the sensual one I've gotten used to seeing at night. *Fuck.* Now I want to
see her again. I need to end the conversation before I change my mind.

**Fletch:**

> You're right about the look, not the
> cuteness. Thanks again, sunshine.
> Have a good night.

**Destiny:**

The emotions I'm trying to squash have pushed to the surface. I look at the phone, anticipating her usual trail of texts popping up. When they don't, I tell myself that's a good thing. *Tonight is going to be great. Just me and Molly and some much-needed peace and quiet.* I set my phone on the table and head upstairs to change.

As I toss my work clothes into the hamper, I see my shirts Destiny slept in the nights she stayed over. I'm tempted to pull one out and see if it smells like her. *What the ever-loving hell is wrong with me?* I pull on shorts and a T-shirt, grab the hamper, and traipse downstairs to the laundry room. After I dump the clothes into the washer, I'm reaching for a detergent pod when Molly walks past the door dragging that damn green blanket from the guest room. I've owned that blanket for years, and she's never taken a liking to it. Destiny uses it a few times and suddenly it becomes Molly's favorite?

What the hell kind of torture is this?

I turn on the washer and head back to the living room. Molly is lying on the couch with the blanket beneath her front paws, gnawing on her antler. I grab the remote and plop down beside her. She eyes me warily. "A lot of help you are, looking at me like that."

She paws at my arm as I turn on the television. I feel guilty for acting like she did something wrong. It's not Molly's fault I'm cutting her off from Destiny and Clementine cold turkey for a night. I pet her head. "Sorry, Mol. This is going to be great. Just like old times. We'll watch an episode of *The Office*." I flip to the show, but as it comes on, I grit out a curse and turn off the television.

Molly looks at me curiously.

"Destiny would be upset if we jumped ahead without her." Molly's ears perk up at Destiny's name. I push to my feet and grab the book I picked up the other night when Destiny and I had dinner at the café and then hit the bookstore. I sit back down and kick my feet up on the coffee table, settling in to read.

Five minutes later I've read the same paragraph a dozen times, and I'm itching to see Destiny. Molly paws at me, looking at me expectantly. "We can handle one night without her."

Molly tilts her head to the side, like she understands every word I'm saying, and barks.

"Yeah, no shit. I miss her, too. But we can't afford to get attached." I set the book down and love her up. My phone rings. "There's our sunshine. I knew she couldn't stay away." As I jump to my feet, I bang my shin on the coffee table. *"Fuck!"* Molly leaps off the couch as I grab my shin, hopping on one foot toward the dining room table. *"Ow. Shit. Damn it."* The phone rings again, and I hurry over and snag it. *"Hey,"* I say, before the phone even gets to my ear.

"Expecting a call?"

*Marshall.* *"No.* What's going on?"

"What are you up to tonight?"

"Hanging with Molly, reading. Why? What's going on with you?"

"There's a concert at the park. I thought you'd want to know your girl's here having a picnic."

I bite back the urge to ask who she's with and try to ignore the uncomfortable feeling gripping me. "I told you she's not my girl. She can go to a concert if she wants to."

"In that case, maybe I'll stick around and get to know her better. Have fun with Molly."

The line goes dead.

*Fuck that.* "Let's go, Molly. We're going for a walk."

# Chapter Nineteen

## FLETCH

Molly and I weave around people sitting on blankets and in chairs near the gazebo at the park, where a band is playing country music. The temperature has dropped since this afternoon, and a damp, earthy scent thickens the air. Children are running around playing, teenagers are gathered in secret-sharing pods, couples are dancing and chatting, and I'm scanning the grounds for Destiny. Molly pulls me toward the right, and I spot Destiny sitting with Marshall, her megawatt smile lighting up the night. There's a big wicker picnic basket beside her, and she's leaning back on her palms, wearing a bright yellow long-sleeve shirt and shorts. Her hair spills over her shoulders, and her legs are crossed at the ankles, giving me a view of her purple-and-yellow checkered socks and the dirty sneakers that I've learned are her favorites. She looks so relaxed with Marshall, my gut churns.

We make a beeline for them, and Marshall's laughter hits my ears like a bomb. They look up just as Molly traipses over the blanket and practically leaps into Destiny's lap.

"Molly!" Destiny loves her up.

Marshall flashes a shit-eating grin as he pushes to his feet. "Destiny, this has been a blast. Thanks for letting me crash your evening, but I've got to take off."

"You can crash my evening anytime." She pops to her feet and hugs him. "I hope we see each other again soon."

Marshall looks at me over her shoulder as he says, "I'm sure we will."

I grip Molly's leash tighter. He gives Molly a pet and walks over to me. "How's it going, Fletch?"

"A'right. Looks like you're having a good night."

He claps a hand on my shoulder and leans in close, speaking low. "Glad you came to your senses."

As he walks away, Destiny throws her arms around me. "I'm so glad you're here!"

I'm intensely aware of how good and right she feels in my arms, but I'm even more aware of how wrong it felt trying to stay away from her. "Me too."

"I would've invited you to join me, but I thought you were working on your lesson plans."

"I was, but Molly got restless, so we came out for a walk." I hate the bitter taste of that little white lie, but I know where we stand. "Then she saw her favorite person, and here we are." I look down at Molly. "Right, girl?"

Molly pushes her snout into Destiny's hand.

"*Aw.* Did you miss me, Mol?" She ruffles Molly's fur. "Can you stay for a while, or do you have to get back?"

"I got enough done. We can stick around."

"*Yay.* We have to celebrate." She takes my hand and pulls me down to the blanket with her. Molly inserts herself between us. "Arjun texted a little while ago. He approved the budget, which means we have a proposal date! A week from Saturday, Paris is coming to Sunnyvale!"

"That's *fantastic.*" I pull her into a kiss, and it's the most natural thing I've done all night.

"I'm so glad you convinced me to use spreadsheets to keep track of everything, because it's all in order. No hunting through my notebooks.

Now it's just a matter of firming up dates, placing orders, and putting my personal touch on all of it. *Fletch*, Get the Yes is going to *get the yes!*"

"I'm so damn proud of you. You've worked your ass off for this. We definitely need to celebrate."

She beams. "Thank you."

"Did you tell your folks yet?"

She shakes her head. "Marshall was here."

The caveman in me beats his chest knowing she trusts me more than Marshall.

"Well, don't keep them waiting." I look up at the clouds. "Listen up, Amors. Your girl's got big news."

"I love how you get me." She tilts her face up to the sky, taking a deep breath. "Mama, Daddy, that client I told you about just gave me the go-ahead to create what I hope is the perfect proposal. I'm as excited as I was when I learned to twirl a baton and as nervous as I was the second it flew from my fingers right before it crashed Mama's lamp to the floor and shattered it to smithereens. Say a prayer for me. I love you."

I picture her as an adorable little sprite with wild blond hair, trying her damnedest to learn to twirl a baton. It kills me that the people who raised her to be the free-spirited whirlwind that she is aren't here to celebrate with her. "You're going to do great."

"I hope so. I want this so much, and now that I'm setting up meetings with other clients, it would be awful if Arjun's proposal went badly."

"It won't. You've got this, sunshine, and I'm happy to help with whatever you need. But if you think you're going to get out of telling me about your baton-twirling days, you've got another thing coming."

She grins, swaying to the country music. "I'll tell you about my foray into baton twirling, but I'm starving. Have you eaten yet?"

"No, but I'm fine."

"Don't be silly. You can share my dinner."

"You just said you were starving."

"Yes, but you know me. I brought plenty of food." She grabs the wicker basket, chatting as she starts emptying it, laying out napkins, a plastic plate, fork, and cup, and a thermos, all of which pique Molly's interest. "My baton-twirling days were a dangerous time. I wasn't very good at it, and it didn't last long."

I move Molly to my other side. "Dangerous for more of your mother's lamps?"

"Among other things." She unwraps a sandwich and a brownie and sets them on the plate, while I take the lid off a container of cut-up fruit and fill the cup with iced tea from the thermos. "Like my neighbor Ronnie Clampton's nose."

"You hit him with the baton?" I set the cup in front of her, and she hands me half of the sandwich, like we've been picnicking together forever. "Sounds like sunshine's got a dark side."

"The fool tried to kiss me after he'd asked Ruby to be his girlfriend the week before." She takes a bite of her sandwich. "You don't mess with a girl's best friend and come out unscathed. I lost baton privileges after that."

"No kidding." I chuckle and take a bite of the sandwich. "So, why baton twirling? Did you know you were going to need a weapon, or did you have dreams of performing in Rosebell's Thanksgiving Day Parade?"

"We didn't need batons to be in our parade. Rosebell is only about as big as a fist. Ruby and I rode on the floats nearly every year."

"I bet you were adorable in a cute frilly dress with flowers in your hair, wielding a baton at rascally kids who tried to climb onto the float."

She laughs. "I didn't learn to twirl so I'd have a weapon. I did it because when I was in fifth grade, Taylor Wrigley moved into town, and I wanted to be just like her. She was fourteen, and I thought she was the most beautiful girl I'd ever seen." As we finish our sandwiches and start in on the fruit, passing the fork back and forth, she gets a faraway look in her eyes, like she's envisioning Taylor. "She had pitch-black hair and bright blue eyes, like yours. She could sing pretty as a songbird and dance like she was born with rhythm and grace running through her veins, and she twirled the baton like nobody's business. I was completely smitten with her, and so was every other kid in town. When Taylor walked down the street, everyone noticed." She takes a drink, then hands me the cup.

"She's got nothing on you, sunshine. You're hard to miss." I take a sip and give it back to her.

"Bless your heart, but I know I'm no beauty queen, and that's okay. Kids used to make fun of me because my mouth was too big for my face, and my mama told me that they were jealous because I had my own unique look, and they were just run-of-the-mill cute."

She reaches for the brownie, and I put my hand over hers, drawing her attention. "You have a gorgeous mouth, and you know I'm a bit obsessed with it. Your mother was right. There are beautiful people everywhere, but I've never seen another woman shine as bright as you."

She gets a dreamy look in her eyes, and her shoulders drop a little. "You've got to be careful saying nice stuff like that, Ryry."

Her use of *Ryry* makes me smile. "Why?"

"Because we've got a good thing going, and I don't need to get all confused about our friendship."

"We're sleeping together, but I can't tell you how pretty you are? That makes no sense, sunshine. Besides, you're the one who said you always say what you feel." I wonder if she'd end this arrangement if she knew how much I'm holding back.

"I know what I said."

"In any case, I think you're safe. I don't recall seeing Grumpy Gus on your checklist."

She studies me, dark brows knitting. "Know what I think?" She sits up taller and picks up the brownie, giving me half.

I lift my chin in question and take a bite.

"I think you're about the best guy friend a girl can have."

"Right back at you, sunshine. Especially now that I know you can bake brownies that rival the ladyfingers at La Love Café."

She nibbles on the corner of the brownie. "My checklist just got a little longer."

"Why is that?"

"Because I have to add CALLS ME A CUTE NICKNAME and SAYS REALLY SWEET THINGS."

"I can't believe saying sweet things isn't already on your list. Shouldn't that be a given?"

She shrugs and pops another bite of her brownie into her mouth. "I never thought to put it on there."

"Maybe you should let me take a look at that checklist to make sure you're not shortchanging yourself."

"You are *not* settin' your discerning eyes on my list again. That list came straight from my heart, and it's private. How'd we get to talking about this anyway?"

"You were telling me about baton twirling and a girl named Taylor."

"That's right. She *was* beautiful, but it was her confidence that I wanted to emulate. All the boys noticed her, and she didn't pay them any mind. Like she didn't even notice them looking at her." She gazes at a couple dancing in the grass and eats the last bite of her brownie, swaying to the music again. "She seemed mysterious and grown-up. When I was young, I found that intriguing. But now I can't imagine being that oblivious to people looking at me. You do the same thing. I've told you that."

"Yes, I remember." She called me out on it that first day in the café. "My guess is that Taylor probably wasn't oblivious to the attention."

"Then why act like it? That's hardly living." She looks at me, and she's got chocolate on the edge of her lower lip. "That's like going to the beach and not putting your toes in the water."

I cup her cheek, and her eyes take on a doe-like quality, enticingly warm and intoxicatingly sweet. I brush my thumb over her cheek, wanting to kiss the chocolate off, but I know I won't want to stop there, and I'm not ready for this part of our night to end.

"It's called self-preservation. Fourteen is an awkward age." I wipe the chocolate from her lip with my thumb and suck it off as I sit back. Her eyes flame, and I fight the urge to haul her into a kiss.

She inhales a ragged breath, her cheeks flushing. "Uh-huh."

She's killing me. "She might have been uncomfortable with the attention, or not into boys, or maybe she'd been hurt by a boy and she chose to keep her distance."

"You think so?" She gulps down the rest of the iced tea. "It would be awful if she'd been hurt that badly at that age. What if one of those boys was supposed to be her best guy friend? Her Ryan Fletcher? She might never have this."

Her dismay is so genuine, I wish I could say, *Look, there she is. She found her best guy friend. Now you can be happy again.* "I don't know, sunshine."

She seems to think about that for a beat. "I hate the idea of her being hurt and lettin' that hurt guide her life. I'd like to go on believing she was just that confident."

I wonder if she's still talking about Taylor, or if she's talking about me. "Then you go on believing it, as long as you never stop sticking *your* toes in the ocean of life and letting your light shine on everything around you."

"There you go, doling out sweetness again." She puts her hand on my leg and lowers her voice. "In case you haven't noticed, I'm all about grabbing life by the horns and wrangling it to my liking."

"I've noticed, sunshine." I can't resist sliding my hand to the nape of her neck, drawing her closer. "It's one of the many things"—*I find irresistible about you*—"that makes you special." I lean in and kiss her, our tongues dancing to our own passionate beat. Her fingers curl into my leg as I take the kiss deeper. I feel Molly moving toward the food, and Destiny startles, breaking the kiss. Molly has knocked over the container of fruit, spilling juice on Destiny's leg, and now my beast is looking at us like, *There's nothing to see here. Go back to what you were doing.*

We share a laugh and clean up the mess.

The band starts playing "Fast Car," and Destiny sings along with them, bobbing her head to the beat. It starts drizzling, and people begin collecting their things.

Destiny holds out her palm and looks up at the sky. "We should go."

She turns to me with a look in her eyes that's full of too many emotions to name, but I know she's thinking of her mother. I haven't danced since I was in college, but I push to my feet and hold out my hand. "Come on, sunshine."

"I need to grab the blanket." She turns to pick it up.

"We're not leaving. We're dancing."

"Dancing?" Her eyes tear up so fast, it takes me by surprise. "I . . . I didn't know you could dance."

I have a feeling she doesn't want to talk about dancing in the rain with her mother, so I pretend those tears aren't making my chest constrict and go for levity. "Try not to look too surprised." I draw her into my arms, keeping hold of Molly's leash. "According to Bridgette's son, Louie, my moves rival Barney the dinosaur."

She smiles, blinking her eyes dry. "I'll be the envy of every woman here."

"What makes you think you're not already?" I spin her around, and since the band doesn't stop with the drizzling rain, we continue dancing. Destiny sings off-key, and I have two left feet, but I'm learning that this woman who wants a guy who moves like Jagger has two left feet, too.

A group of teens laughs at us as they walk by.

I wink at Destiny, and we bring out our worst dance moves, laughing just as hard as they do. When a slow song comes on, I gather her in my arms again, feeling more alive than I have in years.

She gazes up at me with a sweet expression. "Thank you for dancing with me. I was missing my family tonight something awful, remembering when we used to go to concerts like this back home. When Marshall showed up, I kept hoping you would, too, and when Arjun texted, I was dyin' to give you the good news."

I feel bad for staying away. "I'm sorry I didn't come sooner."

"It's okay. I'm just glad you decided to take a walk."

Guilt sneaks up on me. "I have a confession to make about that. Molly and I weren't just out for a walk. Marshall called and told me you were here. That's why we came."

Her lips quirk up. "Because of Marshall? Why? Were you worried you might lose your date for the wedding?"

She doesn't know how close to right she is, but we don't make sense in the long run, so I simply say, "Something like that."

"Well, don't worry about that. What kind of friend would I be if I ditched our date for another guy? Besides, I miss my family so much, I'm looking forward to meeting yours."

My gut twists at the longing in her voice. I want so badly to ease that pain, and there's a solution staring me in the face. "You miss your family, and"—*I miss you when we're not together*—"I'm having dinner with mine next Friday for my father's birthday. Why don't you come with me? My mother's been asking to meet you, and it would be a good way for you to get to know them before the chaos of the wedding."

"It's his *birthday*? We used to have the funnest birthdays. My parents believed your birthday was one of the most important days of the year, because it's not just the birthday boy or girl who has something to celebrate. It's the whole family's special day."

"What did you do to celebrate?"

"For my birthday, they'd wake me up just after midnight, and we'd celebrate with balloons and a mile-high cake, and then I'd get to choose what we did for the entire day. And on their birthdays, my mom would wake me up to decorate for my dad after he went to sleep, and he'd do the same for hers. And no matter whose birthday it was, we'd all stay up until midnight, but I usually fell asleep before then."

"That sounds really special. You must miss it."

"I do, more than you can imagine. But one day I'll carry on that tradition with my own family."

"You're going to make a great mother." That's another thing that sets us apart. No marriage means no kids for me, a good reminder to try to keep things in perspective. "When is your birthday?"

"August seventh. When's yours?"

"November twelfth."

"A Scorpio. That makes sense."

"Why?"

"Because they're as smart as they are loyal and as shrewd as they are stoic. They like to keep people guessing, and they don't rely on anyone else's approval. That's you, my friend, while I'm a Leo."

"Which means?"

"You tell me," she challenges.

I don't even have to think about my response. "You're confident, positive, passionate. Definitely determined, and you have a penchant for colorful socks."

She laughs. "I do."

"Why socks?"

"I don't know. They make me happy."

How can happiness be so simple in the eyes of a woman who has lost so much? "If I let you wear your colorful socks, will you come to dinner with my family?"

"I would love to, but are you sure I won't be imposing?"

"I'm positive."

She takes a deep breath. "Okay, but you have to promise me that if I like them as much as I like you, then when we stage our breakup, we'll do it in a way that doesn't make them hate me. Can we do that? Because it would make me sad to become friends at dinner and then feel like I can never see them again because they think poorly of me."

My gut knots up, and that guilt slithers in again. "I'd never let anyone think poorly of you."

"Then I'd love to meet your family."

It starts raining harder, and I hold her tighter, unwilling to break our connection just yet. The band stops playing, and the din of people shouting and rushing from the park rings out around us.

Destiny looks up at me through rain-soaked lashes. "It's raining pretty hard. Should we leave?"

I spin her again, then pull her in close, earning a smile that gives me the answer before I even ask, "Do you *want* to leave?"

"Not even a little."

# Chapter Twenty

## Destiny

We dance until the rain comes down in sheets and thunder booms around us, and then we run all the way back to our neighborhood, laughing and joking about how Molly must think we're nuts. Fletch's house is closer than mine, but when I run up the walk, he snags my hand, tugging me back to him. Our hair is plastered to our heads, our clothes are drenched, and the rain is relentless. "What's wrong?"

"You said Clementine's afraid of thunder. We'll stay at your place."

I can't believe he remembered. My heart takes a perilous leap. It's a good thing he's holding my hand as we run toward my house, because my head is in the clouds, and my heart is thundering louder than the noises in the sky. Left on my own, I'm not sure my legs would know what to do. Thankfully, running through the driving rain helps me get my head on straight, and by the time we reach my house, I've wrapped all those beautiful, troublesome feelings in a bow and tucked them away.

I'm getting good at that.

We hurry inside, soaked to the bone, and Molly immediately shakes water all over us. I laugh, and Fletch apologizes profusely. I take his handsome face between my hands and go up on my toes to say, "Stop apologizing for her. I know she's a dog, and I'm well aware of what dogs do when they're wet." I kiss the center of his scruffy chin. "Now stop worrying and get those wet sneakers off while I get towels."

As I sink to my heels, he sweeps an arm around me, hauling me back to him, and kisses me until my temperature rises so high, I'm sure we'll go up in smoke. I come away breathless and a little foggy headed.

I must look dazed, because he kisses my forehead and says, "*Towels.*"

"Towels. *Right.*"

After we dry Molly as best we can, she zooms around the house and bolts upstairs. Fletch futilely hollers after her.

"She's just looking for Clemmie."

"I know, but she's still wet, and she's probably standing on your bed right now."

"Then I'll wash my bedding." I wrap my arms around myself, rubbing the goose bumps on my arms.

"You're shivering." He embraces me. "How about a hot shower?"

"I knew you could use that sharp mind of yours for something better than worrying about my furniture."

"Has anyone ever told you you're a smartass?"

"No, but I've heard you say you like my ass a few times."

"I like your ass just as much as I like that smart mouth of yours." He grabs my ass with both hands and lifts me up. As my legs circle his waist, he claims my mouth and carries me up to my bedroom like he carries a hundred and thirty pounds around every day.

I mentally add *Strong enough to sweep me off my feet* to my checklist.

He breaks the kiss as we walk past my bed, where Molly and Clementine are, in fact, cuddled together, and I feel him tense up. I touch his jaw, bringing his attention back to me, and whisper, "Shower," and then I kiss him as he carries me into the bathroom.

We close the bathroom door and let the shower warm up as we strip off our wet clothes. My body hums with desire as his gaze blazes down the length of me.

"My God, you're beautiful, and don't you dare try to tell me I can't say that." He kisses me hard, as if to underscore his authority in the matter.

G.I. Joe has *nothing* on this Ken doll.

He takes the kiss deeper as we step into the shower. Warm water rains down on us, seeping between our lips like secrets. Our bodies slip and slide as we grope and devour, his erection temptingly hard against my belly. I ache for him in ways I never knew I could. It thunders and roars inside me like a creature wanting to be set free, driving me to reach between us and stroke his cock. He growls against my lips, and the sinful sound sends white-hot need shuddering through me. Steam billows around us, and I feed that creature, kissing Fletch's chest, running my fingers over his nipple as I stroke his length with my other hand.

"*Destiny.*" His voice is low and gravelly, dripping with lust as he tangles his hands in my hair and guides my mouth to his nipple. I lick and tease, earning salacious moans that fuel my cravings for him. I graze my teeth over his sensitive flesh, and he grits out, "*Fuck.*" His hands tighten in my hair, sending stings of pain and pleasure slicing through me. I sear a path down his body, greedily kissing and touching every inch of him, until I'm on my knees with his heavy cock in my hand, and he's looking down at me with fire in his eyes.

Water rains down his lean, muscular frame. I hold his gaze as I drag my tongue around and over the broad head of his cock. His jaw clenches, his eyes hungry as a wolf's. I continue teasing along his length and around the crown, loving the way his cock jerks in my hand with every slick of my tongue. When I guide it into my mouth, I do it slowly, sucking just the head, then drawing it out and dragging my tongue around and over it again. I take him a little deeper, sucking and stroking, reading his body, watching his muscles flex, the tension building as I withdraw again. Each time I swallow more of him, he curses. His entire body cords tight, and he cups my cheek with one hand. I know he wants to take control, but he lets me set the pace. I've never enjoyed doing this before, but with Fletch, I'm desperate for it, and I'm getting off on the control.

When I finally take him to the back of my throat, his head falls forward with a *hiss*. I work him slowly at first, my hand chasing my lips, sliding tight and hot along his shaft.

"You look so fucking beautiful with my cock in your mouth."

Chasing that praise like it's candy, increasing my speed.

"That's it," he growls, midnight-blue eyes trained on me. "Tight and fast . . . So good. Cradle my balls."

I do as he asks, and I'm shocked at how much it turns me on. I'm wet and swollen, chasing his orgasm and, incredibly, building my own.

"*Fuck*, that feels good." He tightens his grip in my hair, holding me still, and brushes his thumb over the seam where my lips meet his cock. "Christ, sunshine. Your mouth is exquisite."

His words twine around my heart, and I devour that praise. My desire heightens with every impossibly slow and deliciously deep pump of his hips. "Like that, baby?" he grits out. "Touch yourself while I fuck your mouth." I'm so into him, into *this* and *us*, there's no room for embarrassment. I reach between my legs, and as my fingers slide over my sensitive nerves, I moan around his cock. "That's it, baby. Jesus, you're sexy." He continues thrusting at the same pace, and I match his rhythm with my fingers between my legs, bringing a whole new level of excitement. He pumps faster, and I quicken my efforts between my legs. The lust in his eyes tells me I'm taking us both higher. "Is that okay? Not too fast?"

I nod eagerly, hoping to convey how much I want this. He's letting me in, and I'm learning what he likes. I do *not* want to stop. He puts his hand over my hand that's on his balls and squeezes. "*Yeah*. Fuck, that's good." He brushes his fingers around my lips. "I want to come in your mouth, sunshine. If you don't want me to, it's okay. But I need to know so I can pull out." I give his balls a tug, and the wickedness flaming in his eyes is inescapable. He traces the seam of my lips around his cock again. "That's my girl." *My girl.* I know he's not my Mr. Right, but at that moment, for the life of me, I can't remember why. Then he takes control, burying both hands in my hair, hips thrusting perfectly fast and dangerously deep, obliterating my ability to think at all.

"Keep touching yourself. Think of my mouth on you," he grits out, breathing harder.

Lord, this man could make me come just by saying things like that. I moan around his cock, and he pumps faster. "So fucking good." His thighs flex, and he makes a guttural sound that sends my insides into a flurry as he surrenders to his powerful release, hips thrusting, growls emanating with every hot, salty jet. I stay with him, hanging on the edge of my own orgasm, but I don't chase it. I don't want to miss a second of this fine man losing himself in me.

When his body goes slack, he withdraws from my mouth with a sharp inhalation and tugs me to my feet. His eyes brim with emotions. "You wreck me, beautiful." He crushes his mouth to mine, thrusting his hand between my legs. Two fingers push inside me, and his thumb zeros in on my clit, sending me up on my toes as he works his magic, and I follow him into ecstasy.

And then I'm floating, and the world starts to come back into focus. Warm water slips between us, and he lowers his mouth to my shoulder, biting and kissing, his fingers finding their pace again. I greedily soak in every tantalizing touch and lower my mouth to his nipple. He moans, his fingers quickening, applying more pressure on just the right spot, stealing my ability to focus again. I rest my forehead against his chest, panting, another orgasm just out of reach.

He tugs my head back and crushes his mouth to mine again. My back meets the cold, wet tile, and he kisses his way down my body, palming my breasts, teasing the nipples with his mouth and hands, sending prickling heat racing through me. He nips, licks, and kisses, hitting each of my pleasure points he so patiently and diligently discovered, lingering on them, cherishing them like treasures, until I'm a moaning, writhing mess of desire, begging for more.

He sinks to his knees, sliding his fingers through my swollen sex, visually devouring me as he spreads my trembling legs, holding me open. He flicks that sensitive spot with his tongue, sending shivers of heat racing through me. *"Ohgod—"* His mouth is next, licking, sucking, devouring. He knows just how to get me there. I squirm and moan, scintillating sensations engulfing me as his fingers dip inside, expertly finding that spot that makes my legs weak. I grab his shoulders, my insides swelling, pulsing, reaching for the orgasm that's barreling toward me like a runaway train. *"Fletch. Ohhhh, Fletch—"* The impact sends me crashing into a world of lights and sounds and *us*.

He stays with me until I come down from the peak, and then he rises to his feet, hard again. The feel of his erection against me and the lust pooling in his eyes make me want so much more. I've never trusted any man enough to have sex without a condom, but I trust Fletch. "I need you inside me." I hear the desperation in my own voice, and I don't care. "I'm protected."

The second the words leave my lips, he's lifting me up and lowering me onto his cock. We both moan, and he wraps his strong arms around me. "Don't move, baby. You feel so fucking good. I want to live inside you."

*Welcome home* is on the tip of my tongue, but I swallow it down, telling myself it's the lust talking.

"You're so tight and hot and fucking perfect. It's never been like this."

I pluck those dangerous words out of the air and tuck them away with the other sweet things I've been stockpiling and cover his mouth with mine, trying to outrun the emotions that feel like they're drilling into my soul.

# Chapter Twenty-One

## DESTINY

"I think you should go with a maxi dress. It says confident and classy, without being over the top." Ruby points to a mannequin wearing a green maxi dress. "That's a great color."

It's Wednesday evening, and we're at a clothing boutique, shopping for a dress for me to wear to dinner with Fletch's family, and then she and I are going out for Thai food. We've both been so busy, it's been a while since we've gone out, and I've missed spending one-on-one time with her. I feel like I've worked a zillion hours over the last six days, but it's been worth it. The pieces of Arjun's proposal are coming together nicely, and I've signed two more clients.

"Do you think I can pull one off?" My hips are so narrow, longer dresses tend to make me look like a boy with tiny boobs. "Shorter dresses give the illusion of curvy hips, and they always make my boobs look better."

"Stop being ridiculous. You can pull off anything. You've got a killer body under that T-shirt and shorts."

*I wouldn't say* killer, *but Fletch appreciates it.* Thinking of him brings the familiar flare of something warm and fluttery to my chest.

"And if you don't believe me," she says as we head for the rack with the maxi dresses, "just ask your fuck buddy."

"Can you *not* call him that?" I grab a dress off the rack and hold it up to get a better look.

"Whoa. Testy. Are you sure this dinner is a good idea?"

I feel her keen eyes assessing me and focus on the dress, because I've been asking myself that same question all week. But I want to go, so I brush her off. "Of course. Why wouldn't it be?"

"Because meeting his family is a big deal."

And there it is, the elephant in the room. But the mouse is in the same room, speaking loud enough for us both to hear her. "Not in our case. The reason he asked me to go to the wedding with him was to get them off his back, remember? Meeting them now will help sell that."

"Des, you buy him *socks*."

Have I bought him a few pairs? *Yes.* But it's not like I'm buying his underwear. "He has bad taste in socks. He needed a little color."

"And the love notes?"

"They're not *love* notes. They're friendship notes."

She rolls her eyes. "You hung planters at his house, and you're *still* walking his dog."

"I love Molly. Is there something wrong with that?"

"No, but you really like Fletch."

"*So?* I really like you, too. Is that a problem?" I know it's a stupid response, but I don't want to face what she's trying to make me own up to.

"You don't end up mattress dancing with me every night."

"It's not like we plan it. It just happens." The way we're drawn together is one of the things I love most about us. There's no pressure, no schedule to adhere to. We see each other because we want to and we're on each other's minds. Not out of obligation. But I don't share that with Ruby, because saying it out loud will make it too big, even to me. "And it's not every night. I'm out with you tonight, and I won't see him afterward." I hang up the dress and meet her worried gaze. "You're the one who told me to go for it, remember? Why are you even bringing it up?"

"Because I love you, and when you said you'd protect your heart, I wanted to believe you could. But you're falling for him, Destiny, and I'm afraid you're going to get hurt. I've never seen you like this."

Emotions clog my throat, but I force my words out. "Like *what*? Do you see something bad that I don't?"

Her expression warms. "No. That's the problem. You seem *truly* happy, not just like your normal peppy self. You're different. I can't explain it, but I can feel it, and I'm pretty sure you can, too."

My eyes tear up, and I turn away from the other customers in the boutique.

Ruby moves with me. "I'm not trying to upset you."

"I *know* you're worried about me. But I'm okay. I know what this is, Rube, and I know how it's going to end."

"Do you? Because I feel like you've been fooling yourself."

"Maybe I was, but I'm not anymore. I am falling for him, and I know he's not my Mr. Right. But I also know how quickly life can be snatched out from under us, and for the first time ever—*ever*, Rubes—I feel cherished and special and safe in a man's arms, and I *like* that. I *deserve* that. You're still looking at me like I'm some dreamy-eyed girl, but I'm not. Hear me when I say I *know* he doesn't love me, and he probably never will. He's not capable of the type of love I need. He doesn't believe in it the way I do. But he cares about me, Rube. I can feel it. He cares about me a hell of a lot, and I'll take it for now."

"Of course he cares about you. You're an amazing, smart, warm, fun person, and you don't just lead with your heart. You pour it into everything you do."

"That's just it. What I've realized this past month is that I *have* to be me, and if that means following my heart down a dead-end street with him, then that's what I'm going to do."

"In that case, I'll be waiting for you at the end of that street." She takes out her phone and starts thumbing out a text.

"Who are you texting?"

"John." She doesn't look up. "We need to buy a big, fast truck."

"Why?"

An evil grin curves her lips. "Because after I run Fletch over, I'll need to haul your ass out of there to heal your broken heart so I'm not burying two bodies."

"No wonder I love you. But I haven't died from a broken heart yet, and mine's been put through the wringer twice."

"I'm not taking any chances." She pockets her phone and drapes an arm over my shoulder. "If you're determined to do this, then let's find you a dress that he'll never forget. I don't care how good he is to you. When this sexfest is over, I want him to suffer."

"When did you get so coldhearted?"

"I'm practicing bringing out my mama claws."

"Are you . . . ?"

Ruby shrugs with a hopeful grin.

"Oh my gosh, Rubes!"

"We don't know yet, but I'm *late*, and I've been feeling pukey for two days."

"*Ruby!* I'm so happy for you!" I throw my arms around her. "You're going to be a great mom."

"And you're going to be a great auntie, but if you keep hugging me, I might puke on you."

# Chapter Twenty-Two

## DESTINY

By the time Friday evening arrives, I've picked apart my conversation with Ruby until there's nothing left but bones. I know I'm making the right choice spending this time with Fletch, because every time I get a text from him, or hear his voice, or kiss his lips, my heart sings. But that doesn't mean thinking about the end of our arrangement is easy. Between thoughts of that and being nervous about meeting his family, my stomach has been queasy all day. Which is why I've decided *not* to think about what will happen after his brother's wedding and to enjoy the here and now.

I glance at Fletch as we pull into the restaurant parking lot, with his perfectly combed hair, expertly manicured scruff, and finely pressed black dress shirt and matching slacks, so different from the tousled-haired, thick-scruffed man who makes love to me at night and wakes up wrapped around me like an octopus nearly every morning and the rugged fisherman who whisked me and Molly away last Saturday at five o'clock in the morning to prove there *were* fish in the lake after I teased him about not seeing anything but minnows the weekend before. We had such a great time. It felt like we'd found our own private oasis.

He glances over, catching me admiring him and bringing those hummingbirds to life. I don't know how there could have been a time when he didn't take my breath away.

It's no wonder I'm so nervous about meeting his parents.

He parks and reaches across the console for my hand. "You okay, sunshine? You've been kind of quiet."

"Yeah. I'm just a little anxious about meeting your family." I touch the gift bag in my lap, second-guessing the socks with tiny fishing poles on them I brought as a birthday gift for his father. "I want to make a good impression."

"Sweetheart, that's the only kind of impression you could ever make."

I cock a brow. "Shall I remind you of the park fiasco?"

He grins. "You left quite an impression."

"Not a *good* one."

"And yet look where I am." He lifts my hand and kisses the back of it. "My parents will adore you, and you'll love Beth. She's a smartass, too, and she loves to shop. She'll probably want to know where you got that gorgeous dress."

I look down at the peach maxi dress with a wildflower design that Ruby and I bought the other night. It has spaghetti straps, a fitted bodice, and a slit along one side. When Fletch picked me up for dinner, he took one look at me in it, and he was all steamy kisses and filthy promises as he tried to convince me to skip dinner and let him make good on those promises.

I *almost* caved.

He climbs out, and as he comes around to open my door, I look out the front window at the sky and whisper, "I know this whole thing is complicated, Daddy, but if you've got any advice to make sure I don't ramble or screw up, now's the time to dole it out."

No sooner do I say the last word than Fletch opens the door and takes my hand. As my feet hit the ground, he draws me into his arms and looks up at the sky. "Don't worry, Mr. Amor. I've got her." My throat thickens as he kisses me and whispers, "We've got this, sunshine."

As we head into the restaurant, I know we do, which makes me even more nervous.

We're led through the restaurant, and as we approach his family, Jimmy announces, "There they are."

Everyone gets up to greet us, and they're all talking at once. Jimmy and Chuck act like we're old friends, pulling me into bear hugs before Fletch can introduce me to their parents or Beth. Beth, an apple-cheeked, golden-haired stunner, slides in after Jimmy for a hug and says, for my ears only, "You two are adorable together."

Fletch eyes her as he puts an arm around me, his hand curling around my waist, pulling me closer. "How can you two have secrets already? You just met."

"Don't you know women have telepathic powers?" Beth says with a smirk. "We've been talking about you for weeks."

His family laughs, and he just shakes his head.

"I wish I were in on those conversations," his mother says. She's even more attractive in person. "I've been bugging Ryan to bring you around for weeks."

"She's been a little busy, Mom," Fletch says.

"And she's here now, which is all that matters," his father says. It's easy to see where Fletch and his brothers got their height and athletic builds. With their father's neatly combed hair, perfectly manicured scruff, and serious eyes, it's also obvious that one particular apple did not fall far from the tree.

"Destiny, these are my parents, Mary and Hugh. Mom, Dad, this is Destiny."

"Oh, honey. It is a pleasure to meet you." His mother embraces me warmly.

"You as well. Fletch has told me a lot about you." I turn to his father. "Happy birthday, Mr. Fletcher. I got you a little something." I hand him the gift bag.

"Thank you, Destiny. That was unnecessary, but certainly appreciated."

As his father hugs me, Jimmy says, "*Suck-up,*" and coughs to cover it.

I know he's kidding, but Fletch glowers at him.

"*James,*" his father says sternly.

"What?" Jimmy splays his hands. "It was a joke."

"Bless your heart," I say as sweetly as I can. "Are you jealous? Do you wish I brought you a little something, too? I can run outside and get a lollipop out of my purse if you'd like."

Everyone laughs.

"She's a keeper," Beth says in a singsong voice.

Fletch puts his arm around me, grinning like he thinks so, too.

I turn my attention back to his father. "If you don't like them—"

"Then you can give them to me," Fletch interrupts.

"That's got me curious." His father peeks into the gift bag and pulls out the socks. "They're perfect. I love to fish. Thank you."

"Aren't they *adorable,*" his mother exclaims. "Where did you find them?"

"At the same place I get Fletch's socks. Happy Feet? It's around the corner from the grocery store in Harmony Pointe."

"Yeah, check these out." Fletch lifts his pant leg and shows off the latest pair I surprised him with.

"Is that *Molly* on them?" Jimmy asks.

"*Yes.* Aren't they cute?" I lower my voice teasingly as we settle into our seats. "He has that long-second-toe thing going on. Might as well cover them up with something pretty."

"He gets that from his father," his mother said.

"*Ugh.* Jimmy has it, too," Beth says.

"Don't you want to snip it off at that last knuckle?" I say conspiratorially.

Beth lights up. "Yes!"

"You're not going anywhere near my feet anymore," Jimmy says. "And for your information, that long toe is an indication of how long another body part is. Just ask Chuck. He doesn't have a long second toe."

"All my length went to a better body part," Chuck retorts.

Fletch and his brothers are still tossing barbs when the waiter arrives to take our drink orders. I order peppermint tea, hoping it'll settle my stomach. The waiter relays the dinner specials and leaves us with menus to peruse while he gets our drinks.

"Destiny, where is your charming accent from?" Mary asks.

"I'm from Rosebell, Georgia."

"I don't believe I've heard of that town," she says.

"That's not surprising. It's about as big as a flea's butt. I just moved here a few months ago."

"How do you like it so far?" she asks.

"I'm loving it. My best friend, who I grew up with, Ruby, lives here, and now that Fletch and I are seeing each other, life is even more beautiful."

Fletch's hand circles my shoulder, and he kisses my temple. "Thanks, sunshine."

His parents exchange an approving glance, and I feel a pang of guilt about our ruse. But I'm not going to let it ruin our night, because my feelings are real, even if we have an end date.

"Who is this guy, and what has he done with our brother?" Chuck asks.

"What's the matter, Chucky? Do you need a lollipop, too?" Fletch teases.

I pat his leg. "It's okay. I get it." I look around the table. "I work part time as a pet groomer, and I groomed Molly for a few months before I got to know Fletch better than just a quick hello and a scowl for putting bows in Molly's hair. Which I now realize was a mistake because she likes to eat them. But to be honest, I didn't think Fletch was anything like he is. In fact, I called him Grumpy Gus."

"Now, *that's* fitting," Chuck says.

"It certainly was. He kept himself as walled off as Fort Knox. Just about every woman who sees him lusts after him, and let me tell you something." I lower my voice. "I did *not* see the attraction."

Fletch's head snaps toward me. *"What?"*

"Oh, come on. You know that. I told you I didn't do Ken dolls."

His parents stifle a laugh, but Jimmy, Chuck, and Beth crack up.

Fletch grits out, *"Jesus."*

I pat his leg again. "But I quickly realized the error of my ways. There is so much more to this man than just a handsome face who looks like he walked off the pages of a fashion magazine. The closer we got, the more I learned about him. He's like a Gobstopper. I could lick, and lick, and lick, revealing one layer after another, and never tire of it."

Laughter erupts from his brothers and Beth.

"You laugh, but just when I think I have him figured out, I suck off another layer, and something new springs up." I turn to Fletch, who looks like he's going to laugh, too. "I think I could lick you my whole life and never stop discovering new things about you. *Why* is that so funny?"

He pulls me against him as laughter explodes around the table, and he says, *"Waiter?* Anyone else need a drink?" Which makes everyone laugh harder. Fletch buries his face in my hair and says, "You're talking about licking and sucking me off."

I gasp. *"Ohmygoodness.* I did *not* mean that. I meant—"

Laughter steals my voice, and as Fletch presses his lips to mine, Jimmy says, "No wonder he's smiling all the time," sparking more hysterics.

The heckling continues through drinks and dinner as we get to know one another better, and I can't help but join in. I love seeing this snarky side of Fletch and the way his parents look at him and at each other. They're an affectionate couple. Not overly so, like my parents were, but they share smiles and caring touches, and they take the jokes in stride, both of them joining in with the fun. They ask about what it was like growing up in Georgia, and I get a pang of homesickness while I talk about it, which makes me hyperaware of the gurgling in my stomach.

"Are your parents still in Georgia?" his mother asks.

Why does this question still sting so much? I do *not* want to tear up. Fletch takes my hand under the table, and it makes me feel even more emotional. But I manage to hold myself together. "My mother died when I was eleven, and my father passed away last year. I don't have any other family in Rosebell. That's why Ruby urged me to move here and finally start my business."

Fletch squeezes my hand as his mother puts her hand over her heart and says, "Oh, sweetheart, I'm so sorry about your parents."

"We all are," his father said, and the others chime in in agreement.

"Thank you. But they're still here, shining down on me from above."

"And they're proud as hell of you, sunshine." Fletch kisses my temple again.

"They should be," Chuck says. "Destiny is quite a businesswoman, and she's an excellent baker, too."

"The baking is all my mama's doing, and I have your brother to thank for what little business savvy I have. He has been my saving grace." *In more ways than one.*

"All I did was help you get organized," Fletch says. "The rest is all you."

"Proposal planning is quite a unique niche," his father says.

"You should hear about the proposal she's putting together," Fletch says. "It's going to be phenomenal."

"I would love to hear about it," his mother says.

"Me too," Beth adds.

"It's going to be Parisian themed, and I'm holding it right here on the roof of this restaurant next Saturday night."

"On the *roof?*" Chuck asks.

"*Yes.* I know it seems like a strange idea, but this building has the most spectacular view of the lights of the town. It was a bit pricey to get the roof cleaned, and creating a safe area so my client and his soon-to-be fiancée aren't at risk of falling off means paying to have barriers put up. Not that I think they'll be anywhere near the edge, but you never know what's going to happen when two people are caught up in love."

"That would be a worse proposal than trying to hitch Fletch to his stalker," Jimmy says with a laugh.

"You've got that right. That's why I'm doing it. I'm going to camouflage the barriers with cloth that'll make them look like stone walls and add lights and flowers. I designed beautiful cards to go in the bouquets, and each one has a memory printed on it of a special moment they've shared. I'm excited about those smaller personal touches." I describe my vision for the event from start to finish, and I'm surprised at how interested everyone is. Even Fletch's brothers ask questions.

"And you're doing this all yourself?" his father asks.

"Well, as I mentioned, Fletch has been there to help keep me organized, and he and Ruby are going to help me set up the day of the event."

"I think what you're doing is incredible," Beth says. "I work in marketing, and I can think of a dozen ways you can get your name out there."

"We should talk sometime."

"Definitely, and if you ever want to hire an assistant, I'd love to get involved."

"If I had the means, I'd hire you in a heartbeat." I mean that. I really like Beth. "Maybe someday I'll have more work than I can handle, and then you'll be the first one I call for help."

"You know she's not kidding, right?" Jimmy asks. "That look in her eyes isn't going to go away."

"Well, I sure hope not," I say. "The world needs more people who believe in love enough to help others find their happily ever afters."

Beth lifts her wineglass. "Here's to one day."

"To one day." I lift my cup of tea and take a sip.

"You girls would make a great team," his mother says. "Destiny, will you be there during the proposal to watch it unfold?"

"I wish I could, but I don't want to impose. I hired a very discreet photography and videography duo. I'll get to see the pictures and the video, and use some to promote my business."

"It's a shame you'll miss out on seeing it firsthand," his mother said. "Who's building the replica of the Eiffel Tower?"

"Fletch's friend Piper, and her sister Bridgette is handling the flowers. They gave me great deals."

"How big is the tower?" Beth asks.

"It's going to be about eight feet tall. Piper's building it in levels, so it'll be easier to transport, and she'll set it up on the roof the day of the event. It's almost done. I can show you pictures." I reach for my purse, and remember I left it in the car. "*Shoot.* I'm sorry. I don't have my phone."

"I have the pictures you sent me." Fletch takes out his phone.

"Great. I wanted to show them the pictures we took at the lake last weekend, too."

"You went fishing again?" his father asked.

"Yeah, it was a good time," Fletch says, scrolling through his photos.

"He woke me up at dawn and surprised me with the trip. It was wonderful. We caught a bunch of fish and stayed all day." I look at his brothers and Beth. "Fletch told me all sorts of stories about the trouble y'all got into when you were younger. We saw a gorgeous sunset and then we stargazed with Molly." *It was a magical night.*

Fletch caresses my shoulder with his thumb, and I can't help wanting more nights like that.

"Fletch stargazed?" Beth asks incredulously.

"Guess miracles can happen," Jimmy teased.

"Yeah, yeah, yeah." Fletch shakes his head.

"Destiny made fish and chips using the fish they caught and brought enough for all of us after basketball last Sunday," Chuck said. "Best fish and chips I ever ate."

"Best peach muffins, too," Jimmy adds.

"Y'all are too sweet."

"It sounds like a wonderful weekend," his mother says.

"It was," Fletch says as he scrolls through the pictures on his phone.

I lean closer, looking at the pictures. "There they are. Show them the one of you and Molly in the water. It's one of my favorites." As he passes the phone around the table, I say, "I love the way the sun is glittering off the water like diamonds, and Fletch looks so relaxed, holding his fishing pole in one hand and petting Molly with the other. It makes me happy."

"That is a great picture," Jimmy says as the phone makes its way back to Fletch.

"Which is your favorite, Ryan?" his father asks.

Fletch scrolls to a picture. "This one." He shows me the one of me taking a selfie of us. My hair is damp and messy from a dip in the lake, and I've got no makeup on, but my cheeks are pink from the sun. Fletch is sitting on the blanket a few feet behind me. He's wearing shorts and a T-shirt, and he has his arm around Molly.

"I look a mess in that one."

"Sometimes I wonder if we're looking at the same person. You look happy and beautiful in that picture." He leans in and kisses me, and my heart soars as he passes the phone across the table to his father first. "You can scroll to see the others. The pictures of the tower are right after them."

As his parents scroll through the pictures, his mother holds one up and says, "This is my favorite." In the picture, my hair is in a ponytail, and I'm wearing what I call my bug-eye sunglasses, because they're huge. Fletch is sitting behind me, kissing the back of my shoulder.

That is another of my favorites, too, but I keep that to myself, because it makes me emotional to think about how that tender kiss took me by surprise. It felt more intimate than a kiss on my lips and made me feel like we were a real couple.

Fletch's mother and Beth *ooh* and *ahh* over the pictures of us, and everyone is as impressed with the tower Piper is making as I am, which pleases me to no end.

As the phone comes back to Fletch, his mother says, "It looks like your client is going to have a spectacular event. Do you have a dream proposal, Destiny?"

"Yes, sort of. I hope it'll be something magical that comes from my forever love's romantic heart."

"That knocks you out of the running, Fletch," Jimmy says. "You don't have a romantic bone in your body."

"Yes, he *does*," I argue. "Did I not just tell you about our great day at the lake? Romance comes from more than just roses and candlelight dinners. The first time I met with a potential client, Fletch gave me a special gold pen he had made just for me with *Get the Yes* printed on it in pink, my favorite color. I was so nervous that evening, I thought I might be sick, and he told me how he believed in me and made me remember that there was nothing I couldn't do. Not only that, but after the client signed on with me, Fletch sent me a special bouquet of my favorite flowers. When I signed a new client last week, he sent me flowers again." *With a note that said he heard my father cheering me on from across town.* My throat thickens with the memory, and I push it away to shut Jimmy down one last time in case he still has doubts. "And he does other things, too. Sometimes when I work late, he cooks me dinner, and when Molly ate my lingerie, he replaced it. Your brother is full of romantic bones."

Fletch gives Jimmy a smug grin.

"I'd like to hear more about Molly eating your lingerie," Jimmy retorts.

Chuck elbows him.

"Let's *not* go there," his father says sternly, and turns a kinder tone on me. "You're right about different flavors of romance, and we men have a way of only bringing it out for the most special people in our lives."

"Yes, you do," his mother said adoringly. "Destiny, honey, I understand wanting the proposal to come from your significant other's heart, but you're planning proposals for a living. Do you have something in mind?"

"Not anything specific. Hopefully he'll know me so well, he'll create something he knows I'll love. Like I do for my clients. That's why I ask them so many questions about every aspect of their lives and relationship, so I can help figure out which special moment, or moments, to pick. Like with the Parisian proposal. The couple has wanted to go to Paris forever, but they haven't been able to get there. I'm bringing it to them in a way they'll never forget, and wrapping all their special moments into it. But it could be anything, from re-creating the moment he fell in love with me to something new that he just knows I'll love."

"I hope you're taking notes, Ryry," Chuck says.

Fletch picks up his drink, looking at it instead of at Chuck. "Cool your jets, bro. We just started seeing each other."

My stomach pitches at how easily he says it.

They're all looking at us, and I scramble for something to say to break the tension. "He's right, and we'd both know it if he wasn't. That falling-in-love moment is so special. It's one the other person can't share at the time if they don't know it's happening. But if it's re-created for them, then they get to share it, and it will forever be etched in both their hearts." I know I'm rambling, but I can't stop. "We've all heard stories about how people knew the moment they fell in love. Like when they first heard their person laugh, or saw them dance, or had a meaningful interaction with them."

"We know *that's* not you and Ken doll, given the stalker girl who arranged your first meaningful interaction," Jimmy teases.

Thankful for the levity, I say, "That was not my finest moment."

Fletch drapes an arm around the back of my chair. "It was stressful, but you were pretty damn cute, all flustered and still standing your ground."

Is he trying to give me whiplash?

"I knew I loved Hugh the moment he ran his grandparents' boat into my parents' dock when I was sixteen and he was eighteen," his mother says. "He stood on that boat yelling at me for sunbathing in the grass, like it was my fault he got caught up in gawking at me instead of watching where he was going. All I could do was laugh. Our dock was shattered, and I'm falling to my knees, laughing hysterically. He jumped off that boat and stomped through the water to the grass, staring down at me. And you know what he said?"

"What?" I asked.

She lowers her voice an octave. *"I've been trying to get up the nerve to ask you out, and now my grandparents are going to kill me. I'm heading to Mexico. Want to come?"*

"What did you say?" I ask.

"I said, *No thanks. I'm not done sunbathing, and I'm pretty sure my father is going to kill you when he gets home.* The fool sat down beside me and said, *In that case, I might as well enjoy the view with the time I've got left."*

"Dad, you had game," Chuck says.

"Where do you think you boys got it from?" his father says proudly.

"He came by every day after that," his mother adds. "And he worked all summer to repair my father's dock. I was so in love with him by the end of that summer, I asked *him* to go to Mexico with *me.*"

"I *love* this story," I exclaim. "Did you go?"

"No." His father gazes lovingly at his wife. "I told her she'd lost her chance. I was leaving for college at the end of the summer."

"Then he wrote to me every week and came to see me during every break. He proposed to me on that dock two years later, and we were married there after he graduated from college."

"And I'd do it all over again." He leans in and kisses her.

*That's what I want. Inescapable, unquestionable love.*

"Okay, that's it," Beth exclaims. "Jimmy, we need a do-over proposal."

Fletch chuckles. "You mean you didn't like almost dying when he proposed?"

"Dying?" I ask. "Please tell me you're joking."

"I'm not." He hikes a thumb at Jimmy. "This numbnut put the ring in a piece of carrot cake, and when they served it, instead of getting down on one knee, he went to find the waiter to get a glass of water because he was so nervous, his mouth was dry."

"Meanwhile," Beth says, "I'm chowing down on my favorite dessert, and suddenly there's something sharp blocking my airway. So there I am, choking in the middle of a fancy restaurant, and Jimmy's talking with a waiter. When he finally notices, he knocks into the waiter, making him fall onto another couple's table, and plows over a busboy like he's a linebacker, sending him flying into some guy's lap."

"Hey, I saved you with the Heimlich. The ring shot out of her mouth and landed in someone's soup, like a freaking cartoon." Jimmy laughs.

"Oh my gosh." I cover my mouth, trying *not* to laugh. "You must've been so scared."

"*Nah.* I knew they'd give us the ring back," Jimmy says.

Beth elbows him, but she laughs along with everyone else. "See? Don't you think I deserve a do-over?"

"If you want one, I'm happy to help. But sometimes the universe knows what's right before you do. And you have to admit, that's an unforgettable proposal you can laugh about with your kids. Maybe it was meant to be your story." I glance at Fletch, and he gives me that special smile that makes my chest flutter. Only this time, my stomach burns with the reality of our situation. *And maybe this is meant to be ours.*

◆　◆　◆

# FLETCH

As the night wears on, the conversation turns from proposals to my parents sharing stories about times when we've screwed things up throughout the years, but I'm still sidetracked by what Destiny said about the universe knowing what's right before we do. Could she be right? Could *we* be right? Or is seeing her with my family screwing with my head?

When we finally leave the restaurant, my mother embraces me and says, "She's a special girl, honey. I hope we'll see more of her."

I glance at Destiny as she exchanges phone numbers with Beth, and say, "I hope so, too."

After a round of goodbyes and promises between the girls to keep in touch, we head home. "You have an incredible family," Destiny says softly. "I really like Beth, too. I'd give anything to be able to hire her one day. You're really lucky to have them all in your life."

"I am lucky. Thanks for going tonight."

She doesn't follow it up with her typical upbeat ramblings, and I noticed she didn't eat much of her dinner, which makes me wonder if I messed up by inviting her. "Was tonight too much, sunshine? Being around my family? Did it make you miss yours even more?"

"I always miss my family. I had a really nice time tonight. I'm just tired."

She's quiet the rest of the way back to her place. When I pull into her driveway, she turns to me with an uneasy expression and says, "I'm not feeling that well. I think I've been working too hard and just need a good night's rest. Would you mind if we stay at our own places tonight?"

My gut sinks. "No, of course not." I reach for my door.

"You don't need to walk me up. You should get back to Molly."

I clench my jaw, trying not to react. I shouldn't feel like she's brushing me off, given our *situationship*, but after spending nearly every night together the last couple of weeks, this sure as hell feels like a brush-off.

"Thanks for tonight. Your family is really special."

"So are you, sunshine. Molly and I'll miss you." I lean in and kiss her. "Get some rest."

I watch her head inside without her usual peppy steps and can't shake the feeling that things have changed.

# Chapter Twenty-Three

## Fletch

I wake with the same uncomfortable feeling the next morning and check my phone. I texted Destiny forty minutes after I dropped her off, but she still hasn't responded. She said she was tired, and maybe she was, but I have a feeling that was just her way of letting me down easy instead of saying she needed space.

I go for a long run, mentally replaying last night a hundred times. The more I pick it apart, the clearer I see how unfair it was to ask her to go with me. My brothers can be a lot to handle, but bringing my parents and Beth into the equation probably not only made her feel her losses even more deeply but allowed that boundless heart of hers to take hold. I should have realized it would make things harder for her, but *man*, I wanted her there with me.

Her voice whispers through my mind—*When we stage our breakup, we'll do it in a way that doesn't make them hate me*—making me see how fucked up it was that I thought we might actually have a chance together. As much as it hurts to admit it to myself, if she thought I was her Mr. Right, she would have worded that very differently.

By the time I finish my run and shower, it's after nine, and I still haven't heard from Destiny. Even on the rare mornings when we don't wake up together, we've exchanged several texts by this time. Nothing is sitting right with me, so I thumb out another text to her. *Good morning, sunshine. I hope you got some rest. Molly and I missed you last night.* I read it over and delete the last line. If she wants space, she doesn't need pressure.

*Fuck.* If that's the case, I shouldn't even text her.

This is another reason I don't do relationships. They're messy and complicated and too easy to fuck up. No matter how I look at it, the way she turned me away last night spells trouble. I read the message again and add a more thoughtful line.

**Fletch:**

> Good morning, sunshine. I hope
> you got some rest. I'm about to run
> errands. Need anything?

Ten minutes later she still hasn't responded, and I'm wearing a path in the floor. I call Perfect Paws to see if she was called into work, but they say she's not scheduled until Tuesday. I'm tempted to head over to her place, but I'm not going to be that annoyingly clingy guy. Instead, I sit down to do some work. Half an hour later I'm still unable to concentrate, so I grab my keys and head out to run those errands.

It's almost noon when I finish putting my groceries away, and I decide to call her. It goes to voicemail. "Hey, sunshine. I've been trying to reach you. Give me a call when you get a chance. I'm getting worried." I pocket my phone, trying not to think about how she always returns my texts and calls. But that's like trying not to breathe. This isn't right. She doesn't avoid situations. This is how we got into a mess last time. I grab Molly's leash. "Come on, girl. Let's go see what's up."

A few minutes later I'm knocking on Destiny's door for the third time. Her car is out front, and I'm getting seriously worried. I lift my hand to knock one last time before breaking the damn thing down, when the door opens, and my heart sinks. Destiny's holding a blanket around her shoulders. Her hair is a tangled mess, she's pale, her cheeks are drawn, her eyes are watery and red, and she looks like a fraction of herself. One of my T-shirts hangs nearly to her knees over gray sweatpants, and she's wearing blue-and-yellow fuzzy socks.

"Baby, what happened?" I step forward, but she holds her hand up.

"Don't come any closer. I have puke on me."

"I don't care. Why didn't you call me? Or answer my texts?"

"I didn't want to bother you, and I think my phone is still in my bag from last ni—" Her hand flies to her mouth, and she drops the blanket, hurrying toward the bathroom.

I unhook Molly's leash and go after Destiny. She's kneeling on the floor, clutching the toilet. I hold her hair back as she throws up what little she has left in her stomach. Molly stands in the doorway, watching over her favorite girl. When Destiny stops puking, I rub her back. "It's okay, sunshine. I've got you."

She groans and turns away. "Don't look at me."

"I like looking at you." I flush the toilet and wet a washcloth. "I should have checked on you, but I thought you wanted space."

"I just didn't feel good."

Crouching beside her, I gently turn her face toward me and begin wiping it clean. "You're burning up. How long have you been like this?"

She shrugs. "I went to bed after you dropped me off and woke up a little while later. I've been throwing up on and off since then."

"Have you taken anything for your fever?"

She shakes her head and presses her hand to the side of her face. "Everything hurts. I think I got it from Ruby. She said she felt . . ." Tears spill from her eyes. "Oh no. She's probably not pregnant after all." A sob falls from her lips.

I pull her into my arms. "It's okay."

*"No, it's not."* Tears rain down her cheeks. "She's gonna be heartbroken if she's not pregnant, and she's gonna need me."

"I know, sweetheart, but let's not worry about something you're not sure has happened." I kiss her forehead, keeping her close and rubbing her back, wishing I could put *her* heart on pause so she wouldn't be sad on top of being sick. I frame her face between my hands and wipe her tears with the pads of my thumbs. "Let's get some medicine and fluids in you. Do you think you can handle a tepid bath to bring down your temperature?"

"Maybe."

"Okay. Do you have Gatorade or ginger ale? Coke? Crackers?"

"No, but I'm okay." She tries to stand up, and sways.

I lift her into my arms, carrying her out of the bathroom with Molly on our heels. "You're not okay. But you will be."

As I head for the stairs, she says, "Don't go up there. I puked in both beds."

"It's okay. I'll clean them up." I turn toward the living room.

"That's not safe, either. There's puke in the trash can next to the couch."

"Thanks for the warning, Mount Vesuvius." That earns a small smile. "Let's get you settled, and then I'll clean up and get you into a bath to see if we can bring down that fever."

I lay her on the couch, and can't believe Molly's not going after Clementine, who's curled up at the other end. She's too busy sniffing the puke in the trash can. "No, Molly," I say in my sternest voice as I cover Destiny with a clean blanket. Thankfully, Molly listens and jumps onto the couch with Destiny, sending Clementine up to the back of it. Molly settles behind Destiny's legs, and Clementine stretches out on the top of the cushion behind her. "Do you want me to get them down?"

Destiny shakes her head and rests her cheek on the pillow, closing her eyes.

I tuck her hair behind her ear. "Where do you keep your medicine, sweetheart?"

"Kitchen cabinet above the stove."

"I'll be right back." I grab the trash can and take it into the kitchen.

After giving Destiny Tylenol, I put a cool washcloth on her forehead and a glass of water on the coffee table. I call Marshall as I head upstairs.

"Hey, Fletch. What's up?"

"Are you busy? I need a favor."

"Name it."

"Destiny is sick and I need a few things, but I don't want to leave her. Would you mind picking up some Gatorade, a bottle of Coke to settle her stomach, maybe some tea and crackers?"

"Peppermint tea helps nausea."

*Fuck.* I should've known something was off when she ordered that. "Grab some please, and fuzzy socks if you can find them. The brighter the better, and . . ." I list off a few more things that I hope might help her feel better.

"I'm on it. You okay?"

"Yeah. I just . . ." I stop myself from saying it hurts to see her this way, because while this is probably just a virus, Marshall has suffered much worse. "I'm good. Thanks, man."

I go from room to room, upstairs and down, changing linens and cleaning up puke, and throw a load of dirty laundry into the washer. Marshall texts to say he's out front while I'm filling the bathtub for Destiny. I turn it off and head downstairs. I see Destiny is sleeping and meet Marshall at the front door. "Thanks, man."

He hands me the bag. "How's she doing?"

"She's sleeping, but I'm about to get her into the tub."

"Has she been sick all day?"

"Yeah. It started last night, but I didn't know. I was at my place."

"At least you're here now. I know that look, and I remember the feeling that came with it. As much as this sucks, at least you know that cold heart of yours is still ticking."

I half laugh, half scoff. "Right. Thanks again."

"Let me know if you need anything else."

"I will." I close the door and take the bags into the kitchen. After putting the groceries away, I stuff the rainbow-colored socks in my back pocket and head back to Destiny. I hate waking her, but I think she'll feel better when she's cleaned up and her fever is down. Brushing a kiss to her head, I whisper, "Sunshine."

Her eyes flutter open.

"Think you can handle a quick bath, so we can get you into clean clothes?"

She nods, and I carry her upstairs with her furry sentinels in tow. Molly lies across the threshold to the bathroom, and Clementine watches from behind her as I undress Destiny and help her into the bath. I kneel beside the tub and touch her cheek. "The Tylenol must be kicking in. You don't feel quite as warm as you did earlier."

"Mm." She closes her eyes, and I gently bathe her. "Thank you," she says weakly. "You shouldn't stay. I don't want you to get sick."

"*Shh.* I'm not going anywhere."

Destiny dozes on and off throughout the day, but I'm able to keep her hydrated. Other than a few bouts of dry heaves in the afternoon, the nausea seems to have passed. Tylenol is keeping her fever at bay, and she was able to eat a few crackers and keep them down. It's early evening, and she's cuddled beneath a blanket with her head in my lap, wearing a clean pair of sweats and her new fuzzy socks, which perked her up for a few minutes when I put them on her. We tried to watch *The Office*, but she's still too out of it to concentrate.

"I hope I didn't get your family sick," she says softly.

"You didn't. I spoke with them earlier. They're fine, and they hope you feel better soon."

She falls quiet again, and I run my fingers through her hair. I combed it for her after her bath, but it's tangled and messy again. "Would you like me to read to you?"

"You don't have to. You've already done so much."

"I'd like to, if you're up to it. I think you'll like this story I found."

"You can try." She closes her eyes.

"Let me know if it bothers you, and I'll stop." I pick up *The Guernsey Literary and Potato Peel Pie Society* from the end table, where I put it while she was sleeping earlier, and begin reading the first line of her mother's favorite book. Destiny looks up at me with tears in her eyes. I wink, and continue reading.

*"Fletch."* Her voice is shaky as tears slide down her cheeks, but she's smiling. "Where did you get that?"

"I had Marshall pick it up when he got the other things."

Her forehead falls to my thigh, her shoulders jerking with her tears.

I rub her back, my chest tightening. "I'm sorry. I didn't think it would upset you."

"It didn't." She sniffles and rests her cheek on my thigh again, her tears flowing freely. "I'm happy, not sad."

Relief washes over me, and I continue reading. Eventually her tears stop, and I feel her whole body sigh. A few chapters later, she's sleeping again. I keep reading, because not only am I invested in the story, but I'm also deeply invested in her, and on the off chance that she hears my voice in her sleep, I hope it brings her sweet dreams of her parents.

She shifts, mumbling in her sleep, "He wasn't supposed to be so wonderful."

I don't know if she's dreaming or not, but if she is, I selfishly hope that was about me.

# Chapter Twenty-Four

## DESTINY

My fever broke sometime during the night, and by Sunday afternoon I felt much more like myself, although still as tired as a wet dishrag. I wanted to go over the deliveries for Arjun's proposal and check the designs and spelling for the special-moment signs that I'm having printed tomorrow, but my charming caretaker refused to let me work. He said I'd worn myself ragged the last few weeks making sure everything was perfect, and that my only job today was to rest and recuperate so I'd be in tip-top shape for the event next weekend. Then, while I lay on the couch with Molly and Clementine, *he* went through each of the thirty-seven special-moment designs looking for typos, and after he was done, he went over my spreadsheets with a fine-tooth comb. He compared them to the delivery schedule and even went through the invoices to make sure nobody had overcharged me. When he finished all that, he made me soup and toast for dinner and read more of my mother's favorite book to me.

Now we're sharing a lounge chair in my backyard. I'm sitting between his legs with my back against his chest. His arms are wrapped around me, and every now and then he kisses the top of my head or pets Molly, who is sleeping in the grass beside us. She hasn't left my side, either.

I don't know which of Fletch's skills is stronger, his organization and attention to detail or his caretaking abilities. He's been nothing short of amazing, taking such good care of me and calling in a favor for the things I needed and the things I hadn't realized I needed, like the socks and my mother's favorite book. Listening to him read me the story made me feel like I could get through puking all night if that was the turn I took.

I gaze up at the stars, so full of emotions I'm sure my parents can feel them in whatever realm they exist. I put my hands over Fletch's, and he laces our fingers together. I want to freeze this evening and stay in this bubble of happiness forever.

"How're you feeling, sunshine?"

"Good."

"Are you warm enough?"

"Yes. Your body is like a furnace."

He kisses my cheek. "Around you it is. You've been quiet. Are you thinking about Ruby or your big event next weekend?"

I texted Ruby earlier and was relieved to hear she wasn't sick like I was. She'd called a few hours later to tell me she'd taken a pregnancy test and the results were positive. She's going to schedule an appointment with her doctor to confirm, but we were both in tears.

"I was actually thinking about you. You're pretty good at this care-taking stuff. You inspired another item for my checklist."

He kisses my head again. "What's that? Someone who's good with spreadsheets?"

"I'm definitely adding *that* to my list. I meant caretaking. It's been a long time since anyone has taken care of me like that. When I was young, my mom did, and my dad took good care of me after she was gone, but it was different."

"I would think it would be. Mothers and fathers handle things differently."

My chest aches from a truth I've held in for years. This time, as I look up at the stars, my eyes tear up. *I love you, Daddy. Please don't think*

*I wish anything was different other than Mama not dyin'. I love the way you cared for me, but I want to share my truth with Fletch, because I might never feel this close to anyone again.*

"Are you all right, sunshine?" He presses a kiss beside my ear. "You're squeezing my fingers pretty tight."

"I'm okay. Sorry about that. Can I tell you something without you thinking poorly about my dad?"

"I have nothing but respect for your father and the incredible job of raising you he did. So, unless you're about to tell me that he physically or emotionally hurt you, I don't think you could mar his reputation in my eyes."

"Now you've got me all weepy." I laugh softly and wipe my eyes. "Thank you. He was a special man, and he deserves that."

"But?" he whispers.

"It's not really a *but*. Everything I've told you has been true about how we pulled through after losing my mother, but it was more difficult than I let on. Growin' up without my mom was really hard. I never wanted to make things worse for my dad, so I didn't tell him when I was lonely for her or jealous about other girls doing special mother-daughter things." Tears slide down my cheeks. "We had a big event in Rosebell called the Azalea Festival. Every girl wants to be chosen as the Azalea princess, but you have to be fifteen to enter the pageant. My mom won when she was sixteen, and we used to talk about what it would be like when I was old enough to compete. You know by now that I'm not a dressy girl, but my mama loved that festival to no end. She had dreams of me winnin'. We'd be out shopping for groceries, and she'd stop by the dress shop and we'd look at all the fancy dresses and she'd talk about what it would be like for me to win like she did. And then she was gone, and I . . ." I shake my head, unable to choke out anything more.

"It's okay, baby." He holds me tighter. "Let it all out."

His words break the emotional dam, and my tears flow like rivers. "There were so many times like that when I felt *lost*. When I got my period, which you probably don't want to hear about, but it was scary going through it without my mom. I don't know why I didn't go to my dad or even Ruby's mother, but I couldn't. I went to Ruby, and she told her mother that *she* got her period, so her mom would buy her the products *I* needed."

"That's a good friend."

"Yes, she is. But there were times I couldn't even tell her about because they were too big, and I knew nobody could help me get through them." I swipe at my tears. "Like when I'd get invited to something at school and race through the front door to share my news with my mom, only to have reality take me to my knees." A sob bursts free, and Fletch's chest expands against my back.

He tightens his hold on me. "That's so fucking unfair. I wish I could've been there for you."

I shake my head. "I wouldn't have let you see me that way any more than I'd've let my dad. If he'd known all the feelings I hid from him, he'd've found a way to be with me every second. That's how much he loved me. I am so grateful for his love, and I don't know if sayin' all this makes me a rotten person, but he couldn't replace my mom. He tried so hard, but he couldn't fill the hole her death left inside me. It used to swallow me up from the inside out. There were times I felt like I couldn't breathe, and I was afraid to tell him because he'd lost her, too."

Fletch repositions us, bringing my side against his chest, and holds me while I cry. "That doesn't make you rotten, sunshine. Your father was a smart man. I'm sure he knew nobody could replace your mom and was doing everything he could to lessen the pain, not replace her. A parent is a million different things to each of their children, and every one of those things is unique to that parent and child. You were an only child, so you got all the best parts of her, including all those secret mother-daughter parts."

I'm unable to stop the rush of tears spilling down my cheeks, but I lift my face from his chest so I can see his honest eyes. "You don't think he'd be disappointed in me for feelin' that way?"

"No, baby. You were a little girl trying to deal with a loss no child should have to endure. Sharing those feelings with me doesn't mean you love your father any less than you did an hour ago. It means you finally found someone you trust enough to share them with."

I nod, tears blurring my vision. "I'm countin' on that." I swipe at my tears. "Sorry for blubbering all over your shirt." I touch my forehead to his chest and close my eyes. "Guess you won't be writin' home about this weekend. If you weren't cleaning up my puke, you were dealin' with my tears."

He hugs me. "That's what best guy friends are for."

I tip my head back. "How'd I get lucky enough to end up stuck like glue to a friend like you?"

"I've been asking myself that for weeks."

As I settle in against his chest again, he says, "Which of the stars is your mom and which is your dad?"

"I'm pretty sure the stars I think they are aren't the same from night to night. The sky never looks the same twice, but I try to choose the same ones I've been talking to since my daddy passed." I point to a bright star. "See that bright one? That's him. And see the one to the right of it? That's my mama. She always held his right hand."

"Well, sunshine, they're still shining down on you. Know what that means?"

"What?"

"You've got nothing to worry about or feel guilty about." His voice is low and reassuring. "You didn't hurt your parents' feelings by trusting me." As my heart fills to near bursting, he adds, "But saying you don't know which stars they are? That might've stung," and just like that, I'm smiling again.

# Chapter Twenty-Five

## FLETCH

Destiny spent the week coming up with proposal ideas for her two newest clients and going over every detail for Arjun's event. We worked together the last two nights, organizing and packing the decorations and supplies. By Saturday morning, I know the event is going to be perfect, but Destiny is like an anxious Energizer Bunny, zipping around the house in nothing but my T-shirt, which she slept in, and panties. As I make breakfast, I hear her moving things around in the living room, talking to Molly and Clementine. The proposal isn't taking place until this evening, but the landscaper created a gorgeous stone walkway on the roof of the restaurant yesterday, and we're meeting him there around two, after he's done laying turf on the roof.

I set our food on the table and peer into the living room. The neatly organized plastic containers that were stacked and ready to be transported are now strewn across the floor and on the couches. Destiny is fishing around in a box on the couch as she consults the supply checklist. If anyone had said there would come a day when noisy, chaotic mornings would make me happy, I'd have told them they were nuts. Now I can't imagine a single morning without my sweet whirlwind turning things upside down. She's opened a door in me that I thought was soldered closed. The wedding is next weekend, and as often as I think about trying to make a go of things with Destiny, I know where her head is. *My mama taught me to always say what I feel. Heck, my heart gets tangled up with people and things and moments all the time. If I tried to hide it, I'd probably burst.* Just last night she referenced *when* we break up again, not *if*, and there were no tears or misgivings in sight. I'm not dumb enough to bring it up and risk losing the last week she's already promised me.

"This one's got everything," she says to Molly and Clementine, snapping me back to the moment. "Let's check the other—" She nearly trips over the cat as she turns around. Clementine scampers up the stairs, and Molly follows. *"Sorry, Clem!"*

"Okay. I think that's enough, sunshine."

She opens a box at the other end of the couch. "I just want to check this box one more time."

"We went through each of them three times last night. Why don't you come eat some breakfast."

"I'm too nervous to eat. This is one of the biggest days of Arjun's and Maura's lives, and they're counting on me to make it perfect."

"And it will be. You've made sure of that many times over." I move her hair over one shoulder and wrap my arms around her from behind. "We've got hours before we're expected at the restaurant." I kiss her neck. "You need to relax, sweetheart, or you'll drive yourself batty and flatten poor Clementine in the process."

She laughs softly. *"Relax?* Do you even know me?"

"I know every inch of you." I slide my hands beneath her shirt. "And I know just how to help you relax." I press one hand to her stomach, keeping her close, as I tease her breast with the other.

*"Mm.* More like rev me up."

"Rev you up." I nip her earlobe. "Make you come." I slide my other hand into her panties, teasing her with my fingers until she's slick with desire. "And relaxing will follow." I dip my fingers inside her and roll her nipple between my finger and thumb, squeezing just hard enough to hear her gasp and feel her pussy clench.

"*Fletch*," she says needily, and tries to turn in my arms, but I don't let her.

"Uh-uh, sunshine. I've got you just where I want you." I push my boxer briefs down and step out of them, pressing my cock against her ass. She whimpers and pushes her ass back, grinding against my erection. "Do you want my cock, baby?"

"*Yes—*"

I push her panties down, and she steps out of them. "You can have it after you come."

The air rushes from her lungs. "So unfair."

I bite her earlobe again, and she moans. I move my hand from her breast to her clit. She holds on to my arms, breathing harder as she rides my fingers. "That's my girl. Chase that climax so I can fuck you."

"*Ohgod . . .*"

I grind against her ass, working her faster. She moans and mewls, her breaths coming faster and harder. "*Don't stop . . . Oh . . . ah . . .*" I feast on her neck, using my tongue and teeth. "*Yes . . . so good . . . Fle—*" Raspy pleasure-drenched sounds fly from her lips as her pussy clenches tight and hot around my fingers. Before she hits the peak, I wrap one arm around her waist, angling her toward the arm of the couch, and drive my cock into her in one hard thrust.

"*Yes—*" She grabs the arm of the couch, so fucking trusting. So beautiful and hungry for me, she ignites desires that tear through me, unleashing the possessive beast that wants to carry her off to my cave and never let her go. I grab her hips, pounding into her, her desperate pleas fueling my desires. Greedy emotions coil inside me like a viper waiting to strike. I put my hand on her back, bending her over the arm of the couch, trying to put space between me and those dangerous feelings. But they're inescapable, seeping into my pores, permeating my every breath as we're catapulted into ecstasy, her sensual cries mixing with my lustful curses as we ride out our passion.

# Chapter Twenty-Six

## DESTINY

I'm strangely calm as we set up for Arjun's proposal, which might have something to do with Fletch banging the stress right out of me this morning and maybe also the fact that the most important people in my life are here with me. John came with Ruby and stayed to help. I think he just wanted to stick close to her since she's still feeling nauseous. I told Ruby I could set up without her, but she wouldn't hear of it.

We're making good progress. The turf is laid, the barriers are in place several feet away from the edge of the roof, and the restaurant staff is setting up the table and chairs. Piper should be here any minute to erect the tower, and the floral delivery should arrive soon. I glance across the roof at Fletch, who is stringing waterfall lights with John between the poles we've put up around the perimeter of the proposal area. He looks over and winks.

"Stop gawking, woman." Ruby steps into my line of sight, blocking my view of him, and shoves another bundle of stone-patterned fabric into my hands. "Chop, chop. We have work to do."

"But I like ogling him." We shake out the fabric and spread it over one of the barriers. The effect is exactly what I'd hoped for, giving the appearance of stone walls around Arjun and Maura's love nest.

"You like doing a lot more than ogling him," she says as we retrieve another bundle of fabric.

A male voice booms through the air. "Where do you want this?"

I turn around, and my heart skips at the sight of Jimmy and Chuck carrying a piece of the Eiffel Tower and Beth carrying a cardboard box. "Oh my gosh! You can put it there!" I point to where I'd like the tower. "What are you guys doing here?"

"How am I going to convince you to hire me if I don't learn the business?" Beth answers.

Chuck calls out, "Family helps family," and my heart lodges in my throat.

"If you drop that, I'm going to castrate you," Piper warns as she and Harley, carrying her toolbox, follow them onto the roof.

"Trust me, guys, she'll do it," Harley warns.

Chuck and Jimmy pretend the structure is slipping. Ruby, Beth, and I gasp despite knowing it's only a joke, and Piper and Fletch yell at them. Chuck and Jimmy just laugh.

"If you fuck this up for Destiny, I *will* slaughter you," Fletch promises.

"And I'll be right behind him," Beth chimes in.

"Who are these people?" Ruby asks. "I *love* them."

"Aren't they great? The pregnant blonde is Piper, and the guy with her is her husband, Harley."

"They're Frankie's parents?"

"Yeah, and the other guys are Fletch's brothers, Chuck and Jimmy, and the blond is Beth, Jimmy's fiancée. Beth and I have been keeping in touch since we met, but she never let on that they were coming today."

"She's a good secret keeper. I like that in a friend."

"Speaking of secret keepers." I look at Fletch and call out, "Did you know about this?"

He grins like a Cheshire cat. "They asked if I thought you'd mind a few days ago."

"Mind? I'm thrilled! Come on, Rube. I'll introduce you and John."

After bear hugs, introductions, and some good-natured heckling, the guys carry up the rest of the tower, and the flowers arrive. The rooftop is filled with activity and jovial conversations as we all set up. I'm overwhelmed at how big my small circle of friends has become. As usual, my emotions get the best of me, and tears threaten. A familiar set of strong arms circles my waist, and Fletch's deep voice whispers in my ear, "How's the great mastermind holding up?"

I turn in his arms as tears spill from my eyes, and we both laugh. "Sorry. It's a bit overwhelming, going from having only Ruby and John in my life to *this*." More tears fall, and I huff out a breath and wipe them away. "It's times like these I wish I could hide my emotions. Nobody needs to see me crying."

His brows knit, and he shakes his head. "It's times like these that make you even more beautiful." He kisses me sweetly. "Don't ever change, sunshine."

"Hey, loverboy," Chuck hollers. "You going to help us with this or get a room?"

"Jealous?" Beth teases.

"Nah. He can have the kisses as long as I get the cookies," Chuck says. "But we've got work to do."

"Are you nuts? Don't give Fletch tools, or we'll all be in trouble," Jimmy calls out, sparking a slew of jokes about Fletch's inability to fix things, which has us all laughing.

Three hours later, everyone has left except for me and Fletch. I've gone over the evening's program with Rich and his staff for the last time, the photographer and violinist have arrived and know how to reach me if they need me, and I've confirmed with Arjun that everything is still on track. Fletch is taking pictures as we stand at the entrance to the roof, getting one last look at all our hard work.

Battery-operated candles flicker along the stone path, which is sprinkled with red rose petals and snakes through the lush green turf, leading to the majestic Eiffel Tower. The stunning tower is covered in moss and boasts twinkling lights along the frame and is decorated with red and white roses. The lights of the town sparkle in the distance, just as I knew they would. More candles and rose petals lead to a gold easel holding a large sign with CAFÉ OF LOVE WELCOMES ARJUN AND MAURA TO THE START OF YOUR HAPPILY EVER AFTER written in French above an adorable picture of them taken on the day they met. Just beyond the easel is a table set for two with a bountiful floral centerpiece featuring the most important special-moment card that reads THE MOMENT I KNEW I LOVED YOU—STANDING IN THE RAIN WAITING FOR THE BUS ON THAT GLOOMY OCTOBER AFTERNOON.

Champagne is chilling in a silver ice bucket beside the table, begging for a celebratory toast, and on either side of the entire proposal-area setup, waterfall lights twinkle above stone-patterned barriers draped in greenery and roses, with planters along the bottoms. Each bundle of flowers prominently displays a special-moment card.

*"Fletch."* I clutch his hand, heart racing. "Am I dreaming, or is it as perfect as I think it is?"

"It's every bit as perfect. I knew it was going to be gorgeous, but, sunshine, there are no words for what you've created here."

"We did it. We actually did it!" I throw my arms around him.

"This is all you, baby, and once people get a look at the pictures of tonight, you're going to need to hire a crew bigger than just Beth to keep up with your clients."

"I hope you're right!"

"We'd better get out of here before Arjun shows up."

"I just need one sec." I look up at the sky and feel my parents smiling down on me. "This is it, Daddy. I hope you and Mama enjoy the show."

As we head downstairs, I'm giddy with excitement, but anxious, hoping Maura and Arjun are happy with the outcome. "Do you want to take a walk or grab a bite to eat?"

"Yeah. Let's grab a bite. I know a place right down the street, if that's okay."

"You just spent all day helping me set up. I'll go anywhere you want as long as there's cell service in case there's an issue."

We walk down the street to a tall brick building. Fletch holds the door open for me, and as I step inside, it looks like a regular office building. "There's a restaurant here?"

He eyes me coyly and puts a hand on my back, leading me down the hall to a maintenance elevator. He pulls out a key card and uses it to open the door.

"Fletch, what are you up to?"

We step inside, and he uses the card again. As the elevator rises, he gathers me in his arms and he's all smiles. "You've worked so hard to set this up, I wanted to be sure you got to see it play out. My father works in this building. He pulled a few favors for us. We're heading up to the roof, but don't get too excited. It's just a roof."

Emotions bubble up inside me. "No, it's not. It's a roof you brought me to, to see something that might never have come to fruition if you didn't show up at my door that first day, and believe in me, and teach me how to do it right, and make sure I was protected legally." I'm getting choked up again and take a deep breath. "You, my friend, are incredibly thoughtful, and it will never be just a roof to me. But we might be too far away to see them."

"Maybe, but it's worth a shot."

The elevator doors open, and we step out onto the roof. There's no Eiffel Tower, no waterfall lights or elaborate flooring, but my breath catches at the sight of an enormous telescope with a big red bow around it and a table set for two with a large pizza box in the middle from my favorite pizza place, a bottle of wine, wineglasses, and a vase of beautiful pink carnations. And because I'm me, my eyes tear up.

"How did you do all this when you've been with me the entire day?"

"A gentleman never tells, and stop eyeing my pizza. It's steak and pineapple, my favorite. If you're nice, maybe I'll share."

He's teasing. He picks off the pineapple and puts it on my slices. "That's awfully generous of you."

He kisses me and takes my hand. "Come on, sunshine. I don't want you to miss the big event." We walk over to the telescope. "Have you ever used one of these?"

"I have a vague memory of using a small one in middle school, but it was nothing like this. It didn't have all those gadgets."

"Well, this one is yours, and it's on an equatorial mount. I'll show you how to use all the gadgets later."

"*Mine?* You got it for *me*? For tonight?"

"That's right, Sherlock. Now get over here and look through the lens." He guides me in front of him. "It should be adjusted fairly well already, but you can turn this to focus it."

I peer through the lens and adjust the focus. "*Wow.* I see them! It's like they're right in front of me."

"Do you think I'd buy you a cheap telescope?"

"No. I didn't think you'd buy me *any* telescope. She's walking down the path! Do you want to see?"

"No. This is for you."

"I'm so nervous for her. She's looking around, smiling so big. I think she likes it! They're in front of the tower. He's getting down on one knee! She's crying! I wonder what he's saying. He's standing up and putting the ring on her finger! She said yes! He got the *yes*!" I throw my arms around Fletch again, both of us laughing. "Thank you for thinking of this!" I look through the telescope again, then turn away quickly.

"What's wrong?"

"They're kissing. It feels wrong to watch."

"I've got an idea." He moves the telescope and fiddles with the dials on it. "Take a look through there and see if you can find your parents' stars."

"I think you mean choose stars for tonight." I look through the lens. "I can't get over how clear everything is. It looks like I can reach out and touch the stars. There are two bright ones right there. Look." I step back and let him look through the lens.

"Looks like you found them. The one on the right is your mom, and the one on the left is your dad."

"How do you know which is which?"

"Because your mother always held his right hand, and because I had those stars named for them. The star on the right is Bonnie 'Mama' Amor, and the one on the left is Miguel 'Daddy' Amor."

I can't tell if he's kidding, and then I realize I never told him my parents' names. "How do you know their names, and what do you mean, you had them named?"

"Ruby told me their names. The way you described your parents' love as being all-consuming, I figured their stars would be insepara-ble, so I found two orbiting stars, which are gravitationally bound to, and in orbit around, each other, and I had them registered with the International Space Registry. Now you'll always know where they are, and they're your parents' namesakes forever."

Tears spill down my cheeks as I try to wrap my head around what he's said.

He pulls a black velvet pouch out of his pocket and empties it into his hand. He holds out his palm, showing me a rose-gold necklace with two interlocking hearts on it. "These have their names and the coordi-nates of their stars on them, so you'll always have them with you." He turns them over, showing me the inscriptions.

"You did this for me?"

"I know how important your parents are to you." He moves behind me and gathers my hair over one shoulder, putting the necklace on me. "This way you'll always know exactly where they are. I'll show you how to find the coordinates with your EQ mount so you can see their stars anytime you want."

A sob breaks free, and I wrap my arms around him. "This is the most special thing anyone has *ever* done for me."

"Well, sunshine, you're a special person."

I hug him tighter, my tears wetting his shirt as I choke out, "For someone who doesn't believe in love, you sure do have a big heart."

"Let's keep that between us."

I laugh through my tears, and there beneath the stars that now carry my parents' names, I picture my own special-moment card—*That starry night on the rooftop, when I fell truly, madly, deeply in love with my best guy friend and knew he would never be my Checklist Guy.*

# Chapter Twenty-Seven

## Fletch

The week after Arjun's proposal passes with many highs, including celebrating Ruby's pregnancy with a night out. After work, we take walks with Molly, and every night Destiny looks at her parents' stars, and we fall into bed making love like we might never get another chance. Now it's the night before Jimmy and Beth's wedding, and we're at the rehearsal dinner. The practice run is over, and we're almost done eating, when I'm hit with the strangest realization. There's a universal change that happens to college students the week of their final exams, when reality hits and they realize they probably should have spent more time studying and less time dicking around. Those last days before the exams turn fun-loving players and party girls into anxious nail-biters, scrambling for excuses to tell their parents about why they're going to fail the exam, and turn serious students into laser-focused, neurotic messes. I always prided myself on being the laser-focused guy.

Until now.

As I watched my youngest brother, the ultimate party guy, practice for his big day, he wasn't anxious at all. It's like he's been preparing his whole life to become Beth Peterson's husband, and I know that's not the case. Whereas I've spent a fucking decade preparing myself to be alone, and as I look at Destiny, sitting beside me, telling Beth and her sister about the proposals she's putting together for her newest clients, my insides are churning like a gristmill.

For the second time in my life, I am completely unprepared for what lies ahead.

I never saw the end of my marriage coming. Not that I would've known how to go about preparing for it at the time. But I've known about the expiration date of my situationship, or whatever the hell this life-altering thing is between me and Destiny, since the start, and I feel like the nail-biting party guy who has pushed reality aside, telling myself I can handle the end of us and rendering myself completely unprepared.

My father taps his spoon to his wineglass, drawing everyone else's attention, but I can't take my eyes off Destiny. She is gorgeous in a bright red halter dress, the necklace I gave her shimmering beneath the lights. I want to soak in every second of her that I can.

She leans closer to me, whispering, "I feel you staring at me."

"Good." I put my hand on her thigh, giving it a squeeze. Her smile widens, deepening the adorable dimple that gets me every time.

"I think your dad is going to make a toast. We should pay attention."

"Sorry, no can do," I whisper, and kiss her.

My father clears his throat. Destiny blushes as we look over, and my father lifts his glass. "Nice of you two to join us."

Everyone laughs, and I point to Destiny. "She can't keep her lips off me."

She gasps, eyes wide as saucers. "That's not true!"

I force myself to keep a straight face and cock a brow. "Those *weren't* your lips on mine? Okay, Gobstopper girl." I hold my hands up in surrender and look around the table. "It was all me, folks, all me."

More laughter erupts, and I pull her into another kiss, turning all that laughter into cheers. I hug her, and she whispers, "Ryan Fletcher, you are awful."

"That's not what you said in the shower this morning." I sit back like I didn't leave her slack-jawed, and lace our hands together, giving my attention to my father, who's grinning approvingly. "Sorry, Dad."

"It's all good, son." My father looks around the table. "Would anyone else like to take a minute to smooch before I say a few words?"

"Hell yeah." Jimmy pulls Beth into a kiss, and everyone laughs.

When the chatter quiets, my father's expression turns thoughtful. "People say babies aren't born with personalities. They're born with temperaments, and their character and personality develop over time. I disagree. Each of our sons had very distinct personalities from the moment they were born. Chuck was demanding. He'd cry loud and often, and he had a knack for turning red, which made his mother and I act fast every time he cried. Ryan was a quiet observer. I swear he'd wait until everyone had what they needed and everything around him was calm—yes, I'm talking about Chuck—before he'd vie for our attention. Then came Jimmy, the happiest baby I'd ever seen. I think he came out of his mother's womb laughing. There we were, two young adults raising a ruler, a sentinel, and a jester."

Chuckles rise around us, and Destiny squeezes my hand.

"I remember thinking we were outnumbered, and by the time they were teenagers, they'd run us through the wringer." My father looks at each of us. "And they did, to an extent. But when Chuck was acting like a bull in a china shop and Ryan was trying to rein him in, which was interesting, to say the least, Jimmy never failed to turn the tide with his wild antics and zest for humor. But when the ruler, the sentinel, and the jester were left alone, it was like putting them in a melting pot. We never knew who was going to come out."

Everyone laughed.

"I'm proud of all of my sons and who they've become. Jimmy, I know you're going to make an excellent husband and father. I can say that with complete confidence, because Beth has known how to wrangle you into submission since you were two years old."

"I'll keep him in line," Beth calls out.

"I know you will, sweetheart," he says. "Mary and I couldn't be happier to call you our daughter-in-law. But marriage is hard, and there will be times when you try each other's patience and have trouble remembering why you made your vows. We have faith that you'll go the distance, but as parents, we wanted to give you some profound advice that might help you get through those tough times. The best I could come up with was for Jimmy to learn to say *yes, dear* and sound sincere."

We all laugh.

"As you can imagine, that got nixed pretty quickly," my mother said.

"We were stuck," my father adds. "But then we had the pleasure of meeting Ryan's girlfriend, Destiny."

Everyone looks over, and Destiny's eyes widen again.

"Destiny is a proposal planner, and she told us about special-moment cards she made for a couple representing their most memorable times together. That was a good reminder that love isn't always loud. It can be, but more often than not, it's the smaller, quieter things that create the unbreakable bond. Like doing the things your partner loves, even if you think they're silly, and being there for them when they need you, and even when they don't. It's always, without fail, having their back, which means supporting their dreams and telling them when they have spinach in their teeth." He pauses for the chuckles. "But that doesn't mean one of you should silence your opinions or accept anything you're not comfortable with. Love is arguing and compromising and coming to decisions that are best for both of you."

He turns to Jimmy and Beth. "With all of that in mind, we've put together a brief video collage of special moments that we hope will remind you of why you fell in love. And our advice to you is when you hit those rocky roads, which you will, find the strength and patience to watch this video together. Hopefully it'll be enough of a reminder to practice that same patience with each other. We love you both." He raises his glass, and we all follow suit. "To Jimmy and Beth. May their hearts stay warm and their future children bring them as much joy and worry as they did to us."

There's a round of cheers and glasses clinking as a screen lowers from the ceiling across the room.

As pictures of Jimmy and Beth at varying ages appear, laughing, hugging, and arguing, I put my arm around Destiny, who's wiping her eyes, and kiss her temple, whispering, "Are you okay?"

She nods. "I love this. You don't mind if I borrow your family when I get married, do you?"

*Fucking hell.* Is she serious? "You're not getting married without us, sunshine."

"Good." She leans against my shoulder.

I put my arm around her, keeping her close while we watch the video. A picture appears of our families at the lake. Chuck and I are about seven and five. We're wearing baseball caps, beaming at the camera as we hold up the fish we caught. Beside me, Jimmy, who's probably three, is holding the head of his fish between his teeth. He's waving with both hands, and Beth is trying to pull the fish out of his mouth. We all laugh as the picture fades and another appears of all of us on my father's boat. Beth and Jimmy are crouched behind me, grinning like the evil geniuses they are, as I sleep on the deck. Jimmy is holding a bottle of suntan lotion, and Beth is pointing to my stomach, on which they've written DORK with the suntan lotion.

More laughter ensues.

The next picture was taken that same day, of me and Chuck putting fish down the backs of Beth's and Jimmy's bathing suits.

"I know I've said it before, but you're lucky to have such a great family," Destiny whispers as more pictures appear, and all I can think about is how lucky I am to have this time with her.

As the evening rolls on, we mingle in the banquet room and on the balcony. Beth dragged Destiny away to hang with the other girls from the wedding party a while ago, and her laughter floats around me like a drug I can't resist.

My father sidles up to me, following my gaze to Destiny. "She fits right in, doesn't she?"

"Yeah. She and Beth have gotten close the last couple of weeks."

"And you're not running in the opposite direction."

I swirl my drink around the ice in my glass. "That's the last thing I want to do."

"Don't let your mother hear that, or she'll be planning your wedding."

"I'm smarter than that."

His expression turns serious. "Are you still anti-marriage?"

"Honestly, I don't know where I stand on that anymore, but I'm happy with Destiny, and I'd like to see where we end up." I can't believe how easily that came out, especially now, when we're on the cusp of ending things. *Shit. What am I thinking?* I gulp down my drink. "If you'll excuse me, I'm going to hit the men's room."

I set my glass on the table and head out of the banquet room, following the signs for the bathroom down the hall. I pass the ladies' room and turn the corner into the men's room. Thank God it's empty. I splash cold water on my face and pace the floor, needing to get my head on straight. Destiny's comment about borrowing my fucking family was a damn wake-up call. I don't want to think about her with another guy. My hands curl into fists as I wear a path in the floor. What the hell am I doing? This is bullshit. What am I afraid of? I fucking love her.

That stops me cold.

*Holy shit. I don't just love who you are and being with you. I'm in love with you.*

My chest constricts, and I lift my gaze to the mirror, expecting to see a man I don't recognize staring back at me. But I know this guy. He's spent ten years afraid to put himself out there. Afraid of being blindsided again. Dozens of people have tried to change my mind about love, and not one of them incited a second thought.

Until Destiny.

She blindsided me, but I don't want to run from her love. But will she want to run from mine?

Pacing again, I try to figure that out. There's no way she can fake the emotions I *feel* in her touch and see in the way she looks at me. There's no way this is one-sided.

The devil on my shoulder hisses, *She isn't afraid of love. She can't help but blurt out her feelings, and she hasn't done that with you.*

"No shit, asshole."

Mentally racing through the last few weeks, my own voice slams into me. *I'm not looking for a relationship, sunshine, and I'm definitely not looking for love. So let's be damn sure we're on the same page this time, because I do not want to hurt you with another misunderstanding.*

I told her not to fall for me.

I grab on to that like it's a brass ring. But that damn devil won't relent. *Wake the fuck up, Grumpy No-Love Gus. You're setting yourself up for heartbreak. There might be a fine line between lust and love to most people, but to Destiny Amor, it's a ravine. One not easily crossed, and certainly not by a man who doesn't nail nearly every item on her checklist.*

My gut roils, and I lean my hands on the sink and close my eyes. What the hell am I doing? Do I really want to walk out that door and lay my heart on the line knowing she might trample it?

I lift my gaze to the mirror. *Fuck yeah, I do.* I rise to my full height and square my shoulders. I push through the bathroom door and stop at the sound of Destiny's voice coming from around the corner.

"It's not like that, Beth. He doesn't meet *anything* on my checklist, well, except the things he inspired, but those don't count."

"So what? It's a stupid list."

"It's *not* stupid. I've poured my heart into that list and lived by it for years. Not taking it seriously now is like going to an ice cream shop wanting a three-scoop sundae with hot fudge and butterscotch and all the toppings, and the guy behind the counter hands you a plain vanilla cone."

"Well, if you put it *that* way." Their voices fade as they head out of the corridor.

Gutted, I sink back against the wall, and for the *first* time in my life, I can't remember how to breathe.

# Chapter Twenty-Eight

## Destiny

"I had so much fun with Beth and her sister and their friends," I say as we drive into Harmony Pointe. "Did you see the way Chuck was flirting with Beth's bridesmaid Katie? When the girls and I were on the patio, he came outside to talk to her, and we all thought they were going to start making out. They didn't, of course, but I bet they made plans to meet up later. They'd make a good couple. Don't you think?"

"I don't know."

"Oh, come on. I think they'd be great together. What a fun night. I'm so happy you brought me with you." I gaze out the window as we drive down the main drag. "I really loved what your dad said about you and your brothers and watching that video." I touch the hearts on my necklace. "Do you know how many times I touched my necklace tonight? I really do feel closer to my parents wearing it. Thank you again."

As he pulls into our neighborhood, I realize I've been talking the whole way home. "Listen to me rambling. I didn't give you a chance to get a word in edgewise. What did you think of the night?"

"It was nice," he says as he drives past his house.

"I thought we were staying at your place tonight."

"Change of plans, sunshine." He turns onto my street.

"Oh, okay. Should we get Molly?"

He pulls into my driveway and cuts the engine. "No, she's fine."

The hair on the back of my neck prickles as he climbs out and comes around to open my door. He offers me his hand, like usual, but as we walk up to the door, he doesn't keep holding it, or put his hand on my back, or anything.

"Fletch, did I do something to bother you tonight?"

"No. You're great. Everyone loved you."

"Then what's wrong? This feels like it did the day we scouted locations for Arjun's proposal."

"It's not like that, sunshine."

"Oh, good." Relief rushes through me.

"That was a misinterpretation. This is a decision."

My stomach plummets.

"I think the world of you, Destiny, and I love spending time together, but I can't lie to my family anymore. Pretending we're falling in love when we both know damn well that I don't do love is wrong. I never should have asked you to go to the wedding with me. It was a mistake. It wasn't fair to you and it certainly wasn't fair to my family, and I'm truly sorry for that."

Tears well in my eyes, and I'm trembling so bad, my teeth chatter. I want to tell him he's wrong. It wasn't a mistake. But my mother's voice forces me to hold my head up high. *Smart girls don't beg for love, and true love doesn't require beggin'.* "I guess I didn't do a very good job of changing your mind about love."

"If anyone could do it, it would be you, sunshine. It's just not in the cards for me, but I hope you find who you're looking for."

He leans in to kiss my cheek, and I close my eyes, memorizing the feel of his lips for the last time as my heart shatters like glass. When he turns to leave, I fumble with my keys, hurrying inside seconds before the dam breaks. Sobs burst from my lungs as I close the door, and my knees give out, sending me crumpling to the floor in a wailing, boneless, heartbroken heap.

I gasp for breath between violent, painful eruptions and curl up in a ball, trying to stop the pain, but the sobs keep coming. I cry out in frustration, my voice echoing in the empty house, amplifying my pain.

I don't know how long I lie there sobbing, but it feels like forever. When Clementine finds me and licks tears and snot from my face, I sit up, feeling numb. Like an empty shell of a falling star. I dig my phone out of my purse. Too depleted to get up, I lie back down as I navigate to my father's number. His craggy voice draws more sobs, and when the voicemail tone sounds, my voice cracks. *"Daddy . . . "* I drag air into my lungs and close my eyes, clutching my necklace. "I messed up. I was wrong." I gasp. "Fletch doesn't love me back." Emotions clog my throat, and I just lie there crying into the phone. "I wish you were here . . . I just need . . ." I don't even know what I need. My breath comes in sharp hiccups. "How can it hurt so much?" The time on the voicemail runs out, and that's when it hits me the hardest.

Nobody's comin' to push me back up to the sky.

# Chapter Twenty-Nine

## FLETCH

This is the shittiest fucking night ever. It's been hours since I left Destiny, and the ache of missing her has seeped into my bones. I tried to sleep in my bed, but everything reminds me of her. I have no fucking idea how I ever slept in that damn bed without her. So now I'm on the couch, *not* sleeping, and Molly's pawing me like I forgot to bring her favorite girlfriend home with me. She whines for the millionth time, and I open my eyes.

She's sitting next to the couch with the green blanket in her mouth, staring at me. "I know you miss her. I fucking miss her, too." How could I have misread her feelings for us?

That's not fair. I know she loves Molly.

As if Molly knows what I'm thinking, she whines again, pawing my leg.

I turn onto my back and put my forearm over my eyes, trying to block out my thoughts, but my head is a fucking battlefield. How could she write me off because of a fucking checklist that she probably started when she was fifteen?

None of it makes sense. She looked devastated when I ended things. Did she dupe me? It wouldn't be the first time. Elaina can testify to that.

Molly paws me again.

"I *know* she didn't dupe me," I snap. "She doesn't have a mean-spirited bone in her body."

Molly whines, pawing me again.

I reluctantly turn my head and see paper hanging out of her mouth. "What is that?" I snag it.

It's the card Destiny left on the counter Thursday morning when she headed out early to meet with a potential client. I sit up, glancing at the end table where I keep the cards, and see a bunch of them sticking out. Did I forget to close the drawer, or . . . ?

I look at Molly and raise my brows. She barks and pushes her nose into the card.

I must really be losing it, but I don't fucking care. If Destiny can look for signs, so can I. I open the card, and her loopy handwriting makes my chest ache.

Good morning! It was fun having dinner with John and Ruby last night, but my favorite part of the evening was dessert (you!). Is it just me, or was Molly looking at us like we were doing it wrong? Ha! By the way, don't think for a minute that I'm going to let you get away scot-free for not singing karaoke with me again. That was your last free pass. One of these days I'm going to get you to sing. Stop shaking your head. I am! You can't resist me forever! Have an amazing day thinking of me.
XO,
Sunshine

PS: I know how to get you to sing! The next time you turn me down, I'll turn you down in bed.
PPS: Scratch that. That's punishing me, too.
PPPS: You're still not off the hook! Next time there will be consequences!

The tiny heart over the *i* in Sunshine cuts like a knife, but I know I'm not wrong. There's love in every line she wrote. As I eye the overflowing drawer, my certainty is inescapable. My father was right. Love doesn't have to be loud. Her love is in all the quiet things she does. The notes she leaves me, the treats, the *socks*. It's in the way she talks about Molly needing pretty things. "*I* didn't make the mistake. She did, by writing me off because of a fucking checklist." Fuming, my heart pounding, I push to my feet.

Molly pops to all fours, tail wagging, following me as I pace.

"She loves both of us. I know she does. I don't care what her stupid checklist says. She made it before she met us. I didn't even want a woman in my life before I met her, much less a noisy, messy one. And I sure as hell didn't want love."

I don't even bother with Molly's leash as I head for the door. "Let's go talk some sense into our girl."

I run out the door, and Molly bolts ahead of me, charging down the street and around the corner. I sprint after her, and as I turn the corner, I see Molly running into Destiny's side yard.

*Damn it. Don't take off now.*

I chase after her, staring into the darkness at the field behind Destiny's house, but I don't see her anywhere. "Molly!" Where the hell is she? I spin around, and my heart fucking stops. Destiny's sitting with her legs folded beneath her, her arms around Molly, her face buried in her fur, and Molly's tail is flapping against the patio, right beside the telescope. As my legs eat up the distance between us, Destiny looks up with tear-soaked puffy eyes and a red nose, twisting the knife in my chest deeper.

"I don't know what you did with my parents' stars, but they're *gone*. What else are you going to do? Run over my cat?"

"I didn't . . . *No.* I'm here to tell you that I heard what you said to Beth about ice cream and me not ticking off anything on your damn checklist. And you know what? If I had been looking for a woman when we met, you wouldn't have made the cut, either."

Her lower lip trembles, tears welling in her eyes.

"You're disorganized, messy as hell, and impulsive to the point of being reckless. You talk in tangents and use candy references that sound like you're talking about blow jobs to my *family*. And you love everyone. You'd probably find something to love about the devil himself, and convince the rest of us to love him, too."

She lifts her chin, tears flooding her cheeks. "I *like* who I am."

"I know you do, and you're holding out for Mr. Right. A guy who ticks *all* your boxes. I never wanted to be your Checklist Guy, Destiny. Hell, when we met, I didn't want to be anything more than a guy who was helping you not make the same mistake twice."

I step closer, lowering my voice. "But that boundless heart of yours drew me in with every tangent, every laugh, every wrinkle of your adorable nose. And guess what, sunshine? I fell in love with you and all those things that make you the incredibly special person you are. I can't do anything about not having milk-chocolate eyes or neat feet. But you want killer dance moves? *I'll take a class.* You want rough around the edges? *I'll stop shaving, get my clothes dirty, and use improper grammar.* You want me to learn to fix things? *I'm a fast learner. I'll start hanging out with Marshall more.* You want a guy who's not afraid to talk about his feelings? *That's going to take some time, but I'll work on communicating better.*"

Her brow wrinkles, tears spilling down her cheeks.

"I know you want love and marriage and babies. I didn't think I was capable of loving anyone ever again, but you've proven me wrong, and if you hadn't written me off, who knows what would've happened. One day maybe I'd be able to give you the rest. God knows I want to. I don't know what else is on your list other than a guy who puts love above all else, but whatever it is, I'll do my best to check those boxes, too." I splay my hands. "I'm far from your ideal Mr. Right, but I'm asking you to reconsider that ridiculous checklist and give Mr. Try Real Hard, the Orgasm King, a real shot with no expiration date."

She pushes to her feet, tears flowing. "You're an idiot, Ryan Fletcher." She turns on her heels and walks inside.

My gut seizes.

Molly gives me a disgusted look and trots after her.

*Fuck. What have I done?*

Destiny walks back outside clutching a notebook to her chest, and my traitorous dog sticks to her like glue. "You're a sucky eavesdropper. You should have listened longer," she says with a painful mix of emotions. "If you had, you would've heard me tell Beth that I made a new list, and it wasn't for a stupid ice cream sundae. It was for the whole damn ice cream shop." She thrusts the pink notebook with Mr. Right Checklist scrawled across the front in sparkly gold ink into my hands. "Go ahead. Open it. The changes and all the things you inspired are in caps."

I open it, scanning the modified list.

1. *Not too tall. (Big men, big egos!)* (He's the perfect height!)
2. *Has moves like ~~Jagger~~* Barney
3. *Neat feet* Great hands!
4. *Rough around the edges* Loves the outdoors
5. *Can fix anything* Knows people who can fix things
6. *Dark hair and eyes like milk chocolate* Dirty-blond hair. Eyes like the clear blue sky
7. *Puts love above all else* (He doesn't realize he's in love yet, but I have faith!)
8. *Isn't afraid to talk about his feelings* (Work in progress)
9. *Romantic* in his own special way
10. *Good kisser* Gives me unforgettable kisses
11. *Will dance in the rain* (He did!)
12. *Wants tons of kids* (No, but I would be happy with one. Negotiate?)

As I read, the pain deepens. Did I fuck this up too badly to fix it?

13. ~~Doesn't mind my mess~~ PUTS UP WITH MY MESS
14. *Isn't put off by my tangents and can follow along* (HE CAN!)
15. *Spontaneous after moments of consideration* (HE'S A PLANNER!)
16. *Steady and stable* (HE IS!)
17. *Will love me forever* (I KNOW HE WILL. BUT HE MIGHT NOT REALIZE IT YET!)
18. *Adventurous* IN THE BEDROOM
19. *Loves karaoke as much as I do* SUPPORTS ME SINGING KARAOKE
20. *Loves family* (YES! MINE AND HIS!)
21. *Loves animals* (HE LETS THEM SLEEP IN THE BED!)
22. *Lets me cut his hair* (UNSURE?)
23. *Lets me eat off his plate* (HE'S A GREAT SHARER!)
24. *Honest to a fault* (ALWAYS!)

I wasn't honest when I ended things, but I came clean. Please don't let it be too late.

25. *Comfortable in any situation* (EXCEPT KARAOKE. WORKING ON THAT!)
26. *Looks good in jeans or dressed up* (AND NAKED! HE'S EXCEPTIONAL!)
27. *Give me fireworks* (ORGASM KING!)
28. MUST HAVE SQUEEZABLE PEACH
29. CALLS ME A CUTE NICKNAME
30. SAYS ALL THE RIGHT THINGS
31. *Strong enough to sweep me off my feet*
32. UNDERSTANDS MY NEED TO TALK TO MY PARENTS
33. *Knows what I want and need most of the time*
34. ISN'T AFRAID TO TELL ME I'M WRONG

35. *Helps me be the best I can be*
36. *Makes me laugh and feel loved*
37. *GOOD WITH SPREADSHEETS*
38. *EXCELLENT CAREGIVER*
39. *Ryan No-Love Grumpy Gus Stoic Sam Aloof Adam Fletcher owns my heart, and no one else will ever come close!*

With my heart in my throat, I lift my eyes to hers. "I'm sorry, Des. I shouldn't have assumed. I was on my way to ask you if you wanted to forget the expiration date and give us a real shot when I heard you talking to Beth, and it knocked the wind out of me. It threw me right back to the end of my marriage, and I figured I had missed the signs like I did back then."

"Couldn't you *tell* it wasn't true or there had to be more to it by the way I am with you?"

"I didn't know what to believe. You've been saying things like *when we break up* and talking about when *you* get married."

"Because I'm in *love* with you and I thought you were still against love—"

"You're in *love* with me?"

"Yes, you fool, and I *had* to say those things. I was trying to convince myself that I was going to be okay when our arrangement ended." Her brows knit, her tone softening. "Or maybe I was hoping you'd say you didn't want to break up. I don't know what I was doing."

*I definitely missed those signs.* "Then you can understand why I wasn't sure what to believe." She nods, and I set the notebook on the patio table and take her hand. "I'm sorry for assuming the worst. I love you, sunshine, and I will never stop trying to be everything you want and need."

"Don't you *get it*? You already are." She puts her arms around me, smiling in a way that I am now one hundred percent sure means she loves me. "We just need to learn to trust our feelings and talk to each other straight up when we're scared or something feels off."

"It may take me some time to get this touchy-feely stuff right. I've been out of practice for a decade."

"Shouldn't a guy who teaches a Millennial Masculinity class know more about touchy-feely things?"

"How do you know about that class?"

"My best guy friend taught me the importance of due diligence."

"He sounds like a pretty good guy, even if he's slow on the uptake."

"He's the *best* guy." She winds her arms around my neck. "Can we go back to that part about forgetting the expiration date?"

"I'd like nothing more."

"Does that mean we're officially a couple, and I can call you mine?"

"I'm partial to Orgasm King, but *yours* will do."

As I lower my lips to hers, she says, "Thank you."

"For what?"

"Being there to push me back up to the sky."

It kills me knowing she felt like a falling star again, and I realize that's how I felt without her, too. Lost and far too alone. I go in for a kiss, and Molly shoves her big head between us.

I groan, and my whirlwind beauty laughs. *Like sunshine to a fucking flower*, and just like that, I find myself laughing, too.

# Chapter Thirty

## Destiny

A hint of impending rain hangs in the air and leaves crunch under my feet. I kick them away from Molly's favorite spot in the sun in front of Fletch's fishing cabin, looking for her elk antler. It's mid-October, and we spent last weekend at the Bernese mountain dog retreat and have been at the cabin ever since. I love it here, with its beautiful foliage and pristine lake. But I could love a desert if Fletch and our pets were with me.

I gaze out at the lake, thinking about how autumn swept into Upstate New York with all her cool grace and colorful glory, easing out the dog days of summer. I was sad to see them go, as they brought barbecues and fishing trips, and so many new proposal clients, Fletch should buy stock in pink carnations. I was finally able to hire Beth, who is nothing short of incredible. Between her marketing skills and my proposal expertise, we've grown the business to needing a third person to keep up. After the unforgettable birthday weekend Fletch threw for me, I wish he could be that person. He honored my family's tradition, decorating the house and waking me up at midnight. We spent the dark, early hours of my birthday gazing up at my parents' stars as we shared more birthday memories. Then he whisked me off on a surprise trip to Rosebell. I hadn't realized how much I'd missed my hometown. I loved showing him all my favorite places and my childhood home.

Rosebell will always own a special piece of my heart, but I have a new home now. With the help of Fletch's family and our friends, including Talia and the rest of the lovely Daltons, whom I finally met, I moved into Fletch's house a month after that fateful night when we proclaimed our love for each other. We learned a hard lesson that night, and we no longer waste any time on assumptions.

"Hey, sunshine, did you find Clem's stuffed mouse?" Fletch asks as he and Molly come out the front door. He's carrying Clementine in his crate and checking his phone for the umpteenth time. He's been fielding texts from his family all week. His mother is trying to coordinate holiday plans with all of us and some out-of-town relatives I've yet to meet.

"Yes. Our big fluffy thief hid it in the leaves." I wave the soggy stuffie and kick something hard. I push the leaves away and pluck the elk antler off the ground. "Aha!" I hold it up like a prize. "I told you I'd find Molly's antler."

"I never doubted you would." He sets Clementine's carrier in the back of the vehicle, and Molly jumps in beside it. He loves her up, and as I head over, he thumbs out a text and pockets his phone, flashing the warm smile that is no longer rare and still causes hummingbirds to take flight in my chest.

"Your mom again?" Molly goes in for a slobbery kiss, and I gladly accept.

"No, it was John. I texted him earlier to let him know we'd be late for dinner. He was just saying it was fine."

We were supposed to leave an hour ago, but I convinced Fletch to take one last walk by the lake with me and Molly because it's just so pretty here. It's almost five, and it's a two-hour drive. "I'm glad they're willing to wait." I pull Molly's head from my face. "Okay, stuffie thief, that's all you get right now." I give her the antler and put Clementine's toy in his carrier, giving him some extra love before Fletch closes the back door.

"Ready to go home, beautiful?"

*Home.* What a magical feeling it is to share a home overflowing with love again. Our own private buffer from the rest of the world.

"I wish we could stay another week. I like having you all to myself." Between my business and Fletch's teaching schedule, we have less time together than we had over the summer, but it makes the time we do have that much more special.

"I was thinking the same thing." His arms circle me. "We'll come back again soon, but we have to go."

He kisses me so thoroughly, I go up on my toes, wishing we could cancel dinner and stay for more, but that wouldn't be fair to Ruby and John. Fletch holds me tighter, making that growling noise I love. "I will never get enough of you," he rasps against my lips, and kisses me again. "To be continued."

"I'm holding you to that."

He helps me into my seat, and I get one last kiss before we get on the road.

I don't know what it is about road trips that makes me chatter up a storm, but on the drive home, I talk about how much fun we've had this week, how much I enjoyed the Bernese mountain dog retreat, and I throw out ideas for Fletch's birthday next month, all of which he nixes.

"Are you turning into Grumpy *No Birthday* Gus?" I tease.

"No. I just don't need a party." He reaches across the console and takes my hand. "Everything I need is right here in this Rover—" A loud sound cuts through the air, and the Rover veers to the right. Fletch grabs the steering wheel with both hands and slows us down as the telltale *flap, flap, flap* of a deflated tire rings out. He maneuvers to the side of the road, puts on the flashers, and cuts the engine. "Are you okay?"

"Yes, I'm fine. It's just a flat." We both look at Molly, who's looking at us like, *Are we there already?*

We climb out, and sure enough, the right front tire is flat. "Shit." Fletch takes out his phone, thumbing out a text. "I'll let John know we're going to be later than we thought and call roadside assistance."

"Don't be silly. I can change a flat in no time."

"I don't even have a jack."

"Of course you do."

His brows slant. "I think I'd know if I had a jack."

"Mm-hm. Says the man who pays a guy to mow his lawn." Unable to resist teasing him, I push up my sleeves and look up at the gray sky. "I know, Daddy, but he does other things so well."

"Hey."

"Open the back, Mr. Fix It. I'll give you the lesson my daddy gave me when I was thirteen."

"Thirteen? Really?"

"Yes. Some of us liked getting our hands dirty." While he puts the leash on Molly, I set Clementine's carrier in the grass. "Your jack and tire are right under this flap." I lift the flap in the back and take out the jack and the lug wrench. I reach for the tire, but Fletch stops me.

"I'll get it." He hands me Molly's leash and takes out the spare, setting it on the ground. "Give me the jack."

"Do you know how to find the jack point?"

Those expressive brows knit. "The what?"

I giggle and hand him Molly's leash, then head for the flat tire. "Come on. We won't use the jack until the lug nuts are loose, but let me show you how to find the jack point." Fletch crouches beside me, and I explain what the jack point is. I'm showing him how to find it when the sky opens up, and rain pours down on us.

I laugh; he curses.

"It's just rain."

"We're going to be even later. Now we'll have to stop at home and change before dinner." He pushes to his feet, pacing with Molly as I take off the hubcap.

"We have to drop off Molly and Clem anyway."

He sighs heavily and thumbs out another text.

"Why are you so worried about dinner?" I wipe the dirt from my hands on my shorts and struggle with loosening the lug nuts.

"I don't like keeping people waiting. Let me do that."

I hand him the lug wrench. "Don't take them all the way out yet."

He looks at me like I don't know what I'm talking about, but he does as I ask and gets up to answer a text as I jack up the Rover. We take off the tire and crouch to put the spare on, but I slip and land on my butt in the mud. "Shit. *Sorry*, baby."

He grabs my hand to help me up, and I slip again, nearly pulling him down with me, which makes me laugh. I'm trying to wipe the rain from my eyes when I notice the rear tire has deflated, too, and "*The tire*," is all I get out before another burst of laughter steals my voice, so I point to the deflated tire.

"What is so—" The color drains from his face.

That's when I notice Molly rolling in the mud, and I lose it. I'm laughing so hard, Fletch starts laughing, too. He pulls me to my feet, and I hold my arms out, looking up at the darkening sky. "We hear ya, Mama! It's time to dance!"

I twirl around, dancing in the mud with Molly. "Dance with us, Fletch!" I spin around, and Fletch is down on one knee, holding his fist like it's a microphone as he starts singing to the tune of "Marry You" by Bruno Mars, only the lyrics are all his own.

> "It's a rainy night, and I had it all planned out
> Hey, sunshine, it was the perfect proposal for you
> But this is the way things go
> And I definitely want to marry you."

"Are you . . . ?" Tears roll down my cheeks as he pushes to his feet and takes my hand.

"Yes, I am. This isn't how I had planned to propose to you, and I know it's not what you dreamed of, but I don't want to wait another second. Destiny, you came into my life like a whirlwind, and I have been swept up in you ever since, with your funky socks and boundless heart and that stunning smile that reels me in deeper every time I see it. I fell in love with you the way night takes over day, without warning, wholly and completely."

"*Fletch*" comes out in a whisper.

"I love the way you laugh, and cry, and *love*. The way you make the world a better, brighter place and make me want to be a better man every day of my life. I want forever with you, baby. I want to raise creative, impulsive children who aren't afraid to grab life by the horns and wrangle it to their liking. Maybe one or two of them will have my careful side, but it'll be second to the rest."

"You want *kids*?" My voice cracks.

"I want it all with you, sunshine. I want to carry on your family traditions and make our own, and when we're old and gray, we'll look back at all our special moments and the family we raised, and we'll laugh about all the things we did wrong and celebrate the things we did right. Destiny Grace Amor, will you do me the honor of marrying me and becoming Mrs. Try Real Hard?"

I laugh and cry. "*Yes!* I want forever with you, too!" I launch myself into his arms, and he spins me around as we kiss. When he sets me on my feet, he slides the most beautiful diamond ring on my finger. It has a round center stone and two breathtaking halos, like a flower. "You had that in your pocket this whole time?"

"Yes. I've been planning tonight for a month. My family and all our friends are waiting for us at the Lucky Lizard, which is filled with pink carnations. I was going to get up onstage and sing the real words to that song to you and ask you to marry me in front of everyone you love. We were going to toast with Sparkling Sunshines, which is a drink I had them name after you. It's strong and sweet and fizzy with a kick."

I laugh through my tears. "Perfect."

"I should've known it wasn't going to go as planned when I asked your father for your hand, and a bird pooped on my head."

*Oh, my heart!* "A bird pooping on your head is *good* luck."

"Really?"

I nod. "I can't believe you asked my dad for my hand."

"I'm just glad he didn't spill the beans, but I can't believe you didn't have *that* on your checklist."

"I didn't even know I wanted that to happen, which just goes to prove that my real Mr. Right loves me so much, he can read my heart."

"Always and forever, sunshine. Even after we're up there in the sky partying with your parents."

# A NOTE FROM MELISSA

Destiny had suffered so much loss and managed to still keep her hopes up for love and for the career she'd always dreamed of. I knew she needed someone special to appreciate all her wonderful qualities and all that she had to offer. When Fletch stepped up to the plate, I was a little skeptical, because he was so closed off to love. But I quickly realized that wall of his was no match for his *sunshine*. I had so much fun peeling away their layers and bringing them together. I hope you enjoyed their story as much as I enjoyed writing it.

If this is your first Melissa Foster book, you might enjoy reading the Dalton siblings' love stories in my Sugar Lake and Harmony Pointe series. All my romance novels are part of the Love in Bloom big-family romance collection. Each story is written to stand alone without any cliff-hangers or unresolved issues and may also be enjoyed as part of the larger series. Characters from each series make appearances in future books, so you never lose track of engagements, weddings, or births. You can find more about my Love in Bloom series on my website (www.melissafoster.com) and download reader checklists, series orders, and other free and fun book-related information on my Reader Goodies page (www.melissafoster.com/rg).

Be sure to sign up for my newsletter to keep up to date with my new releases and to receive an exclusive short story (www.melissafoster.com/news).

Happy reading!

~Melissa

# ACKNOWLEDGMENTS

Writing is my passion, but as much as I love the process, long hours spent in a writing cave might leave me batty if not for my wonderful family, friends, and fans, who inspire me on a daily basis. I am so grateful for their support, and while there are too many to list, I'd like to throw extra gratitude out to those who helped ensure I had the correct meaning of Destiny's surname. That should have been easy, but there are always nuances in language related to geographic areas, and I wanted to make sure to get it right. Luckily, Leticia Teixeira, Inêz Cotovio, Raquel Duarte, Luisa Filipe, and Lisa Filipe were happy to help. I'd also like to send a shout-out to Leslee Lovell and Justinn Harrison for their patience when answering my dog-grooming questions and to Beth Noble, AKA author Sawyer Bennett, for all things Bernese mountain dog related. If you enjoyed reading about Molly, you might want to check out Sawyer's *Atticus: A Woman's Journey with the World's Worst Behaved Dog.*

I'm forever grateful to my wonderful editor Maria Gomez and the rest of the Montlake team. My books would not shine without the editorial expertise of Kristen Weber, Penina Lopez, and my capable proofreaders. Thank you all for helping to bring readers the best books possible.

If you'd like to get a glimpse into my writing process and chat with me about my love stories, please join my fan club on Facebook, where I chat with fans daily, some of whom have made it into my stories (www.Facebook.com/groups/MelissaFosterFans).

To keep up with sales and events, please follow me on Amazon and sign up for my newsletter (www.MelissaFoster.com/News).

# ABOUT THE AUTHOR

*Photo © 2013 Melanie Anderson*

Melissa Foster is the *New York Times, Wall Street Journal,* and *USA Today* bestselling and award-winning author of more than one hundred books, including the stand-alone romantic comedy *Hot Mess Summer* and several steamy and emotional series such as Silver Harbor, Sugar Lake, and Harmony Pointe. Her novels have been recommended by *USA Today*'s book blog, *Hagerstown* magazine, the *Patriot,* and others. She enjoys discussing her books with book clubs and reader groups, and she welcomes an invitation to your event. Melissa also writes sweet romance under the pen name Addison Cole. For more information, visit www.melissafoster.com.